Whispers in the Shingle

Whispers in the Shingle

An Eighteenth-Century Suffolk Smuggling Tale of Love and Lawlessness

BRIDGET M. BEAUCHAMP

The Book Guild Ltd

First published in Great Britain in 2023 by
The Book Guild Ltd
Unit E2 Airfield Business Park,
Harrison Road, Market Harborough,
Leicestershire. LE16 7UL
Tel: 0116 2792299
www.bookguild.co.uk
Email: info@bookguild.co.uk
Twitter: @bookguild

Typeset in 12pt Sabon LT Pro

Printed and bound in Great Britain by CMP UK

ISBN 978 1915352 842

British Library Cataloguing in Publication Data.
A catalogue record for this book is available from the British Library.

Cover image: 'Blakeney Point, Norfolk'
by kind permission of the artist Keith Judge, with grateful thanks.

In loving memory of my mother Dorothy,
who thrilled me with tales of smuggling,
along the lonely Suffolk coastline,
where I spent my childhood.

'Watch the wall, my darling, while the gentlemen go by...'

– Rudyard Kipling

Main Characters

Katherine (Kate) Goldsmith – young girl from Orford
Jack Howell (alias Will Pallant) – craftsman, sailor, smuggler
Ellen Goldsmith – Kate's mother
John Goldsmith – Kate's eldest brother
Thomas (Tom) Goldsmith – Kate's younger brother
Rebecca (Becky) Goldsmith – Kate's younger sister
Joseph Goldsmith (deceased) – Kate's father
Lieutenant Harry Goldsmith – officer in the Preventive Service and Kate's uncle
Dick Halesworth – skipper of smuggling lugger
Nate Halesworth – son of Dick Halesworth
Ben Fosdyke – old smuggler
Mike Chapman – owner of the *Zephyr* and the *Storm Petrel*
Edward Sawyer – miller's son
Daniel Bird – innkeeper at the Crown and Castle Inn, Orford
Isaac Smith – warden at Orford Castle
'Mad' Willie Mumford – reclusive fisherman
Stephen Hammond – captain of the *Zephyr* and the *Storm Petrel*
Joe Willis – first mate and foreman
Charles Sawyer – miller, Edward's father
Mr and Mrs Joseph Baxter – proprietors of the Vulcan Arms, Sizewell
Patrick (Pat) Harvey – smuggler from Hadleigh
Pip – cabin boy and deck hand
Kit Pallant – Kate's son

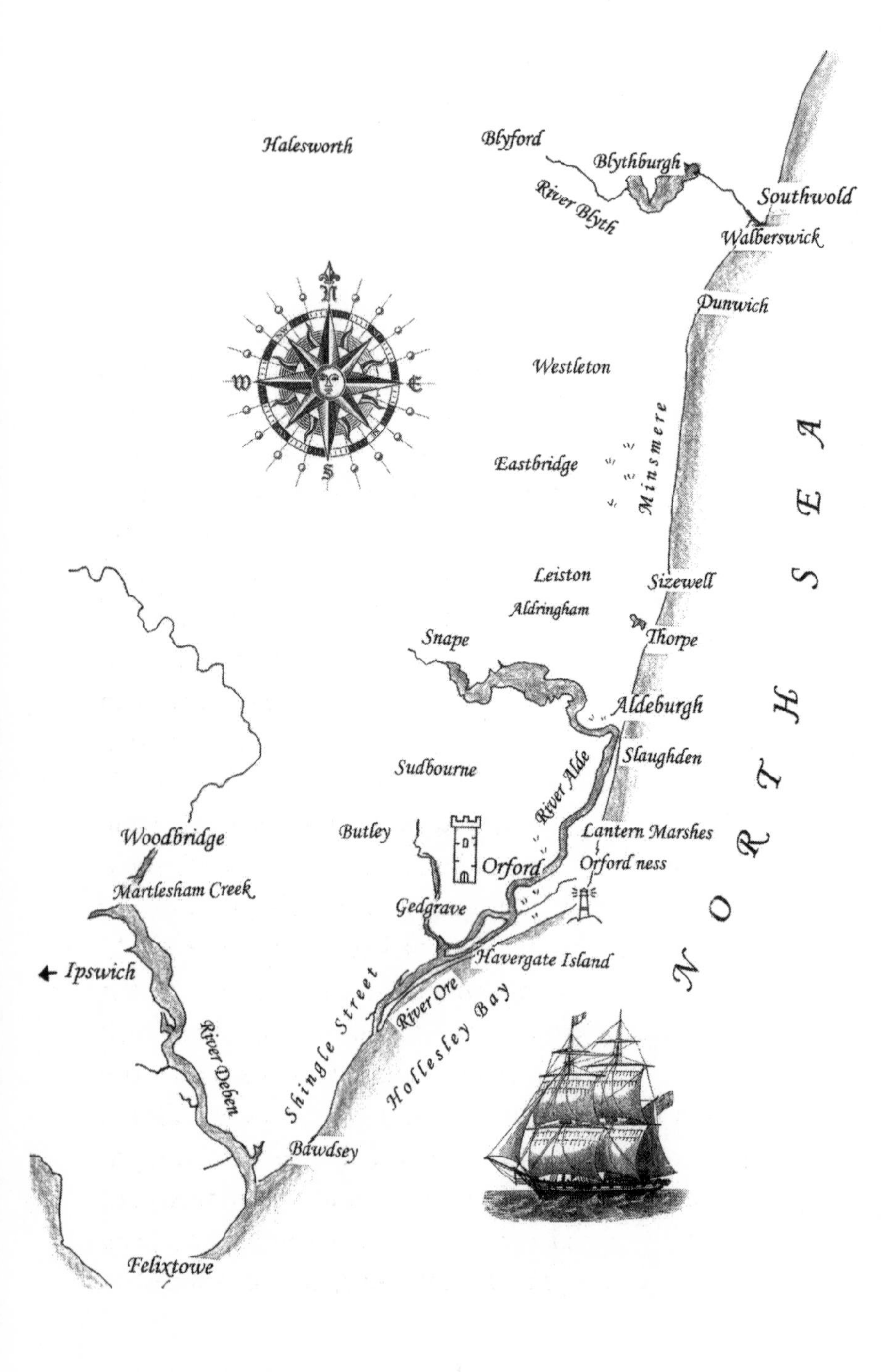

Halesworth
Blyford
Blythburgh
River Blyth
Southwold
Walberswick
Dunwich
Westleton
Minsmere
Eastbridge
Leiston
Sizewell
Aldringham
Thorpe
Snape
Aldeburgh
Slaughden
Sudbourne
River Alde
Butley
Lantern Marshes
Orford
Orford ness
Woodbridge
Martlesham Creek
Gedgrave
Havergate Island
Ipswich
Shingle Street
River Ore
Hollesley Bay
River Deben
Bawdsey
Felixtowe
NORTH SEA

Chapter One

Kate hurried down Orford's Quay street, past the rows of red-brick cottages, down to the quayside and out across the water meadows, following the shoreline of the River Ore, where dunlin and redshank skittered over the mudflats and black-tailed godwit probed the wet surface with their long, straight beaks. Across the river, the low-lying expanse of Lanthorn Marshes and the shingle spit of Orford Ness separated the calm waterway from the North Sea breakers, relentlessly pounding on the exposed seaboard, where no high ground deflected the cold blast of air ripping across this flat Suffolk landscape. Reverberating across the estuary, the bell of St Bartholomew's Church rang out, sending a flock of sanderlings urgently skywards, their bright wings flickering against a dark, menacing sky heralding an approaching storm in the west, and to the north, the white sails of Aldeburgh Mill stood out in stark relief, catching a last ray of sun before it hid behind a curtain of blue-grey rain-saturated cloud.

Her young man had promised to meet her tonight at the old fisherman's hut, now long abandoned but still affording enough shelter from the elements, to keep a passer-by or misplaced sheep dry, if not altogether warm, amidst a tangle of broken nets, buoys and rotting timbers. Its owner had long since died and no-one had claimed the dwelling since, except as a temporary refuge. As always, with the mistrust afforded solitary folk, reclusive and taciturn old George the fisherman had gained a reputation for sorcery and devilry; his ghost was said to have been seen appearing at the window on dark nights, when ethereal lights would glow briefly then disappear through the mist.

Kate was not afraid of George, either real or spiritual. As children she and her siblings would go down to watch him mending his nets or wave to him rowing out in his tiny skerry to set his lobster pots. He would show them his latest catch and regale them with far-fetched fishing tales, which thrilled, astonished or horrified them in equal measure. Relaxed in the innocence of their guileless company, he enjoyed their unconditional acceptance of him, so removed from the suspicions and distrust of the local adult population. The children would happily share with him a currant bun or a slice of fruit tart, baked by Mother and packed in wicker baskets as a snack for her ever-hungry brood. '*Anything to keep you occupied and out from under my feet*,' Mother would say, as she shooed them out of the door, with instructions to be home by the time the church clock struck five. John was the eldest, then Kate, a year behind, followed by Thomas and lastly Becky, but as always it fell to Kate to be mindful of her younger siblings when they were away from the house. John, now approaching manhood, remained content to leave child-minding to the womenfolk like his father before him. Aware of his position at the head of the family since their father's death, he used his superiority over his siblings as a useful asset towards asserting his authority and achieving his goals. Becky and Thomas would bend to his will without question, so it was left to Kate, who was nearest his age, to challenge him when he became too preponderant.

This evening, after helping her mother clear away the evening meal, seventeen-year-old Kate had wrapped herself in her cloak against the freshening breeze and set off alone towards the river. The Alde Estuary lay broad and low, sheltered by the long shingle spit at Slaughden, before it became the Ore, bifurcating around Havergate Island and running down to North Weir Point, where it spilled out into the cold North Sea waters of Hollesley Bay. Behind the spit, the river formed a wide stretch of calm water, frequented by numerous sea birds and waders, its meandering course ambling past Orford and Aldeburgh and up to the moorings at Snape and beyond. A deep channel midstream afforded passage to the larger craft bringing goods from London and Felixstowe, however, by nightfall, the river was deserted and dark and folks kept away from its shores, fearful lest they should witness clandestine goings-on that might compromise their safety.

Everyone knew this was the smuggling coast, the ruthless reputation of the so-called free traders, assuring the silence of honest folk, content to go about their daily lives unimpeded. The cost of betrayal was too high a price to pay. Caught between the law, with its threat of imprisonment or the hangman's noose, and the lawless, whose retribution was to be equally feared, the people of these parts preferred ignorance to intrigue. However, with wages pitifully low and life a daily struggle, many a young man would be tempted by the rich pickings to be had along this lonely Suffolk coast after the sun went down. The punitive government customs tax on luxury goods and excise duties on domestic consumption, levied as a means to pay for costly wars in Europe, assured that many a local businessman was not averse to turning a blind eye to the goings-on and indeed benefitting from keeping their silence. The plight of the poorer classes of unskilled labourers living in grinding poverty and deprivation appeared to be ignored, fuelling widespread resentment and dissent, in turn giving rise to defiance and lawbreaking – their only hope, when all they had was endless, crushing inequality.

Publicans, farmers, mill owners and even the gentry could be 'persuaded' to allow night-time access to their cellars or stables in return for a keg of duty-free spirit or bundle of tobacco. In some cases, compliance with the free traders was assured by the threat of damage to livelihood or even lives. This made the job of upholding the law doubly difficult for the Preventive Service, with very few folk willing to impart what they knew.

Approaching the hut, eager for its relative warmth, Kate stepped over a puddle formed before the threshold and pushed open the excuse for a door, hanging half-heartedly on one rusty hinge, before kicking it with her boot as it scraped reluctantly over the floorboards. Forcing the door closed against the wind, she threw back her hood and pulled her long hair out from her collar, arranging it over her shoulders in eager anticipation of her young man's caress. She knew he loved to feel its silky softness against his work-roughened hands, the contrast serving to emphasise her femininity. Sitting herself down on a crate in the dusty fisherman's hut, Kate watched apprehensively through the broken windowpane. Dark clouds to the west hung ominously in a swirling curtain of angry blue, the breeze catching the surface of the river, obliterating the reflection that a short while before had mirrored the rushes on the far bank. As always, her keenness was a mixture of excited expectation and trepidation. Jack was late. The church clock had already struck the quarter hour before she heard the familiar thudding of galloping hooves approaching and shortly afterwards the door was thrust open vigorously.

'Forgive me, my dunlin, I got caught up at Sudbourne,' Jack Howell explained, breathless, throwing his hat down and grabbing Kate eagerly around her slim waist.

'Oh, no matter, Jack! You are here now. I'm glad you came.' Kate gazed up at her sweetheart adoringly as he leant down and kissed her firmly on the mouth. This was no polite kiss of a hopeful suitor, fearful lest he should frighten away too soon the object of his intentions; no, this was the kiss of desire, of unquenchable passion, of moral abandon, a fusion of lust and love that neither one could stop or would stop if they could. Time stood still as they kissed and caressed with the energy and impulsiveness of youth. As they took breath, Jake stroked Kate's long mahogany-hued tresses falling down her back and wound them round his fingers, pressing her towards him and burying his head into her neck. Her skin smelled of rose water, soap and the freshly baked bread her mother would soon be laying out on the supper table. After a while, he stood back and smiled, looking his lover up and down desirously, her plain woollen dress laced tight at the waist accentuating her figure, ensuring he could not resist touching the rise of her breast gently with his lips.

'My pretty Kate, you render me defenceless and I surrender,' he whispered tenderly into her cleavage.

Kate laughed shyly, then frowned as she voiced a concern that had been playing on her mind. 'Oh, Jack, I heard the coastguard were waiting for the free traders at Shingle Street last night. I was afeared you would not come... you weren't with them, were you?' She leaned, back focussing her gaze upon him anxiously. Her uncle Harry who, like his late brother, was also in the Service, oft visited Joseph's widow, partly out of kindness but more pointedly because Ellen was still a handsome woman for whom he had long felt affection. He would keep Kate's mother informed as to the success or failure of their night-time operations in the war against free trading and had told her of the night's undertaking, Kate listening intently for any news that might involve her lover.

Jack knew this question was coming. Gazing steadily into his lady love's storm-blue eyes, framed by long dark lashes, marvelling at the unblemished whiteness of her soft skin, running his hand appreciatively down her curves, he tried to distract her from the lie he was about to tell.

'No, my dunlin,' he lied hesitatingly, knowing she would be unconvinced. 'But would it have mattered so much if I was?' he added, attempting to soften the blow of truth, which he knew he must soon confess, if he wanted no secrets between them.

'Oh, Jack, I can't stop you, but I wish you wouldn't. It's so dangerous – if you get caught with them, you'll go to prison or hang... if you are not killed first, that is!'

Jack released her from his grip, suddenly peevish, turned his back to her and peered out of the window, eastwards towards the estuary. It was easier not to look at Kate when she pricked his conscience. She always made him feel bad about deceiving her, but he was in too deep now. Poverty had driven many an honest man to risk all on the *Sandpiper*, but having tasted the thrill of the danger and the rewards to be had, he wanted more. It made him feel alive. He was young and strong, could wield a cutlass or aim a pistol with skill, and with the bravado of youth and a reckless courage, born of self-preservation, he knew he was more than a match for the conscripts in the Preventive Service. He and his band had had luck on their side last night, having received a last-minute tip-off that the excise were waiting for them, quickly diverting their loaded craft southwards towards the safety of Woodbridge Haven.

'I can't betray my friends, Kate. I've known Dick and Nate since I w'or a lad – Dick's like a father to me and Nate's as good as a brother to me.' He took a deep breath of resignation.

'I understand that, Jack, but it doesn't mean you have to run with them, does it?' Kate moved towards him and wrapped her arm around his chest, pressing her head against his back affectionately. She hated to arouse his anger, hoping that some gentle persuasion would soften his resolve.

'You don't understand, my dunlin, I can't turn my back on them now, I know too much – besides, how else would I manage on an apprentice wage?' He stared, unfocussed, out of the window.

'You'll make a fine ship builder one day, Jack, can't you be satisfied with that?' Kate pleaded.

'Aye, mebbe when I'm old and grey, but I'm a young man, Kate. There's a big world out there. There's riches beyond your wildest dreams. I've watched my parents toil the land all their lives, and for what? To end their days in the poor house, relying on the generosity of kind folk and the few pennies they get for their labours?' He scoffed. 'After Father died, Mother ended up in Nacton Workhouse and it killed her. That's not the life for me, you *must* know it.'

'Yes, I know, Jack, I'm sorry,' Kate commiserated before her face brightened. 'There's always the Navy?' she ventured. 'My brother is thinking of joining up. It's a better wage than labourin'.'

'Huh,' he sneered dismissively. 'I'd only be swapping one hardship for another! My life would be just as punishing on the deck of a warship but without the rewards. Why settle for a conscript's tot o' rum when you can have a barrel as a free man!' He chuckled.

Kate knew in her heart Jack would never be content with a life of servitude. They were more alike than she cared to admit, but she felt she had to try to keep him grounded, if only to keep him alive.

'I don't want to lose you, Jack,' Kate whispered as she clung to him, nestling her cheek into his back, closing her eyes in silent prayer.

'You won't, my dunlin, I promise.'

Just then, Kate felt Jack's body stiffen, as in the gathering dusk a light blinked twice out of the gloom upriver and almost immediately another flashed in response down near the mouth.

'Yes!' he exclaimed abruptly, and Kate knew she had lost his attention. 'I have to go,' he announced, turning around to kiss her firmly but hurriedly, retrieving his hat from the dusty floor and yanking the door open. The rush of cold air made Kate shudder, not only from the goosebumps on her skin but also at the thought of him engaging in the iniquitous activities of his dubious friends.

'When can you come again?' she asked hopefully as he untethered his horse.

'Soon, my dunlin. I will let you know. Don't you fret now,' he added, landing a peremptory kiss on her upturned brow.

Kate stood in the doorway as he re-mounted and rode off up the path, just as heavy droplets of rain began to patter down on the old tin roof. She watched him disappear into the murk, pulling her cloak around her shoulders, running back towards the village, her shoes now saturated, her wet hair channelling droplets down her back as the sodden woollen cloth clung to her skin.

'You'll catch your death, my girl,' admonished her mother as Kate came in. 'Have you been out with Edward?'

'Yes, Mama,' Kate lied as she flung off her dripping cloak and stood before the fire, shivering and holding her palms towards the flames. Thirteen-year-old Becky, busily folding clothes ready for ironing, raised her eyebrows quizzically at her sister but said nothing.

Poor Edward, Kate thought ashamedly as a pang of guilt struck her conscience. He was a good man and she knew he wanted to court her and offer her a comfortable life as a miller's wife, but agreeable as he was, there was no spark, no frisson of excitement in her breast when in his company, not like there was with Jack. She closed her eyes, her senses still fresh from her lover's embrace. Jack was everything she found desirable in a man: ruggedly handsome with dark, brooding looks and piercing blue eyes; his body toned and muscular; his shoulder-length black hair tied loosely back; his open shirt revealing a smooth chest, tanned from the sun's rays reflected off many a well-scrubbed deck. When he held her, Kate felt safe and protected, and when he kissed her, she was putty in his hands.

He was a couple of years older than Kate. They had met by chance when she had accompanied her brother to Chapman's boat builders on the River Deben at Woodbridge to enquire after work. Jack had caught her eye and she had shown interest in the craft he was working on while John spoke with the foreman. They had both felt an instant attraction and it was not long before they agreed to meet at old George's hut, but something told Kate to keep their relationship discreet. That 'something' gave her a thrill, awoke in her an excitement, an element of danger that was irresistibly compelling. He was a man for whom she knew a life of routine and sensibility was as unappealing as it was for her. She knew her mother would disapprove of such an attachment, especially now it was assumed she was stepping out with Edward. *Level-headed, passionless, lacklustre Edward!* she sighed inwardly to herself, feelings of self-reproach uncomfortably pricking her conscience.

Like a polar opposite to Jack's swarthy looks, Edward Sawyer was slight of build and fair, hazel-eyed, with sensibly short-cropped hair, a classic well-proportioned face, somewhat pale from years working inside the mill but agreeable enough to attract the attention of several young girls in the village. He was reputable and uncomplicated, a good match for any prospective bride, being poised to inherit the family business; however, he had fallen for the dark-haired beauty from River Cottage and was set on wooing her, much to her mother's approval. 'A miller's wife is as good as any life for my eldest daughter,' Ellen had announced proudly to her neighbours.

Kate knew she should be grateful for Edward's addresses, but she had tasted the thrill of a secret liaison, and the irresistible lure of malfeasance and masculine prowess afforded by a man who aroused feelings in her she didn't know she had, was an enticement more than she could resist. The temptation was too great. Jack was dashing and brave and he wanted her – not as a dutiful wife who would keep house, cook his meals, mind his children and accompany him to church on Sundays. No, he craved a lover, impassioned and responsive, abandoned and spirited, living life to the full, fiercely loyal to her man and appreciative of his desires – Kate longed to be that lover, to taste the danger, to feel the passion, to feed the soul. Her life had just begun and she was determined to sample its many delights before being shackled by the bonds of domesticity and motherhood, arriving all too soon to young girls of her age.

It was not long before Kate had begun to suspect there was more to Jack's life than his apprenticeship at the boatyard. He was often away for nights on end and she had seen him carrying an elaborately crafted flintlock pistol and had marvelled at his expensive boots and gold timepiece. He had brought her a pair of pearl earrings of the finest quality, trinkets far beyond the buying power of his employ, and when Kate had asked about them, he told her they had belonged to an ageing relative. She had hidden them amongst her things, away from her siblings' prying eyes and her mother's certain admonishment and inevitable interrogation as to their provenance. One night, after repeated questioning, Jack had had to admit to Kate he was acquainted with some free traders and been rewarded for certain services. He knew he couldn't deceive her for long; neither did he wish to. He wanted her to accept him for who he was, good or bad, and he had learned enough of her character to know she would be discreet. Kate understood he must now remain her secret, but she suspected he was more involved with the illicit traders than he had so far professed.

Kate's father Joseph had been in the Preventive Service but had been killed by a shot fired from a free trader's gaff-rigged lugger racing for cover towards a shallow inlet where the Revenue brig could not follow. Kate's mother was left to bring up the children alone and bitterly railed against her husband's killers, vowing to have nothing to do with the so-called 'gentlemen of the night' or their contraband. If Ellen knew her daughter was seeing a man in league with these lawbreakers, with their reputation for ruthlessness and murder, there would be hell to pay. However, Kate herself held no grudge. Her father's death was long before Jack was old enough to work, and the men who killed him had long since disappeared or been apprehended, no proof of who had fired the fatal shot ever having been acquired. Her father was simply doing his duty and was well aware of the risks he faced in the Service.

Already Kate sensed herself and Jack were soulmates, bound together by their shared love of the inland waterways they knew so well, where waterfowl nested amongst the reed beds, crowded in summer with yellow flag iris, horsetail and marsh marigolds, while the air reverberated with the haunting boom of the bittern. Nearer the sea, the plaintive cry of oyster catchers, the woeful two-toned whistle of the curlew, the raucous shriek of the gulls filled the air; all the sights and sounds of this place dwelled within them, pervading their inner being, a vital force, as much a part of them as the life blood coursing through their veins. The huge skies, ever-changing vistas of tone and multiform, vast watercolour paintings ethereal and elusive, a cloud here one moment, gone the next; shafts of sunlight colouring the landscape in every hue before the mist rolled in from the sea and rendered everything in monotone. Kate had always been struck by the colours and forms of nature, an ever-changing palette of shades and contrasts etched on her memory, enriching her consciousness. The familiar sounds of this coastal lowland were like a heartbeat, a reassurance that this place was home – there was something comforting about the hiss of the shingle as the tide dragged it back and forth, like an intake and exhalation of breath as the ever-shifting stones clattered and clinked, worn smooth over millennia; fragments of granite, sandstone, quartz, limestone and flint sighed and shone in the wet surf, the clear saltwater gurgling and percolating down into the damp sand along the water's edge.

The mudflats along the Deben, the Ore and the Alde glistening in the late afternoon sun, where dunlin and redshank flocked in droves and crabs scuttled to the shelter of an upturned boat, its rotting timbers bleached by the sun; the beaches at the river mouth where the North Sea crashed and foamed; the pungent mats of sugar kelp and oarweed strewn on the tideline in shining brown ribbons, the green hair like fronds of grass kelp and black glistening bladderwrack generously studded with tiny blisters of air, as if from a pestilence – all perennial elements that made up the cherished habitat they knew and loved.

As children Kate and her siblings would go foraging for treasure, whelk shells, scallop shells, razor shells, limpets, cuttlefish bones and skates egg cases, dead crab and starfish, pieces of amber worn smooth and fragments of green glass from some broken bottle long lost. They would search amongst the clumps of sea holly, sea kale and yellow-horned sea poppies, collecting pieces of driftwood for the fire, worn smooth and grey like old bones, skeletons of craft long wrecked, each one with a story to tell. They would watch red-sailed Thames barges making their way up and downriver, heavy in the water with cargos of grain or coal, and out from Aldeburgh they would occasionally thrill to the sight of the graceful Preventive Service brig, carvel-built for speed with its long bowsprit, patrolling the coast in full sail. They could hear the shouts from the sailors busy on deck echoing across the bay, the ship's bow cutting through the surf with ease as the children watched and waved in greeting, despite knowing their tiny figures were too far distant to be seen or heard by those on board.

On foggy days the sea mist crept in like a damp blanket, silent and cold, the eerie foghorn booming from one of the twin Orford Ness timber light towers, resounding along the hushed coastline, adding to the mystique, the flat sea sloshing gently on the shingle, the dimness rendering solid shapes into ghostly apparitions appearing and disappearing into the murk. By contrast, when winter storms battered the coast and bitter nor'easterlies whipped the waves into a seething mass of spume, ships caught in the gale pitched and rolled amidst the slate grey water. Heaving waves topped by successions of charging white rollers, tumbling ever shorewards, angrily spewing out spray and spindrift, as fierce breakers roared and curled, crashing over the tideline, scattering pebbles high onto the foreshore.

The children would thrill to the noise, giggling joyfully as they leaned into the wind, almost pushed off their feet by the gale, their hair blown across their faces, the air rudely pulled from their lungs as their voices were snatched away, and when the storm abated there would be a new hoard of flotsam and jetsam to scavenge. Arriving home, eager to show off their trophies and vie with each other for the best find, they would empty their pockets out onto the kitchen table, much to Ellen's disgust, brushing sea spiders and sand particles off the surface onto her clean floor. Kate would get out her Sunday school book and make detailed drawings of the things she found on the plain end pages, attempting to recreate the forms as accurately as she could, fascinated by the intricacies of shell structure and plant profiles. She had inherited her mother's craftsmanship and her father's eye for detail, for amongst his effects, he had left sketches of the many sailing craft frequenting these waters, in his quest to identify black marketeers, and Kate was keen to emulate his artistic expertise.

Growing up on this wild windswept seaboard, these childhood memories would become part of an inbuilt subconscious, a persona indivisible from the landscape these youngsters inhabited. Now in adulthood, Kate had been drawn to one of her own kind, both children of this East Suffolk seacoast, she and Jack were cast from the same mould, the same sense of identity, the same roots. It felt right and it felt natural, almost as if it were meant to be, as if their destinies had been mapped out and laid down by some higher power fulfilling a master plan. As Kate climbed into bed that night in the small upstairs chamber she shared with her sister, extinguishing the lamp between the beds, Becky sat up, leaning on her elbow, and whispered with the smug satisfaction of one who had guessed a secret.

'I *know* you weren't with Edward tonight!' she goaded.

'What makes you think that?' Kate replied defensively, turning her back, attempting to appear unconcerned.

'Because I saw him! He stopped by to ask if you were at home, so I told him you weren't.'

Kate's stomach churned. Her lie was already unravelling. 'I just met up with him later,' Kate refuted quickly, but Becky wasn't buying it.

'No, you *didn't*!' she announced triumphantly. 'I saw him come out of the King's Head with some men just before you got back.' Kate swore silently to herself and turned towards her sister, knowing there was no point in prolonging the pretence.

'Look, Becky, I wasn't doing anything wrong. I was just walking down by the river. Please don't tell Mama, you know how she worries,' she pleaded, wishing her sister would drop the subject.

'What's it worth?' Becky smirked triumphantly.

'I will do your chores tomorrow, alright? Pleeeease, Becky!' Kate implored, hoping to appeal to her sister's better nature.

'Alright,' Becky chirped happily, diving under the covers, her objective achieved.

Damn! Kate thought to herself crossly, immediately blaming Edward for calling upon her unannounced and then Becky for blackmailing her. *Why did he have to come tonight and then involve Becky?* she thought peevishly. *But then, why shouldn't he come, poor man?* she admonished herself. He wasn't to know she had another lover. A stab of remorse pricked her conscience at her deception, consuming her with shame momentarily before her thoughts turned back to Jack and the feelings he aroused in her. She sank between the sheets and smiled to herself as a warm glow of desire enveloped her, reliving his passionate kisses and firm embrace as he held her to him. She wondered where he was tonight, comforting herself with a somewhat vain hope that he was tucked up in his bunk at the shipyard, though logic told her it was unlikely. The wind rattled the windowpane and she shivered to think of him out in this storm. She offered up a quick prayer for his safety and before long her fretful thoughts were subsumed by the welcome relief of sleep.

Outside, the night was dark; there was no moon. Storm clouds whipped the sea into angry peaks and barrelling breakers crashed onto Shingle Street, dragging stones to and fro, as an unlit craft surged towards the beach. Jack watched, huddled down in the lee of an upturned boat, its rotting timbers affording little protection against the sou'westerly gale, his men lying in wait upon the shingle bank, tense and silent. They had gambled that the excise would not expect a second attempt by the traders the following night, but it was well to be vigilant. By the end of the night they would be soaked through, their energy spent, but the rewards of a few hours' discomfort would be more than worth it. He pulled his collar up round his ears, straining his eyes to make out the outline of the approaching three-masted lugger in the darkness, the beams from the Orford light towers to the north affording a brief glimpse of the familiar silhouette above the waves as it passed by the aligning beacons.

As the *Sandpiper* beached on the ebb tide, Jack jumped up, signalling silently to his men to form a line up towards the bank, where a dozen or more packhorses were held steady by more hushed figures, their backs to the wind, keeping watch upriver towards Aldeburgh and west over Oxley Marshes. Gradually kegs, crates and bundles passed down from the craft to men standing knee-deep in the surf, were passed man to man along the line before being loaded onto panniers or strapped to the backs of those who had broad shoulders. Nobody spoke; each man knew his role and carried it out without command, not that they would have been able to hear much tonight over the roar of wind and tide. It was a successful drop this time, and before long the hushed figures of the tub men and their fully laden beasts melted into the night.

By morning the lugger was refloated on the incoming tide, fishing gear ostensibly at the ready for another day's honest toil, no footfall evidence of the night's activities remaining at the water's edge; the damp sand washed smooth and glistening, the shingle banks deserted now, save for the wheeling gulls, and a pair of townsfolk with a handcart collecting driftwood spewed up by the storm.

Chapter Two

The townsfolk of Orford were in an upbeat mood for the next couple of weeks, starlight undertakings having been profitable for both trader and customer. The innkeeper Michael Barker at the King's Head had an extra ten kegs of wine and spirit, stacked behind his stable of weary horses, at a fraction of the legal cost; the grocer Edwin Godbold counted two sacks of salt, a crate of soap, a chest of tea and some chocolate that according to his stock-take he didn't have before; and even the Reverend Day found a couple of bottles of claret and a pouch of Jamaican tobacco had mysteriously made their way into the vicarage cellar. Up at the grand house on the edge of Aldeburgh, Squire Bedingfield happily presented his delighted wife with a bolt of the finest rose-tinted silk, together with a roll of Flemish lace, and congratulated himself on his marriage boosting bargain with a tun of Spanish Port wine. *Simply payment for service*, he assured himself. His horses had been returned to him in the early hours, the stables having been left conveniently unlocked some hours before. He was not the only man of property to benefit. Despite the fact Lord Orford's Norfolk regiment were stationed in the town, the citizens of this pretty fishing port with its distinctive sixteenth-century Moot Hall were able to carry on their clandestine activities with impunity, due to the involvement of the majority of the population in one way or another.

At River Cottage, Orford, its front door opening directly onto the street, Kate busied herself with her daily chores, helping her mother keep house, prepare meals, wash clothes and sew seams. Ellen was a skilled dressmaker and had taught Kate the basics of cutting and stitching cloth which kept the family fed for a while, but now that they had learned all they could from their basic charity-funded Sunday-school education, the children needed to find regular work. Kate's eldest brother John had signed up to join the Navy and was soon packing his bags, and Thomas had signed up to follow his father in the Preventive Service, much to mama's delight, though she worried for his safety. Kate had asked Daniel Bird, the landlord of the Crown and Castle, for serving work to supplement the sewing and to get her out of the house, while Becky found live-in work in the kitchens over at Sudbourne Hall, which to Kate's relief meant she would sleep alone at last, free from awkward questions and threat of bribery.

It had been two weeks since she had heard from Jack. Kate was worried. She began work at the Crown and Castle, much to the relish of the steady stream of regulars who now had a pretty face and youthful figure to leer at over their jugs of ale. Disdainfully ignoring ribald comments that oft were directed her way, Kate busied herself clearing tables and serving, feigning disinterest but at the same time listening carefully to any gossip that might be useful.

On a trip in Uncle Harry's trap to buy supplies at Woodbridge, Kate called at the boat builders but was told Jack was away on the *Zephyr* with Captain Stephen Hammond and Joe Willis, the first mate and boatyard foreman, procuring sailcloth and tallow from Dutch merchants.

The following morning she rose early before going to work and walked out of the town to the old elm tree with the hollow trunk, standing alone beside the road to Sudbourne. After a furtive glance around her surroundings, to ensure she wasn't being observed, she felt inside for the familiar leather pouch she and Jack had devised to convey missives, shuddering at the thought of the many spiders and woodlice inhabiting the void but the bag was empty. Her heart sank. *Why hasn't he sent me a message?*

Another week went by without word until late one afternoon an old sailor entered the inn, seating himself down in a dark corner. His face was rough and rugged, unshaven, a grubby kerchief encircling his neck, his skin as brown as the leather overcoat he wore and beneath his felt hat, an untidy mess of long, lank greying hair, his left earlobe pierced by a gold earring. Kate was immediately struck by the pair of penetrating steel-grey eyes staring out from under his lowering brow: cold, compassionless eyes that seemed to seek out her very soul with a disarming directness.

As Kate stepped up to ask his preference, he grasped her wrist purposefully.

'Be you Kate Goldsmith?' he rasped, as Kate tried to pull away from his iron grip.

'Who wants to know?' she replied defensively.

'Jack Howell has a message for her.'

'Oh... Jack!' she started, her guard immediately dropped. 'Where is he?'

The sailor ignored the question. 'Are you she?' he repeated, not relaxing his grip.

'Aye, I am, Kate. Tell me!' she ordered, irritated, trying not to raise her voice. She wondered why Jack had not left a message in the elm tree. She realised he must have learned from one of the regulars that she now worked at the inn.

'He says to tell you half past ten o' the clock tonight, you know where.' The sailor shoved a penny piece towards her. 'Ale,' he commanded, before letting go of her wrist, the pressure of his strong fingers momentarily constricting her blood supply and leaving their fleeting imprint on her skin. Kate rubbed her benumbed wrist back into life, thanked the man politely and went to fetch the ale, her heart racing as she felt his eyes upon her and wondered why Jack had sent another in his place and how she was going to meet him. She would have to go straight to the hut after work, but she knew her mother would wonder where she was. She realised with regret that Becky was not there to cover for her, so she decided she would go home first and slip out after bidding her mother goodnight. The hours ticked by interminably until the last customer departed and the landlord locked the door, enabling Kate to hurry home.

Ellen was sewing downstairs by the kitchen range, her head gradually drooping as she fought to keep awake. She jumped as the door, which could not be seen from the kitchen, opened and a rush of cool air blew into the cottage.

'Is that you, Kate?'

'Yes, Mama,' Kate replied as nonchalantly as she could, hurrying up the stairs to her room, calling out, 'Goodnight, Mama,' before shutting her door loudly. Kate waited and, after a suitable interval, crept downstairs slowly, avoiding the loose board at the bottom that she knew would creak and give her away. Lifting the latch as carefully as she could, she slipped outside, shutting the door behind her with equal deliberation. Luckily her mother's hearing was not what it was and she did not look up from her threads.

Running through the dark street, down to the river path and along to old George's dwelling, Kate was glad the moon was up and she could see her way clearly. The church clock had already struck the eleventh hour and she worried Jack might have left. A dim light showed in the window and her heart leapt. *Yes, he's still there!* She pushed open the door with relief and immediately fell into Jack's arms. He smelt of the sea and sweat and something else. His long hair was loose and unwashed, and he had several days' growth of stubble on his chin. He kissed her with a long, voracious kiss, which she returned with passion, but something about the way he was holding her, pressing his wrist bone into her back, concerned her.

She pulled back from him. 'Where have you been, Jack? I've been worried.' It was then that she noticed his heavily bandaged hand, swathed in a bloodied cloth. 'Oh, what's happened, Jack?' She gasped in alarm.

'I've lost a finger, my dunlin, that's all.' He breathed in, wincing as she took his injured hand in hers. 'Caught it in the anchor chain coming out of Flushin'. We've been picking up supplies for the boatyard.'

'Oh, Jack!' Kate exclaimed in horror. 'Let me look at it,' Kate demanded, as she unwrapped the makeshift bandage to reveal a bloody stump where his forefinger should have been and beside it a deep gash in the middle finger, exposing the bone. Kate gasped, fighting to keep her stomach stable. 'An anchor chain did this?!' She stared at the disfigurement, aghast.

'Aye, they're lethal when they're runnin'.' Jack knew his lie was somewhat implausible given the clean-cut nature of the wound and inwardly cursed at his lame excuse, for Kate was no fool.

Kate frowned, unpersuaded. His explanations would have to wait, but at least for now her motherly instincts came to the fore and she examined the lesion. She knew he would tell her eventually, but for now she would allow him his deception, which she knew was purely to allay her fears.

'It needs cleaning, Jack. Mister Chapman should have sent you to the doctor. Please go to Doctor Ward about it. I hope you will still be able to work.'

'I'll be alright,' he reassured her. 'Good thing it's my left, eh?' He chuckled wanly, attempting to make light of the situation.

'Do you have any spirits?' Kate asked tersely.

He drew a silver hip flask from his coat and sat down on a crate. Kate poured some liquor from the flask onto his wound, Jack sucking his breath between his teeth as the liquid penetrated the cut. She then tore a strip from the hem of her underskirt and tried to clean the wound gently. She tore another strip of cloth and used it to bandage the stump and middle finger, fashioning a sling with a further long remnant of fabric.

'Keep it upright and please see the doctor, Jack!'

'Yes, Nurse.' He grinned obediently, grabbing her with his other arm and pulling her down on his lap. 'Don't stop me kissin' you, though!' They kissed and Jack ran his free arm yearningly down her figure, his rough stubble scouring her cheek, heightening her desire for his rugged masculinity. Kate could feel he was aroused in response to her caresses and it gave her a shiver of excitement to think she had the power to tantalise and excite this handsome young exemplar of manhood.

They heard the church clock strike midnight, although it seemed as if time had not gone by anything like that quickly. They stopped kissing, Jack stroking Kate's hair absentmindedly. She could tell he had something to say.

'Look, Kate, I may have to keep away for a while, just until it heals, my dunlin.' He knew he could not be seen out and about with such an injury so soon after the fight on the shingle. 'Chapman has got me fetchin' and carryin' over to Holland for this new brig we're building.'

'He should let you off to recover,' Kate suggested, knowing it would be to no avail.

'He won't do that, we're behind as it is. You must go, my dunlin, it's late.' He patted her buttock affectionately as she got up. 'Don't you fret about me, I'll be alright,' he said dismissively, standing up to place the flask back in his pocket.

'Jack, who was that man who came to the inn to tell me to meet you?' Kate asked, curious.

'Oh, that's old Ben. Been at sea nigh on forty years now. Knows these waters like the back of his hand. He's as strong as an ox and a crack shot wi'...' He stopped suddenly, realising he had said too much, especially to Joseph Goldsmith's daughter.

'Is he in the employ of Mister Chapman?' Kate's suspicions were building.

'No!' Jack snapped, immediately regretting his curt reply. 'Look, enough questions for now, my dunlin. You'll be missed if you're not already. I'll come wi' you as far as the jetty.' He took the lantern, Kate linking her arm with his, the lovers walking silently together in the moonlight, Kate feeling excluded by Jack's reticence and Jack wishing he had told her the truth about his injury. They embraced again at the landing before Jack turned and strode back along the path into the blackness.

'Be careful, Jack!' Kate called after him, the futility of her wish echoing unavailingly in her ears.

He waved in response and broke into a jog, his long coat billowing out behind him like a black sail. He cursed at himself for lying to Kate. He knew his excuse sounded pathetic and unrealistic, and he knew she was suspicious. *I'm gonna tell her next time*, he vowed. She deserved to know, and as much as he didn't want to lose her affections, neither did he wish to keep lying to her, especially if they were to build a future together.

Kate sighed despondently as he disappeared into the night. She knew he was lying about his injury. That cut looked more like a cutlass wound than a ragged laceration from a dragging chain. She understood he was simply attempting to protect her so she would not become party to any incriminating knowledge. It was best she did not know what he got up to and could therefore tell no lies if questioned, but she felt hurt that he could not just be straight with her.

The cottage was in darkness when she reached the door. Mother had gone to bed but had secured the bolt on the inside. Kate cursed inwardly but then remembered the pantry latch was broken and the window could easily be pulled away from the frame. Stealthily skulking round the back of the rows of cottages, she found a crate by the kitchen door and, standing upon it, pulled open the casement and heaved herself up through the opening, dragging herself across the draining board and down onto the stone floor, pausing every few moments to listen for any movement upstairs. With Ellen's regular snores assuring Kate's impunity, she eased the window back into its frame and crept up to her room, thankful Becky was not there to extort even more recompense for her silence. Lying in her bed, the moonlight streaming in from the low window, casting a distorted shadow across the coverlet, Kate was uneasy. She could still smell the blood from Jack's lesion in her nostrils and knew the wound would mark him out. Questions would be asked and suspicions raised, though no doubt such an injury could easily be explained away as a work accident.

The morning dawned fine and bright. It was a clear, warm April day, the blackthorn blooming in a haze of delicate white along the bare hedgerows, its black stems contrasting strikingly with its chalky blossom and below on the grassy verges pale yellow primroses flowered in profusion. Along the Ore and the Alde the sheltered marshy inlets echoed with birdsong, ducks, coots and moorhens paddling about amongst the rushes and sedges, tending their nests amongst the long stems. It was a perfect day for a picnic, Ellen informed her daughter, announcing contentedly that Edward would call on her this afternoon. He would bring the pony and trap and they would go out for a ride, with a basket of mother's fruit tarts and a quart of ale for sustenance. Kate knew she would have to accept the miller's invitation for appearance's sake and anyway, she decided, it would be a welcome distraction from her worries about Jack.

Later that morning, however, Uncle Harry called in to see his sister-in-law, who offered him some vegetable broth, homemade bread and a hunk of cheese for his midday fare while they sat in the kitchen chatting. At first Kate ignored their pleasantries until, without warning, she heard words that stopped her mid-step.

'We had a set-to with the free traders last night,' Harry was saying. 'Chapman's ship, the *Zephyr*, and that lugger *Sandpiper* met two miles off Woodbridge Haven. The *Zephyr* had been out from Flushing with a cargo of sailcloth and tallow, and we saw her meet with the lugger to discharge some goods, huh...' He sneered derisively. 'Clearly not her authorised cargo! We followed the lugger past Bawdsey Point and up to the Ore, just as it got dark. Our men were waiting on the shore at Havergate Island, tipped off that it was the off-loading point. As they came ashore, we managed to down a couple of the traders with pistols and then it became a hand-to-hand cutlass fight. My God, they've got some strong fighters! It was as much as our lads could do to hold 'em. We wounded a few and I know I got one of 'em with a slash to his hand, but they ran off and we couldn't catch 'em. Good-lookin' lad, he was, but I reckon he lost a finger, m'ebbe two.' Harry chuckled. 'They left the goods, though, so we won the day,' he gloated, pleased with himself at the prospect of a handsome profit, for revenue officers seizing goods, he told Ellen, were entitled to half the proceeds at the next customs auction.

Kate stood transfixed, her mind racing. *I knew it*, she thought as her heart sank. Jack was with them and that was how he'd sustained his injury! *Oh, Jack, why didn't you tell me!* If she needed any confirmation he was mixed up with the *Sandpiper*'s men and their night-time activities this was it. The laceration would give him away or at the very least place him under suspicion. She felt sad and somewhat annoyed that Jack had not trusted her enough to be frank with her. *He must surely know I would never give him away?* she brooded. Kate slipped into the pantry and shut her eyes, steadying herself against the kitchen door, her heart thumping in her chest. After a few moments' composing herself, she managed to complete her chores in a daze of preoccupation, before readying herself for her afternoon outing with Edward. She washed and changed into a clean dress, brushed her hair and tied it back with a scarlet ribbon, for, not wishing to disappoint her mother, she would do her duty and play the part of the young miller's companion, despite it being the last thing on her mind. So long as she was seen to be courting Edward there would be no reason to suspect another suitor. For now, it suited Kate to maintain the pretence for appearance's sake, but she fully intended to let Edward down gently if he broached the subject of marriage.

As arranged, just as the church clock struck twice, Edward drew up in the trap, jumped down and knocked firmly on the door. He was smartly dressed in a well-fitting grey coat and breeches, clean white shirt and tricorn hat, his hair neatly trimmed. To any other young woman, he would be the perfect match, but to Kate he was just too predictable, too sensible, too fresh-faced and vernal to be anything other than boringly cautious and lacklustre, but he had come to court her and she felt it rude to spurn his well-meant efforts. She must let him down gently, she resolved, wishing her mother wasn't quite so enamoured.

'Go on, you answer it, Kate.' Ellen smiled contentedly as Kate lifted the latch.

Edward grinned boyishly, removing his hat, taking Kate's hand and kissing it respectfully. He felt proud of himself for being the first admirer to formally court Mrs Goldsmith's attractive daughter and was determined to keep her ostensibly 'spoken for' to deter other would-be suitors.

'Good afternoon, Kate, Mrs Goldsmith,' he said formally, nodding to Ellen, taking Kate's basket from her and placing it in the trap before helping her into the front seat.

'Edward.' Kate nodded in acknowledgement, inwardly comparing his pallid, youthful complexion to the rugged appeal of her swarthy lover. Watching him sit beside her, urging the pony forward, returning his smile politely as he glanced her way, she wondered why on earth she was doing this. Despite his debonair looks, she felt no attraction or empathy with him, nothing to excite or enthral her. *Still*, she argued with herself, *Edward is a good, honest man and he would look after me, I'm sure. Perhaps I could grow to love him?* It would be so easy to settle down to a domestic life as Mrs Sawyer, the miller's wife. She could see it now, children at her feet, food on the table, horses in the stable, her husband a pillar of local society, socialising with wealthy merchants and their wives. *Oh God!* she moaned inwardly, dismissing the image forming in her mind, vowing never to be that person, although trotting along in the sunshine with an upstanding respected member of the community it did not seem so bad a life to contemplate. So many of the local girls would give anything to be in her shoes, a fact borne out by the envious glances that came her way as they passed through Orford.

Edward was expounding animatedly on a new mill his father was erecting near Blythburgh. He was full of enthusiasm for the project and barely acknowledged that his pretty companion might not find the subject quite so absorbing. Kate listened politely, but her mind was full of Jack and his injury, Edward's words merging into a monotonous drone from which she only registered the odd word. Her suitor, so absorbed in his own conversation, failed to notice his companion's lack of response. After a few miles he pulled on the reins, halting the pony at the top of a gentle hill and edging the trap to one side of the road, forcing Kate's attention back to her present situation. She gazed around at the scene. The sun beat down warmly; it was a perfect spring afternoon. Stretching before them, the ground fell away to the east, affording a panoramic view of the coastline, past Aldeburgh and away down to Felixstowe.

What am I doing here? Kate thought guiltily, as Edward extended his hand and helped her down from the trap, before laying out a blanket on the grassy hillock. Kate busied herself by unpacking her mother's picnic basket, uncomfortably aware of his scrutiny. Usually she would have appreciated the beauty of her surroundings, but today her mind was in turmoil. The couple sat for a while, each deep in their own thoughts as the heady, sweet scent of the abundant golden yellow gorse blossom permeated the air, attracting bees and butterflies to its rich nectar-filled florets. Ellen's gooseberry tart went down a treat, as did the ale, though it had warmed considerably on its journey. 'Your mother's an excellent cook,' Edward remarked. 'I'm sure she's taught you a few things.'

'Yes, she has,' remarked Kate dully. She immediately took his comment to be a carefully veiled reference as to what he would expect of a wife and felt irritated by it. Not wishing to be reminded of a woman's domestic obligations, she changed the subject, remarking on the view and pointing out the buildings they could make out: St Bartholomew's church, Orford Ness light towers, Orford Castle, Butley Priory, Friston Mill, Aldeburgh Moot Hall and lighthouse.

Edward appeared to be preoccupied. He kept looking at Kate as she gazed out across the heath. She wished he wouldn't study her when she wasn't looking. It made her feel self-conscious and awkward, as if she had to live up to some imagined vision of the perfect chaste and dutiful maiden he doubtless had in mind for a wife. She hated her profile, with her slightly turned-up nose, which she thought made her look like an elf but which men thought was endearing and childlike, her natural beauty undiminished by its imperfection. All at once Edward grasped her hand earnestly. *Oh no!* she thought. *He's going to propose! What can I say? I don't want to marry him, but am I being foolish? Am I going to turn down someone who is more than I deserve?* She thought of all the girls who would swoon with delight at such a prospect.

'My dear Kate, you know how fond I am of you. I make a good living and could look after you. Kate, will you do me the honour—'

Kate sprang up, flustered. 'Don't say any more, Edward, please! I... er... I'm not ready for anything serious,' she pleaded.

Edward looked crestfallen. He stood up and took her hands in his as she looked away, embarrassed. She could not look at his face and see the hurt and disappointment she had caused.

'Kate, I'm sorry if it's too soon for you, I understand that, but please, don't say no just yet. Think about it, Kate.'

'I'm sorry, Edward, I can't... forgive me.' She studied her feet guiltily.

He fell silent for a moment. 'Is there someone else?' His voice hardened. He suddenly realised that of course he would not be the sole admirer of this Suffolk beauty. He had heard the lewd remarks from the regulars at the inn and knew she was a prize worth winning.

'N-no...' Kate replied, the untruth pricking her conscience uncomfortably. 'Of course not.' She could not admit she was involved with another man, especially one of such doubtful respectability. Neither could she let him to think she was a woman of loose morals.

'Well then...' He sounded relieved. 'Look, Kate, I've told you how I feel. Will you do me the favour of at least considering it? I can offer you a good life and you would want for nothing, I can assure you.' His tone softened with an impassioned plea. '*Please*, sweetheart...'

Kate knew this was the moment she must tell him 'no', not give him any false hope. Steeling herself for the confession she had dreaded, she took a deep breath. 'Edward—'

But in that brief hesitance he'd remembered something. He touched her hand to silence her, reached into his pocket, took out a small case and held it out to her. 'I bought you a gift, Kate. Please take it as a token of my affection,' he interrupted.

'Oh no, Edward!' Kate felt humiliated at his gesture, which she knew she did not deserve. 'I can't take it, Edward, not *now*!' She shook her head, but he pressed it into her hand.

'Please, Kate, open it, at least do me *that* courtesy.'

At the obvious slight on her conduct, Kate opened the box with trembling hands to find a delicate single-strand pearl bracelet with a silver filigree heart at the centre. 'Oh, Edward, it's lovely! Thank you! But—'

'It's not a bribe, Kate. I was going to give it to you anyway. Please wear it to remind you that you hold my heart in abeyance!' Edward smiled and took the bracelet from its case, fastening it carefully around her tiny wrist.

She stared at his pale, well-manicured, well-scrubbed hands and shuddered. There was something cold about him that made her skin crawl. His touch felt clammy, his slim fingers and weak wrists more effeminate than masculine. By contrast an image of Jack's severed finger and rough seaman's hands flashed before her. Despite the disfigurement, her lover's caress was always warm and responsive, virile and stimulating, and Kate knew which one of her suitors she craved, and it was not the man standing in front of her. As the guilt churned in her gut, she heard her mother's words of courtship advice repeating in her ear: *Don't go toying with men's emotions, Kate, unless you want to get yourself a reputation.* And yet here she was doing just that with Edward!

'Oh, Edward!' Kate felt a lump in her throat constrict her words and a tear welled in her eye. It was too late now. How could she tell him she was not interested when she had just accepted such a gift? She wished she had told him the truth before he had even asked her, despite the hurt it would prompt, but she had not wanted him to think badly of her. Although she had not encouraged his attentions, she knew she had not discouraged them either, which he would understandably take for affirmation.

They sat back down for a while, supping the warm ale until the freshening breeze signalled time to go, self-consciously making small talk, each aware of the gulf now yawning between them, Kate fingering the bracelet uncomfortably, acutely aware of the obligation it held. On the way home in the trap they sat in pregnant silence, Edward broodily disappointed and Kate wracked with guilt at the hurt she had unintentionally caused. When they reached River Cottage, Edward helped Kate down from the seat, grasping her hand tightly, almost covetously.

'I will ask you again at harvest-time, Kate, when you have had more time. If the answer is still no, I will ask no more.' He was sure once she had had time to consider his proposal at leisure, she would accept him. *After all, who else has offered her such a prize?* He smiled self-importantly, kissing her hand before reluctantly letting it fall.

'Thank you, Edward,' Kate replied sincerely, relieved that she could still feel she had left him some dignity. *Harvest time is over three months away – plenty of time to defer judgement day!* She ran into the house and threw herself down on the bed. She thought immediately of Jack. Jack, the handsome sailor who made her laugh, who excited her senses and who thrilled her with his touch; Jack whom she adored; Jack the smuggler! Now she was wearing Edward's bracelet, the symbol of his heart next to her pulse! Trusting, sensible, polite Edward, who had done nothing wrong. *How could I?* she chided herself. *Now I've betrayed them both!* She felt wretched and guilt-ridden and at this moment didn't like herself very much.

Chapter Three

The days went by with no word from Jack, nor Edward for that matter. Kate had made her way to the elm tree on several occasions but found no messages therein. Trade at the Crown and Castle was brisk and she kept her eye out for old Ben or any other likely-looking seaman who may have word for her. Once or twice, she had enquired of a plausible candidate if he had any message for her and was rewarded with a vulgar suggestion, enough to make her blush and send Mr Bird in her stead with the liquor.

One May Sunday after church, Kate was charged by her mother with the task of delivering two aprons and a newly repaired dress of Kate's which she had altered for Becky, now employed up at Sudbourne Hall. The midday sun beat down on the road to the hall, as Kate set out on the two-mile walk to the two hundred-year-old manor house, with her bundle tucked under her arm, and it was a relief to reach the shade of the woodland as she neared the estate. The grounds of the manor were unkempt and the building was in a poor state of repair; the sills of the stone-mullioned windows crumbling and thick stems of ivy forcing its way through crevices in the walls.

Making her way round to the tradesmen's entrance, Kate knocked timorously.

After what seemed like an eternity, the door opened and a scullery maid poked her head out. 'Yes?' she demanded, looking the visitor up and down superciliously.

Kate explained her errand, and after a peremptory 'Wait here', the door closed once more. When Becky appeared, her face flushed from the heat of the kitchen, her apron smeared with flour and grease, she embraced her sister warmly, taking the parcel from her and exchanging it for a welcome tumbler of Cook's special lemonade water.

They sat on a stone bench outside and Kate filled Becky in on the local gossip while she gratefully refreshed her parched throat with the cool, sweet liquid. She decided not to mention Edward's proposal at this stage, although she had shown her mother Edward's gift which had, of course, delighted Ellen. There was no point in submitting to another lecture on the merits of a good marriage until after harvest-time and she knew Becky would be equally dismayed at her reticence. Her little sister had always held a soft spot for Edward and, now she had turned fourteen, saw herself as a potential rival for any eligible suitors calling at the Goldsmith's cottage. If she thought Edward was available, Kate knew she would immediately set her sights on him. Not that Kate wanted him for herself, far from it, but she judged her sister too young and immature for an adult relationship and, as the elder sister, felt some responsibility for her welfare.

As they chatted, watching the stable lads sweeping manure-soaked hay from the stalls, Becky abruptly lowered her voice, shifting closer to Kate.

'You know, Kate, I hear things at night here. I sleep with Agnes in the attic directly over the stables and we see lights, horses, carts and men coming and going in the dead of night. In the morning the horses are lying down asleep and there are tracks in the mud where a heavy wagon has stood which wasn't there the day before.' Her voice dropped to a whisper and she leaned in towards her sister. 'I think those night traders come here! I asked Johnny the stable lad about it, but he just said, "You didn't see nothin' if you know what's good for you!" ... Kate, do you think I should tell Uncle Harry?'

Kate stiffened. 'No!' she said forcefully, making Becky start and look quizzically at her. 'Do *not* tell anyone, Becky! It's dangerous! Keep out of it, don't look out and whatever you do, don't mention it to Uncle Harry. He probably knows about it anyway and will be making plans. Promise me, Becky!'

'Oh, alright, but—'

Just then a loud female voice boomed from the kitchen, 'Becky? Where's that girl got to?!'

Becky leapt up and ran to the door. Kate returned the tumbler to her and kissed her quickly on the cheek. 'Come and see Mama when you can, Becky – we can talk again then.' Kate nodded, holding her sister's gaze, referring, unspoken, to her sister's disclosure.

As Kate walked away from the manor, she glanced over to the stables, immediately averting her eyes as the lads returned her stare. She wondered how many of them were party to these clandestine activities and whether Lord Seymour was aware, or even complicit, although she deemed it unlikely in his political role. She thought about Jack. *Had he not mentioned Sudbourne that night when he was late coming to the hut? Is he mixed up in this? If Becky tells Harry I will have to warn him.* 'Silly girl!' she spoke aloud to herself. *If she thinks this is some sort of game of seek and find, she will get a queer shock if she is branded informer on the midnight traders!* Kate knew they were not all as restrained as Jack: many hardened fighting men, born into poverty, desperate and ruthless, and not averse to cruel and bloodthirsty punishments when it came to exacting vengeance or ensuring silence from the population. They had to be that way, for the law would not discriminate or categorise. A smuggler was a smuggler, no quarter given, and now Kate was directly involved with them, like it or not.

At the shipyard, Jack's wound healed gradually with the administrations of Doctor Ward and he was able to perform his tasks competently, if a little awkwardly at first. The doctor had questioned the nature of the injury but accepted Jack's account of an accidental slip of the hand at the sawmill. Fortunately for Jack, injuries of this nature were commonplace in the carpentry trade, missing fingers being almost a badge of office. Mike Chapman kept his young craftsman ashore for a couple of months until his wound no longer hampered him, or at least that was the excuse given for his non-appearance.

Not having had word from Jack for some while, Kate made sure to accompany her mother on her next trip to Woodbridge to purchase some more threads for her needlework. Uncle Harry as always, transporting them in his trap, welcoming the opportunity to be of service to his sister-in-law, while at the same time enjoying her company. While Ellen and Harry walked about the town, Kate made her way down to Chapman's yard, ostensibly, as she told her mother, to deliver a message from Daniel Bird to the foreman. She entered the huge building and gazed up at the graceful form of the new brig taking shape on the slipway. The shed was warm and smelled of new wood, tar and fresh paint. A teenage lad standing beside the keel amidst a carpet of coiled and crimped shavings, looked up from planing an oak plank.

'T'boss ain't here, miss,' he said, assuming she wished to speak with Mr Willis.

'No, I came to see Jack Howell. Is he here? I have a message for him,' Kate lied.

'Aye, he's up there.' The lad inclined his head towards the upper deck of the brig. 'Jack!' he called loudly. 'There's a lady here to see ya.'

The hammering that had been going on since Kate arrived abruptly ceased and Jack appeared at the stern rail. He grinned when he saw Kate and slid down a ladder hooked over the ship's side with the agility of a seasoned seaman. Kate noticed he wore a leather glove over his left hand, padded out where his forefinger should have been. He looked tanned and healthy in a loose linen shirt over navy breeches, his long hair tied back, his deep blue eyes exhibiting the smouldering sensuality that never failed to melt Kate's heart.

'Kate!' he exclaimed, appraising her face and figure appreciatively; then, signalling to the boy to get on with his work, he took Kate by the arm. 'Thank you, Jem, I've got this.'

He ushered her down past the slipway out of the boatshed and down to the river's edge out of sight and earshot. They sat on some old rope coils away from the shed doors and he put his arm around her. 'I'm sorry I couldn't get away sooner, Kate, I've been busy. Chapman wants the *Storm Petrel* ready for launch in a month. He's got a big shipment comin' in from France and the *Zephyr*'s fully contracted. How are you, my dunlin?' He squeezed her hand, kissing it firmly, whilst surveying the shore for anyone watching.

'Oh, Jack, I've missed you! How's your hand?' Kate asked, observing him covetously. *How handsome he looks!* When they were apart, she always forgot quite how compelling his physical presence was until he stood before her in the flesh: a presence that never ceased to turn her to jelly and marvel at her good fortune in snaring such a prize. She wanted to show him off yet at the same time keep him only for herself. At that moment she couldn't really care what he was mixed up in. All she saw was that he was the most compelling, charismatic and desirable man she knew.

'It's fine, my love, no problem now. I hardly miss it – my finger, that is!' He smiled.

Kate decided to be honest with him. 'Jack, Uncle Harry spoke to Mama about a fight with the free traders at Havergate Island. He said he cut someone's hand with a cutlass.' She took a deep breath. 'It *was* you, wasn't it?'

Jack knew there was no point in lying to her anymore. *May as well come clean.* He stood up and tossed a pebble into the water, watching it skim across the surface, disturbing a group of redshanks probing the muddy shallows.

'I suppose you're going to lecture me on the error of my ways, eh, Kate?' he said bitterly, knowing any denial was pointless. 'You know, we lost a whole night's cargo that night, besides one man dead and two injured! God knows it's hard enough makin' a living, but to go through all that for nuthin'...' His voice trailed off, as he relived the battle on the shingle, his fight with the exciseman, saw again the flash of the blade that disfigured him and how he, transfixed with shock, was yanked away from danger by one of his comrades as he stared in disbelief at the severed finger lying at his feet. He half expected Kate to finish with him there and then but was rewarded by her words.

'No, Jack,' Kate sighed sadly, 'I won't lecture you. I hate what you do, but I will stand by you. I love you, Jack, but from now on don't lie to me anymore. I'm not going to tell anyone, you know that. You know how my father died. It would kill my mother to learn I was seeing someone mixed up with the free trade.'

'I know, my dunlin, and I'm sorry, that's why I didn't say nothin'.' Jack heaved a sigh of relief at unburdening his secret and being assured of her loyalty. He had taken a risk telling her, but she had guessed anyway and he knew she would not betray him, much as she disagreed with his motives.

He turned back to her and pulled her to him with a grateful kiss of passion which she readily returned, savouring his body warmth and the pleasing smell of wood shavings and wax. It was then he noticed the bracelet. Kate had quite forgotten she was still wearing it.

Jack grasped her wrist. 'What's this, Kate?' he enquired, suddenly peevish, jealousy catching him unawares with a depth of feeling he had not conceded until now.

'Oh, Jack, it means nothing!' Kate tried to assure him, pulling her arm away, annoyed with herself for not removing it earlier. 'Edward Sawyer gave it to me. He wants to marry me, but I'm going to refuse him.'

'Edward Sawyer, the miller's son?' Jack asked incredulously. 'You've not been seein' *him*?'

'Well, yes, but *only* because Mama wishes it. If she thinks I'm stepping out with Edward she won't question my whereabouts when I go to meet *you*, Jack.' She looked up at him imploringly, wishing he would understand.

Jack ignored the explanation, his mind fixed on the fact another man was giving Kate gifts and clearly expecting something in return. 'If it's pretty trinkets you want, lass, I can get you plenty o' those!' he retorted resentfully, turning his back and gazing out over the river, feigning sudden interest in a heavily laden Thames barge making its way slowly upriver with a cargo of coal, its red sails reflecting soft focussed in the placid water of the Deben.

Kate clutched his arm. 'Oh, Jack, of course not! It's *you* I want! *Please* understand! Can't you see it's a perfect cover-up? Stops folk gossiping about who I may or may not be seeing! Edward means nothing at all to me. I don't find him in the *least* bit attractive.' She lowered her voice. 'Not like I do *you*, Jack. I haven't even kissed him... not properly.' She turned him to face her and the hurt in his eyes twisted like a knife in her gut.

'So when are you gonna refuse him then?' he asked moodily, the compliment unheeded in the face of his jealousy.

'He's given me 'til harvest-time to answer him. I'll tell him then.'

'You gonna tell him about us?'

'No... well, maybe I should, to stop him pursuing me further. *Should* I tell him, Jack?'

'Up to you, lass,' he replied grumpily, as though it mattered not. 'You'll have to tell your ma, though, too. It'll soon get round you've refused him, unless, of course, you're ashamed o' me.' He realised as soon as he had said it, he sounded immature and defensive. *Grow up, Howell!* he scolded himself silently, remonstrating with his bruised ego.

'Of course, I'm not ashamed of you, Jack! How could I be? You're hard-working, skilful, brave and quite the handsomest man in Suffolk!' Kate smiled and was relieved to see Jack break into a smile too.

'Well, it's a good thing I'm seein' the prettiest lass in Suffolk then, or else there'd be some stiff competition!' he joked, his puerile comment passed over, his irritation soothed, his vanity boosted by her compliment. 'But seriously, though, my dunlin, folk will talk and try to discredit you out of jealousy, and I don't suppose Sawyer will be too pleased when you turn him down.'

'I don't care what people say... or him!' Kate continued. 'T'will be a relief not to be sneaking around anymore. Jack, you *must* know I love you and no-one else?' She reached for his hand and held it tenderly against her cheek.

Before he could reply, the clock of St Mary's struck three. Kate looked up. 'I've got to go! Mama will wonder where I am.'

'Oh, Kate, you are more than I deserve!' Jack sighed, embracing her once more with a kiss of unconcealed passion, regretting his outburst of possessiveness, his pride restored by her flattering words. They walked slowly around to the front of the boatshed and said their farewells, Kate turning to wave before running up the path, her cheeks aflame with lustful ardour, her lips still tingling from his kiss.

'Where have you been for so long? Harry's waiting to take us back,' Ellen admonished her daughter testily as they met outside the drapers.

'Forgive me, Mama. I had to wait for the foreman at Chapman's,' Kate lied breathlessly, her flushed cheeks and sparkling eyes casting seeds of doubt in Ellen's mind. She knew better than to question Kate further to avoid more falsehoods. She would find out the truth in good time; she always did.

Chapter Four

August and harvest-time came round sooner than Kate wished. It had been a warm summer and the crops had ripened well. Kate joined the women of Orford and its environs at the annual harvesting, always a welcome boost to the family's modest income. This year, however, Kate's usual upbeat demeanour was soured by her promise to Edward hanging over her like a sentence. She hated confrontation and always shied away from facing an unpleasant scene, but she knew it had to be done, if only to prove her sincerity to Jack. She dreaded Mama's reaction but now she had turned eighteen she was an adult. *Surely free to make my own choices?* she determined assertively.

Toiling all day from 5am under a hot sun, gathering up the scythed crops into sheaves, binding it together before stacking it in stooks to dry, the labourers sweated from their backbreaking work, briefly punctuating the long hours with welcome stops for ale, bread and cheese. The women broke the monotony by singing or gossiping, the younger ones eyeing up the farmhands, who vied with each other to complete their tasks manfully and earn the respect of the womenfolk. Kate, however, had no interest in any of the young men who tried to catch her eye – none of them were a match for her Jack, although she was not averse to sneaking a furtive glance at the abundance of sun-kissed muscular-bound torsos of those who had discarded their sweat-soaked shirts. It was nature's way, she conceded ruefully – desire rising in the veins of her newly fledged adulthood like sap through a sapling; however, she was content to reserve her affections purely for her man and hoped he would do the same for her.

At the harvest supper, held on Orford village green, everyone was in good spirits, the landowners providing their hungry workers with fine fare and victuals: folk songs given a boisterous airing, musicians playing lively jigs with fiddle and pipe, children excitedly chasing each other round the trestle tables and young folk dancing. It was a rare treat for the poorer folk and nobody was going to turn down the chance of a good blowout at their master's expense.

Kate spotted Edward arriving with his father and another young man, and her heart sank. Any minute now he would expect an answer. She was still wearing his bracelet, but with the intention of returning it to him, and busied herself fetching and carrying jugs of ale and fruit pies until she could put it off no longer. With the food all served, she sat down to eat, though somehow her appetite was lacking. She knew Edward was watching her and as their eyes met he inclined his head towards Quay Street. With another rendition of 'Oh No John' breaking out from the inebriated workers, he took Kate's hand and led her down to the quayside, the folk song's prophetic words almost mocking in their appositeness to her situation. Kate shivered despite the warm night, attempting to make small talk and delay the inevitable. However, her determined suitor was not swayed from his mission; he wanted his answer.

'Well, Kate?' Edward demanded as they reached the jetty, turning to face her and taking both her hands in his.

Kate flinched; his fingers were limp and sweaty to the touch, and she was glad the darkness hid the distaste on her face.

'Do you have my answer? Will you marry me?' he asked keenly, fully expecting an affirmative response.

Kate took a deep breath and pulled her hands away; she could not look at him. 'Forgive me, Edward, the answer is no. I cannot marry you.'

There was silence, apart from the muted echoes of singing and laughter coming from the market square, and she wondered for a moment if he had heard what she said. Just as she was about to repeat her answer, Edward's face hardened, his eyes narrowed, his jaw clenched and Kate braced herself for an outburst. As she expected, his response was brusque, all softness immediately gone from his voice, immediately confirming to her she had made the right decision.

'Cannot?' he snapped. 'There is no impediment as far as I can see, Kate.'

She knew she would have to mention Jack now. If she gave any other reason, he would dismiss it as trivial and persist in his advances until she would be forced to admit the truth with the one answer that would halt any further claims on her affections.

'I am sorry, Edward, there's someone else.'

Another silence. He turned away. A questioning *hoo-hoo, hoo* from a tawny owl perched high up on an oak branch was all he needed to add to the humiliation rising in his breast.

'But you told me there was nobody! So you lied!' he argued defensively, staring into the gloomy wastes of Lanthorn Marshes.

Yes, I did lie, Kate thought defiantly, as she stared at his back, seeing his fists clench, *but only to spare your feelings!* She knew what was coming next.

With simmering rage and chagrin, he spun round to face her. 'Who is he?' he demanded, snapping with such force it made Kate start.

'He's a carpenter from Chapman's, I'm so sorry, Edward.' Kate twisted her hands uncomfortably.

'I see,' he retorted, tight-lipped. 'How long has this been going on?'

'Quite some time. I... I didn't know what to do, Edward, forgive me.'

'What's his name?'

Kate did not want to name her lover, but she knew it would not stay secret for long. *Best get it over with.*

'Jack. Jack Howell.'

Edward swore under his breath. 'Jack Howell who sails with Dick and Nate Halesworth on the *Sandpiper*?' He swore again.

Kate did not reply, which he took for confirmation.

'You know they're suspected of free trading? Not been caught in the act yet, but it's only a matter of time. You know that man I was with tonight at the supper? He's in the Service and knows which fishing luggers are suspect. Honestly, Kate, are these the sort of men you want to be mixed up with?' he asked, his anger now turning to incredulity.

'Jack's a boat builder, he wouldn't...' Kate defended weakly, her voice receding and her brow creasing, as she wrestled with the guilt of what she now knew about Jack.

'Jack's a boat builder!' Edward mimicked scathingly. 'How convenient! Honestly, Kate, with your father dead and your uncle in the Service I would have thought you had more sense! Have you told your mother?' Without pausing for a response, he scoffed acerbically, '...No, of course you haven't!', answering his own question.

'Not yet, but I will,' Kate confirmed meekly.

'I'll save you the trouble!' Edward turned on his heel and strode off towards the village.

'*No*, Edward!' Kate sprang after him. 'Let *me* tell her, please!'

Edward ignored her plea but stopped walking as he remembered his gift. He grabbed her wrist as she reached out to him and roughly unfastened the bracelet. 'You won't be needing this anymore. I'll find someone who appreciates it!'

'Edward!' Kate called after him. 'I'm sorry!' She sank to her knees, sobbing. *Why does he have to be so bitter?* she agonised, upset by his sudden coldness and abashed by her own actions.

'Goodbye, Katherine,' he called flatly without turning his head.

Kate ran back to the cottage and wearily ascended the stairs to her room. She could not face the merry-making, or the stares that would come her way from Edward's father and exciseman friend, whom he would surely tell straight away. The news would soon be all over town and it would not be long before he would have a string of hopeful valentines hoping to ensnare the heir to Sawyer's Mills. This very minute he was no doubt bewailing her refusal of marriage to Mama. She could see Ellen's face, shocked and angry, sympathising with him for her daughter's behaviour and attempting to initiate a reconciliation. *Surely Kate did not mean it? Give her time, she is young*, she would say placatively. The merry-making continued long after the children had been ushered to their beds, each successive ditty increasing in its lewdness, until one by one the revellers fell into drunken stupor. For Kate, however, the expected tirade came on cue at breakfast time the next morning.

'I'm ashamed of you, Katherine! My own daughter thinks she's too good for Edward Sawyer! You know how hard it is to make ends meet? Since your father died, I've struggled to put food on the table, and the one chance we have to better our lot and you turn it down? How can you be so selfish?' Ellen slammed the steaming pot of porridge down on the table and ladled it roughly into Kate's bowl, splashing the mixture carelessly.

'I'm sorry, Mama, but I don't love him. I don't want to be Edward's wife.' Kate's eyes filled with tears.

'If you were gentry, you'd have no choice, girl. You'd be forced to wed the most suitable match. Love wouldn't come into it.'

'Well, we're *not* gentry, Mama!' Kate argued, but Ellen ignored the indisputable assertion.

'So, who is this boat builder you've got your eye on, then? He'd better not be mixed up in anything unlawful! Your father would turn in his grave!'

Kate knew her mother would use Father's death to prick her conscience and clearly Edward had not been able to resist revealing Kate's choice of suitor.

'Jack Howell from Chapman's. He's a skilled craftsman with good prospects,' she answered quietly.

'Hmm, I will ask Harry if he knows of him. Well, as long as he's respectable and can look after you. Has he proposed?'

'No, Mama, he's still on an apprentice wage.'

'Well, don't get serious with him then, Kate. Keep your options open. I will keep an ear out for any eligible young businessmen and Harry will no doubt know a few young officers in the Service who would be pleased to pair up with you.'

Kate stared into the porridge congealing unappetisingly in her bowl.

Ellen regarded her daughter's tear-stained cheeks and felt a pang of regret for her harsh words. She was young once and had tasted the sweet fruits of young love. Despite her disappointment for the match she had harboured such hopes for, Ellen understood, though she would not admit it to her daughter. Her voice softened. 'You're a pretty girl, Kate. Use it to your advantage. You could have your pick. If you weren't, you would have to take what you could get and be satisfied.'

Kate knew her mother was right. *Am I being selfish? Should I do my duty and settle for security and a life of comfortable monotony, regardless of love? Yes, God has granted me fair features, but does that mean I have to throw them away?* Age and loss of looks would come soon enough. No, Jack was all she wanted. If God willed he was destined to die by the King's sword, musket ball or hangman's noose, then so be it. She would take from life what she could while it was there for the taking; she lived for the moment, the here and now, not the dreary prospect of a secure but humdrum future as the wife of a local businessman; that's why she and Jack understood each other perfectly.

Chapter Five

Relieved now that her secret was out, Kate relaxed into her work at the inn and in her spare time obediently assisted in her mother's darning and dressmaking business, hoping to win back Ellen's favour. She could not wait to tell Jack they need sneak around no more and were officially stepping out together. She wanted her mother to meet him, for she would surely be impressed by his good looks and charm, but since the launch of the *Storm Petrel* she had not seen him.

She soon learned from local gossip that Edward was pursuing several young girls and was happily enjoying the attention of more than one marriageable female. *Good luck to him*, she thought, relieved her refusal had not dampened his ardour or sunk him into depression. In fact, the speed of his recovery confirmed to her she had made the right decision and he was not as devastated by the rebuttal as she had imagined. It seemed clear he simply wanted a pretty young wife to parade around as a trophy to boost his bruised ego. Had she known he was seething inside and avowing revenge on Jack Howell, she might not have felt so comforted.

As the autumn colours emerged and the nights drew in, there was increased activity within the Preventive Service. Dark nights and longer hours of darkness were just what the free traders needed to carry out their operations, and the watches were stepped up. Bills were posted, reminding townsfolk of the penalties for receiving and concealing goods, and rewards were increased for those willing to identify miscreants, but despite the temptation, few felt able to jeopardise their safety and security, preferring instead to turn a blind eye and live a peaceful, if impecunious, life.

Becky had called on Ellen and Kate one Sunday, being her fortnightly day off, bringing with her a surplus mutton pie from the hall kitchens, kindly donated by Mrs Barrell the cook, whose somewhat apt name was the frequent butt of jests, considering her portly figure.

'Please thank Mrs Barrell, Becky,' Ellen said, barely disguising a smirk of mirth at the unfortunate appellation.

'She must have rued the day she met Mr Barrell,' quipped Kate.

'I'm sure she loved him very much!' rejoined Ellen, before all three descended into giggles.

Becky explained that to save embarrassment on all sides Mary Barrell was simply addressed as 'Cook' within the household, Lord Seymour's family included. More mirth ensued before the conversation soon turned to Kate's rejection of Edward Sawyer. Becky had heard all about the harvest supper and how Edward's proposal of marriage had been refused.

'How could you refuse him, Kate?' Becky asked her sister with astonishment. 'He's handsome and rich! ...

or he will be one day! I wish he'd ask me! I'd have him!'

'Becky!' Kate exclaimed, irritated at her sister's immodesty.

'What's wrong with that?' Becky exclaimed indignantly, her mouth full of pie.

'You're too young for a start, young lady!' Ellen remonstrated in support of Kate.

'No, I'm not! Plenty of girls marry at fourteen – besides, I *know* he likes me!'

'Really? And how did you work that one out?' Kate queried, aware that the miller had not been celibate since their parting and was actively flirting with several girls at the same time. She worried for her sister's reputation and virtue, should she appear too eager.

'He told me!' Becky pronounced proudly.

'When did he tell you?' Kate stopped eating and stared at her sister.

'A few days ago when he came to the hall to deliver some flour. I offered him a drink and we got chatting. He said I was just as pretty as my sister, if not prettier!' she replied smugly.

'I'm sure he was just being polite, Becky,' Ellen interjected palliatively, glancing at Kate's expression. A thought struck her that perhaps she could wed her younger daughter to the miller's son instead, but from her elder daughter's stony face she thought it best to keep that idea to herself for the moment.

'Well, *I* like him,' Becky continued. 'If he asks me out, *I* won't refuse him,' she said pointedly.

Kate scowled at her sister for stoking the fire of her mother's disapproval.

'Kate's seeing a boat builder at Chapman's now, Becky.' Ellen attempted to steer the conversation away from Edward without success.

'Oh, yes, I heard that too. Edward told me some of Chapman's men are in with the free traders.' Becky smirked smugly at Kate.

'Rubbish, Becky, that's just tittle-tattle!' Kate remonstrated sharply, enough to make Ellen look up at her suspiciously. Kate caught her mother's eye and looked away, fearful her guilt would betray her. She could have hit Becky. It had taken more than a week of singing Jack's praises to bring Ellen round to accepting her new suitor and in one sentence Becky had cast doubt on his integrity. The trouble was, her sister could not realise how close to the truth she had come. Now Becky was flirting with Edward, which would not end well, Kate brooded. The thought of her sister taking up with one of her cast-offs was distasteful and smacked of consanguinity, despite the fact they had not entered into an engagement. Besides, she had seen another side to the miller's son that made her feel uncomfortable.

She got up and busied herself with clearing away the dishes, attempting to curtail any further discussion about her sweetheart and invite any further probing from her mother, as to his worthiness.

Uncle Harry arrived later that afternoon together with Thomas, who was eager to show off his new uniform to his mother and sisters. He changed into his blue naval frock coat, knee breeches and white stockings, topped off by a black bicorn hat, strutting pompously around the kitchen, his pride only matched by his mother's. Becky hugged him and flattered him, but although Kate made all the right noises, she felt a weight in her stomach that one day her little brother might encounter her lover on the shore some dark night, the consequences of which were too horrible to imagine. She knew Jack would hesitate to harm Thomas, but her brother had never seen Jack face to face, who to him would just be another lawbreaker and therefore a legitimate target, and if it came to a fight Tom would be no match for a seasoned fighter like her lover.

Harry gave Ellen bills to post around the town, which she agreed to do. 'Anything to help in the fight against smuggling.' She smiled at her brother-in-law. In return Harry offered to take Becky back to Sudbourne on his way home, although it was a two-mile detour, but he knew he could cut across through Butley on his way back to Woodbridge.

Ellen and Kate waved off their visitors later that afternoon, Becky sitting contentedly on the front seat of the trap, wedged between her brother and uncle, satiated on mutton pie and her mother's delicious apple tart. For a while the conversation was trivial, but Becky had something on her mind that was troubling her conscience. Nestled between her two relatives, she felt safe and protected, and Harry would be sure to thank her for the information she was about to impart, despite her promise to her sister, as after all, she persuaded herself, she was simply being an honest citizen.

'Uncle Harry?'

'Yes, m'dear?'

Becky went on to explain to him what she had told Kate about the late-night goings-on at the Hall. 'Should I tell the housekeeper?' she concluded.

Harry abruptly pulled on the reins and halted the pony. 'No!' he said forcefully, surprising Becky with his acerbity. 'Do not say *anything* to anyone!' He echoed Kate's words. 'You could be in great danger, Becky. When does this happen?'

'About once a month, Uncle. I mean, why in the middle of the night when they can't see where they're going? Do you think it's those free traders?'

Harry ignored her question. 'Do you know when they might be expected next?'

'No, but I did hear the groom mention something about Sunday week, but he stopped talking when he saw I was looking.'

'Now, look, Becky, do *not* say another word to anyone. I want you to keep this just between me and yourself, alright? I will deal with it. Understand?'

'Yes, Uncle Harry.'

'Good girl.' He snapped the reins and the pony jerked the trap forward. Harry let Becky off at the main gate. 'It's best I don't drive in,' he said. 'You don't want anyone to think you have brought the coastguard to spy on them!' He chuckled. 'Seriously, though, Becky, do not speak to anyone about what you saw.'

'No, I won't, Uncle Harry. Goodbye, thank you for the ride.'

Harry turned the trap back down the road and Becky waved before making her way to the kitchen. She felt relief at unburdening herself to Uncle Harry. He would know what to do.

'We're going to have to put a watch on the hall,' Harry said to Thomas as they drew away. 'We've suspected them for some time, but unless we catch them in the act, we can't prove anything. If we turn up to search the house, the goods'll be gone before we've even got to the gate! I only hope Becky keeps quiet. If the traders find out she's been spying on them, well… it doesn't bear thinking about.'

'Sudbourne's quite a way from the coast. How would they get the goods there?' Thomas enquired as they passed through the woods.

'I imagine they'll bring it up the Alde Tom. They'll either off-load at Slaughden and carry it across the spit to the river or sail it up the Ore from North Weir point.'

'Do you think the Marquess of Hertford knows about it?'

Harry took a deep breath. 'I'd be surprised if he did. He's never in residence and if he were, the smugglers would be foolish to try to carry out their business right under his nose. It will most likely be some of the estate's employees who are involved.'

'Will you question them?'

'What? And alert them to our intentions?! There's no point, Tom. They would only plead ignorance and the family has powerful friends in high places. If any of them are involved, they'd close ranks, the goods would be long gone and we'd get nowhere. No, we're more interested in the traders themselves than those who might benefit from their unlawful activities. Cut the roots and the tree won't grow. Simply prune the branches and it just sprouts elsewhere.'

Two weeks later, Becky was awoken from her sleep. She sat up with a start and stared into the darkness. It sounded like a shot.

Chapter Six

Down at the Coastguard House at Aldeburgh, the customs and excisemen were readying themselves for a night's work patrolling the shore. They knew that the newly launched brig the *Storm Petrel* was off-shore out from Bawdsey Point with a full cargo of goods from Calais awaiting possible rendezvous with a lugger. Captain Hammond was commanding the new craft, leaving Joe Willis to take his place in command of the *Zephyr*. The brig had been followed at a discreet distance by a Preventive Service cutter awaiting just such an assignation; however, Michael Chapman's latest ship was fast under a full head of sail and the cutter lost sight of her before she slowed two miles out from North Weir Point. The night was promising to be dark and stormy, perfect cover for smuggling, and both law breakers and law enforcers knew it.

What the King's men did not know was the location of the drop – it could be anywhere from Felixstowe to Southwold – but their usual informant had been killed at Shingle Street, ostensibly by the servicemen but more likely by the smugglers who had discovered a traitor in their midst. His body had been picked up afterwards, a musket ball wound shattering his skull, his brains spilling out onto the sand, the gun appearing to have been discharged at close hand. Harry knew his men had not been fighting at such close quarters as to have inflicted such a wound. Their informant was only a young man, naive and foolish, tempted by the lure of the King's pardon and promise of indemnity. When Harry had first heard mention of the lad, he had remarked sadly that the youth was simply signing his own death warrant and sadly he was right, though repulsed at the thought of who could commit such a cold-blooded murder of one so young.

Tonight, the Service had to determine where to station the men. They couldn't patrol the whole Suffolk coastline, which was why so much smuggling activity went undetected, but with Becky's information Harry judged it could only Sudbourne and would likely be via the Alde that the manor house could be accessed unseen. He figured that a large haul could be better hidden in a vast estate, where it could be distributed at leisure, out of sight of gossiping townsfolk. The Deben was under the watch of the Woodbridge garrison, so his money tonight was on the Alde, which was always quieter, its long and winding course just the cover needed for a night's subterfuge. Besides, the river would be calmer than the tempestuous conditions out in the bay. He decided to station his men on the river side of Slaughden spit, with rowing craft at the ready, poised to intercept the smugglers as they landed on the far shore with their contraband. Quantities of tea and liquor had recently been found buried in the shingle at Orford Ness recently for possible later relocation and the smugglers would know not to land on the seaward side for a while.

Out in the North Sea, on the deck of the *Storm Petrel*, there came a shout from the lookout; a light from the ramparts of Orford Castle Keep was seen flashing once, then twice through the murk. This was the signal they needed. Sails dropped and anchor chain released, the brig hove to about two miles off Orford Haven. She lay low in the water, her hold heavy with cargo, enough of it legitimate to ensure her authenticity, bound for Ipswich, Felixstowe, Woodbridge and Southwold but concealed within her bulkheads, a plenteous amount of illicit goods to make a healthy profit for her owner and for the many anonymous recipients of her luxury payload. Captain Hammond scanned the coast and could just make out the bow wave of the *Sandpiper* scudding towards him, illuminated briefly by the shafts of light from both Orford light towers. There was no sign of the King's ship to the south and he figured they would be waiting nearer the mouth of the Orwell to board and inspect his ship's cargo legitimately bound for discharging at Ipswich.

Ninety minutes later, having picked up its load from the brig, the *Sandpiper* raced through the tide at North Weir Point, her shallow draught skilfully negotiating the narrow passage between the Orford Ness peninsular and Shingle Street. Entering the quiet lower reaches of the River Ore, the lugger snaked along the channel past Havergate Island and Orford Quay, a dark-sailed shadow silently skimming the water, showing no light, her tackle greased and muffled, her name blacked out, her crew tight-lipped and alert, scanning the banks for signs of activity. Jack stood on deck with Dick and Nate Halesworth, the father-and-son owners of the *Sandpiper*, and focussed his spyglass on the shingle spit but could see no movement. Stacked at the stern of the lugger were barrels, bales, chests, tubs, bolts and casks containing spirits, tobacco, tea, coffee, salt, cloth and soap. Staring into the darkness, the crew were taut and edgy, poised to react instantly at the first sign of discovery, but so far all was quiet.

Pulled up onshore, once the river had snaked past Aldeburgh and entered the S-bend, there were half a dozen jolly boats, small rowing craft propelled by four oarsmen, oars muffled, ready to off-load the contraband onto the packhorses and wagons standing in readiness on the west bank. Jack and his shipmates were armed with flintlock pistols, clubs and cutlasses, some bought from suppliers in the Netherlands but many seized during battles with Revenue men. Some of these recruits were little more than boys, certainly no match for the seasoned and skilful night traders fuelled by years of hardship and conflict, for whom the rewards were too great to pass up and the punishment too unappealing.

Across on the east bank of the Alde, the excisemen waited on the shingle bank, lying prostrate amidst the damp stones, the cold penetrating their uniforms and chilling the bones.

'I hope Goldsmith's right about this,' the sergeant grumbled. 'Gonna catch me death out here before much longer!'

All the servicemen could hear was the crashing of the waves on the shore behind them and the lapping of the river in front, there being no cover to protect them from the relentless wind. Billowing storm clouds hurtled past, a yellow glow where a ghostly moon briefly shone through a thin veil of water vapour, only to disappear a moment later. As their eyes adjusted to the dark they could make out the far bank of the Alde: the river one minute a wide band of silver in the elusive moonshine, a dark black void the next. Harry trained his spyglass downriver. *Yes!* He could just make out the outline of an approaching lugger, snaking silently upstream, showing no light. Becky's information had been correct and his hunch about the location accurate, although he couldn't be sure where they would drop anchor. He ran along the shingle, crouching down to alert his men, instructing them to wait until the lugger passed before manning the boats. They would follow her upstream and wait until the drop was well underway before intercepting the smugglers.

On board the *Sandpiper*, Jack was more nervous than usual tonight and although he had been fortunate so far, there was always that feeling that his luck would eventually run out. After Jack's parents died, he had become close with Nate, his childhood playmate, and Dick, Nate's father, had taken Jack under his wing, teaching the two boys the rudiments of sailing, fishing and trading. Dick had recommended Jack to Michael Chapman at the shipyard, recognising the young man's skill and craftsmanship in carpentry. Jack felt he owed Dick for his kindness and if the fisherman was mixed up in illegal trading, Jack would not be the one to betray his benefactor and had soon become a trusted and valued member of the crew.

Now, after several years of night-time activity, he found he actually enjoyed the thrill of the free trade and the huge profits to be had, rendering him able to consider buying his own property or starting up in business. He hoped to share a future with Kate, and leaning against the ship's rail he was suffused with a warm sensation at the thought of caressing her soft skin and womanly curves. He was relieved she had guessed the truth about him and he would no longer need to lie to her. She would be his partner in life and in crime until they could start a successful business and grow rich and old together. He smiled to himself contentedly at the prospect before a cold gust brought him sharply back to actuality. His wound was troubling him with a dull ache and he felt the odd sensation that his finger was still attached, until the stump came into contact with a hard surface and reminded him somewhat painfully that it wasn't. He shivered as the wind whined through the rigging, the lugger's shifting direction luffing the sails with a vibrating shudder. The drop was imminent. *So far so good*, he thought, dismissing his earlier qualms as they turned into Westrow Reach.

Almost immediately a light blinked on the larboard shore. The crew trimmed sails and hove to, dropping anchor midstream. The waiting tub men rowed the small boats out to the *Sandpiper* and swiftly and silently, barrel by barrel, crate by crate, her cargo was discharged. As the last few items were being unloaded, Jack climbed down into one of the craft and pushed off towards the bank. Suddenly a musket shot rang out, echoing across the marshes. Jack swore and cocked his pistol, resting it on his arm, aiming in the direction of a number of small naval craft that were seen rapidly approaching across from the Slaughden bank. His comrades did the same and several rounds of shots fired from the lugger found their targets amongst the excisemen. *How did they know we were here?* Jack brooded as a musket ball whizzed past his ear. *No time to think about that now!* he decided, ducking behind a crate as another shot hit the side of the jolly boat, sending wood splinters flying.

Dick Halesworth swiftly weighed anchor, set the sails and turned the lugger about, heading downriver, leaving the rest of the gang to fight it out, knowing they would soon disperse amongst the maze of pathways, scrub and marshy inlets. It would be hard for the soldiers to follow, confused by the unfamiliar heaths and wetland, and they could easily be picked out in their bright uniforms. The remaining smugglers were keeping the soldiers pinned down midriver, as volleys of shots were exchanged, but gradually as the traders ran out of gunpowder, they turned and fled away from the river, a good quantity of contraband having already gone, loaded in panniers on the waiting horses. Jack and old Ben were with the last group of men to disembark from the *Sandpiper* and therefore the last to reach the shore. Jack reached for his cutlass as the first soldier lunged at him and they set to thrusting and parrying vigorously for what seemed to Jack like an eternity.

The man he faced was an accomplished swordsman and Jack was lucky to parry each blow. However, he was stronger and as their weapons clashed, Jack slid his blade down his opponent's blade and caught the soldier on his forearm with a heavy blow, as the release of tension drove his weapon downwards. As the man went down Jack barely had time to draw breath before another was at him, slashing purposefully, the razor-sharp edge just missing Jack's face as he leapt away from the falling steel. He jumped forward for a return thrust, but just as he did so, his foot encountered a rabbit hole, his ankle buckled and he fell forwards. The soldier raised his cutlass for a decisive strike but immediately a fountain of blood erupted from the man's wrist where his hand should have been and his legs gave way under him. Jack leapt to his feet and reached for his weapon, staring down at the young man writhing on the ground. He looked up. Ben had come up from behind and landed a disabling blow, severing the soldier's hand. Jack stared, cursing with surprise, then broke into a grateful smile.

'Well, if you're gonna go pussy-footin' around, Jack...' the old sailor quipped dryly; then, glancing upriver, he clinched Jack's forearm. 'We best get goin', lad, there's more o' 'em comin'.'

Jack looked down at the injured man, a part of him concerned for a fellow human being now disfigured for life, before Ben wrenched him away. 'Come on! Leave 'im! He'll live!' Jack forced his gaze away, straining his eyes upstream, and could make out two craft carrying more Preventive men approaching from the direction of Snape. Harry, meanwhile, had left the reinforcements to battle it out with the remaining smugglers and was leading a party of men across the heath, intending to cut off any stragglers making for the hall.

A group of Jack's men were still fighting on the bank, but some had broken off and run, seeing they were about to be outnumbered. Jack and Ben followed them, making their way swiftly and quietly across the heath towards Sudbourne, skirting the marshes to their right. Jack was limping from his twisted ankle, but with adrenaline pumping he ignored the aching joint and lumbered on, following the older man.

'M'ek for the Chequers Inn,' Ben urged. 'T' landlord's an old mate. We can lay low in the cellar 'til mornin'.' The pair jogged along in the darkness, the sound of musket fire diminishing behind them as they drew away from the river.

'I hope Dick, aaargh… got the *Sandpiper* away… aaargh,' Jack reflected as he ran, grimacing each time his foot took the full impact of his weight.

'He'll be a'right. He'll most likely take 'er up t' Butley as far as he can,' Ben reasoned. 'They won't follow him up there. Even if they did, ther'll be no goods aboard and Dick'll claim he were just out fishin'.'

After a couple of miles' sprinting over the heath, Jack lolloping awkwardly behind his companion, the pair neared Sudbourne and stopped to rest, concealing their weapons under some gorse bushes.

'How did they know where the drop was?' Jack rasped, breathless from their sustained flight.

'Damned if I know,' his companion spat contemptuously. 'Mebbe someone at the hall has a loose tongue?' he suggested.

Jack didn't reply, his mind still dwelling on his throbbing joint and his near-brush with death on the riverbank.

'Thank you, Ben. I thought I were mincemeat then!' Jack breathed heavily as he sank down to rest, removing his boot and rubbing his swelling ankle.

'Aye, I'm yer guardian angel, lad!' Ben chuckled, giving Jack an affectionate slap on the back. He had grown fond of the young man, who exhibited the spirit and drive he would have liked in a son, had he ever begotten one.

Behind them the sound of gunfire had ceased and there was no sight nor sound of any pursuing servicemen, just the moan of the wind blasting across the scrub. Ben shared the last of his hip flask with Jack before they got up and joined the Snape Road in the direction of the Chequers Inn.

The pair were almost upon the inn when suddenly a command rang out. 'Halt, in the King's name!'

'Christ! They've been waitin' for us!' Ben exclaimed as he and Jack were immediately surrounded, half a dozen muskets aimed straight at them.

Jack swore under his breath, blaming his present condition for not thinking clearly. *How could I have been so careless?* They should have known the road would be watched.

'We've got two more of 'em, sir,' said a young corporal proudly, as Harry Goldsmith approached with several more recruits, muskets aimed and ready.

'Good work, Corporal. Fetch me a light, will you?' As the lamp was handed to Harry he held it up to his captives.

'I know him.' A soldier stepped forward, pointing at Jack. It was Edward's friend from the harvest supper. 'He's Jack Howell from Chapman's boatyard, and that's old Ben Fosdyke the fisherman, who sails with the Halesworths.'

Harry's eyes narrowed and he studied his prisoners, his gaze now resting on Jack's gloved hand. The young man before him looked familiar. He seized the glove and wrenched it off Jack's hand. 'Just as I thought! How do you explain this then, Howell?' He grasped his wrist roughly.

'A work accident,' Jack said sullenly.

'Oh, yes, a likely story!' scoffed Harry. 'You lost that finger at Shingle Street – I know because I took it off!' he exclaimed triumphantly.

'Dunno what you're talking about,' Jack snapped defensively, although he too had recognised his combatant from the fight on the shingle.

'No? Tell that to the judge, young man. You'll go down for this. Get 'em in the cart with the others.' Harry gesticulated to his men. 'Good work, lads.'

Just at that moment, a shot rang out, and then another and another. A party of smugglers had re-grouped and come to rescue their comrades. Two soldiers went down and the rest ran for cover, letting go of their charges. Jack and Ben, who were being held beside the cart, jumped up on the seat and snatched the reins, the terrified ponies breaking into a gallop, sending them and the captured smugglers hurtling towards Orford, leaving a volley of gunfire behind them. At the intersection with the road to Chillesford they veered off to the right, down the track towards Sudbourne Hall, where, using the wooded parkland for cover, they managed to halt the wagon, calm the horses and cut the ropes restraining their cohorts, one by one dispersing into the half-light of the approaching dawn.

'That was close! I thought we were goners then!' Ben chuckled with relief to his companion as they jogged through the woods.

Jack was exhausted. 'I'm done in, Ben,' he said as he stopped in his stride to take a breath. Not just his ankle but his hand was also pulsing where his half-healed wound had been knocked. 'Should we go to the hall?' he suggested. 'They lent us their horses so they'll surely hide us. It's a big-enough place! Kate's sister works in the kitchens. She might help us.'

'No! The law'll be all over it this mornin' lookin' for the rest o' t' goods. It's best we keep away, today anyway. T' less folk know the better. Sister or no sister, we can't be sure she'd keep her trap shut!'

Ben's words made sense and all at once the thought struck Jack that maybe Becky had seen something and reported it to her uncle, unaware of its significance. *Best keep that to myself*, he concluded, as Ben continued, reminding him of their situation.

'Besides, they know 'oo we are now – there'll be a price on our 'eads soon enough to tempt the most 'onest o' folk!'

Jack swore as if the reality of his situation had just hit home. 'I can't go back to Chapman's. That'll be the first place they'll look!' He swore again.

'I know where you can hide out. I'll tek you ther' and then I'll find the *Sandpiper*. We need to lay low for a while,' his companion rasped, as they turned back in the direction of Orford.

Chapter Seven

As the morning sun broke over Lanthorn Marshes and a flock of oyster catchers probed the mudflats with their long, straight, scarlet beaks, the grey-haired sailor and his young companion approached the looming tower of Orford Castle Keep, ascended the steps and knocked on the main door of the twelfth-century fortress. The circular fortification abutted by three rectangular towers stood on raised ground overlooking the River Ore and was now the only remaining structure left in situ after the demolition of the outer walls. Much of the original stonework from the perimeter complex had been re-used by generations of owners of the Sudbourne Estate for new building projects, but so far, the keep was mainly intact, apart from a few crumbling stones on the ramparts. Still in the ownership of the Seymours, it functioned as a useful storage facility for supplies and building materials, with the upper floors utilised for accommodation when required, albeit basic. The caretaker Isaac Smith, a fisherman acquaintance of Ben's, held the keys and acted as both lookout and signalman. He used a spout lantern, designed to cast a long, straight, pin-pointed beam through its opening, which could be covered by hand for signalling, the 360° view from the battlements affording due warning of friend or foe approaching from land or sea. Jack had laughed when Ben told him about the resident warden.

'D'ye know everyone in Suffolk then, Ben?' he quipped.

'Aye, pretty much,' his comrade corroborated pragmatically.

Just as well. Jack smiled to himself, thankful that this cold-eyed old seadog was his friend and not his enemy and still feeling beholden to him for his timely intervention on the banks of the Alde.

After repeated knocking, Isaac Smith, rudely awoken by the early morning wake-up call, unbolted the heavy door and peered out. 'Wha'd'ye want at this hour?' he croaked crossly before acknowledging Ben. 'Oh, it's you, you'd better come in then.'

Ben explained the situation and, after some initial reluctance, Isaac agreed to shelter Jack for adequate recompense.

'If anyone comes callin', I'm denying all knowledge, mind.' He looked Jack up and down before showing the pair down some steps into the lower floor of the castle. It was dark, save for a single small lamp illuminating crates, kegs, bales, piles of wood and rope, nets, lobster pots, old wheels, and oars stacked against the circular walls. In the centre of the room was sunk a deep well, enclosed by an iron railing. 'You can bed down here, but I'll show you somewhere you can hide if the excise come callin'.'

He led Jack through a side door behind the fireplace, into a small chamber where, by the light of his lantern, they could make out some sacks of an unknown commodity leaning against the walls. Isaac moved several sacks to reveal a trap door neatly set into the wooden floorboards.

'Ye' can stay down here, 'til it's all clear. I'll put the sacks back to hide the trap,' he said, pulling up the trap door. A ladder fixed to the wall led down to a dungeon-like void with no windows, dank and dark but solid and soundproof, about fifty kegs of liquor stacked against one wall. 'You're not the first to have made use o' it,' Isaac commented sullenly.

Jack thanked Isaac, and he and Ben returned to the storeroom, as the caretaker replaced the bags. Jack sank down heavily on a pair of bales, a wave of fatigue and relief sweeping over him.

'Get word to Kate for me, would you, Ben? Ask her to bring food,' he urged his friend, before collapsing back on the bales to fall instantly asleep.

Leaving the Crown and Castle that night, Kate was startled by a sudden whisper from the shadows as she crossed the street towards River Cottage.

'Miss!' the voice hissed.

She stopped, peering into the blackness. 'Who is it?' she enquired, straining her eyes to make out the shape in the gloom. The iron grip she had felt before took hold of her arm.

'Message from Jack,' Ben hissed. 'He's in t'castle keep – bring food, tell no-one.'

Before Kate could answer, the disembodied hand released her arm and where the shadow had been was now just a void. She shuddered. Something about that man unnerved her, and the way he slunk around without making a sound was disconcerting, his sibilating voice implying menace, whether intended or not.

Lying in bed later, her thoughts were full of questions. *What has happened? Is Jack injured again? Why is he in the castle? Why does he need food?* It wasn't long before she knew why.

The Orford folk were full of gossip about the fight on the Alde between the Service and a band of smugglers and how some had been captured before an ambush facilitated their escape towards the grounds of Sudbourne Hall. She knew then Becky must have told Uncle Harry about the goings-on at the stables, but what she did not yet know was the fact Jack had been identified and was now a marked man. She was relieved to hear that despite many injured, no man on either side had been killed outright. *But then why is Jack holed up in the keep*, she puzzled, *when he could surely have returned to the boatyard? Keep calm*, she reasoned to herself, *I will find out soon enough.*

Leaving the inn the following night, her basket heavy with a meat pie, a hunk of cheese, half a loaf and a quart of ale, Kate's hooded figure hurried through the old castle walls a short distance from the inn and up the steep incline towards the towering mass of the keep. A partially clouded moon bathed the eastern elevation in an eerie luminescence while the shadowed rear of the castle stood out in black silhouette against the silvery ribbon of water it overlooked. Kate trod her way carefully around the looming walls, until she found the steps that led up to the entrance. Hastily mounting the stairway, she reached the pointed archway which would have originally housed a portcullis, before tapping gently on the thick oak panels of the weighty wooden door now barring the way. She heard the bolt slide across on the inside, and as the gap inched open, an arm pulled her quickly into the building.

'Jack!' she exclaimed, wide-eyed, as he took the basket from her, laid it down and embraced her ardently with an eager kiss of passion. Taking a breath, she pulled away from his arms to look at her lover in the dim light of the single lantern mounted in the lobby, observing his mud-stained clothes and unshaven, unkempt appearance. He did not appear to be badly injured, thank goodness, despite what looked like spatters of blood on his shirt and a swelling around the ankle, and her initial relief quickly turned to inquisition. She wanted answers.

'What are you doing here, Jack?' Jack took her hand and led her into the first-floor chamber lit by the smouldering embers from the capacious fireplace, then down a flight of stone steps into the dingy basement, sat her down on a bale and described the night's activities.

Kate listened, staring at him, horrified at the picture he painted and the slow realisation of his situation. Her eyes filled with tears, and the dread in her stomach of just such a scenario, now settling like a lead weight, all her dreams of a future with Jack now dashed. He was a wanted man; she could see bills being posted by her mother with Jack's name picked out in large type and no doubt those of other men who had been identified.

My mother! Oh, God! Ellen knew Jack Howell was the name of her daughter's suitor and her worst fears would be realised when Harry imparted news of his latest clash with the free traders. Ellen would be outraged. *Her own daughter a smuggler's moll, the very villains who murdered my father!*

'Oh, Jack, what are we to do?!' Kate wailed.

'Don't fret, my dunlin.' Jack swept her up in his arms again. 'We'll think of somethin'.' He kissed her wet cheeks tenderly and stroked her long dark hair, nestling his face into her neck as she wept. 'I'd like to know who gave us away, tho',' he remarked icily. 'Their life won't be worth a jot once the lads get wind of it.'

Kate stiffened and her stomach somersaulted. *Becky! Her revelations to Harry about late-night activities at Sudbourne!* Although she would not have known when it was to happen. Harry must have set a watch on the hall and worked out for himself the smugglers' likely tactics. Becky would no doubt be boasting to Edward about her part in the operation. *Edward!* She nearly uttered his name out loud as further comprehension struck her like a thunderbolt. Edward, whose friend was in the Service and who would soon be relaying Jack's involvement to the very person with a personal grudge to bear against his rival in love. Not only was Jack a fugitive from the law, but because of her, he would also be a target for private vengeance from her former suitor. She decided not to mention the fact to Jack yet. He already had enough to worry about.

'Jack, will you be safe here? Isn't this castle part of the Sudbourne estate?' Kate enquired uneasily, concerned as to who might turn up unexpectedly and give him away.

'Aye, my dunlin. That's why Ben brought me here. The caretaker's been helping us. The landowner lets us use the tower for signalling and he stores his goods here. We supply the gentry and they turn a blind eye. They're not the only ones to take advantage of the free trade, my dunlin. They're as averse to the cripplin' duty charges as anyone else!' He decided not to tell her about the secret cellar. The less she knew the better for her and for him.

Kate agreed to bring food as often as she could from the inn. Trade was brisk and the small amount would not be missed from Daniel Bird's kitchen, she told Jack. When she could, she promised him, she would try to bring him one of mother's delicious fruit tarts on the pretext of eating it herself. However, the prospect of a few missing tarts was nothing compared to the explosion of ire she knew she would face from her mother, now her suitor was branded a wanted man. Kate sighed resignedly, inwardly admonishing herself, *Well, you've made your bed now, my girl!*, before her thoughts turned to more immediate concerns.

'I'll get you a clean shirt, Jack. You can't keep wearing *that*.' She frowned, observing the mud and blood-spattered garment, a segment of sleeve flapping loosely where it had been slashed. 'There'll be some of John's that won't be missed, and I can wash and mend that one for you.'

'Thank you, my dunlin, but don't take any unnecessary chances. I'll be fine until I can arrange to get out of here. It's a risk for Isaac the caretaker to have me here, so I can't stop too long.'

'Where will you go?' Kate asked anxiously.

'Dunno yet, maybe Holland for a bit. I may need your help to get my belongings from Chapman's, though. I'll let you know, my dunlin.'

Fortunately for Kate, Uncle Harry had been too busy to visit Ellen for some days, giving Kate welcome breathing space and a chance to take stock of her predicament, while her mother still remained in blissful ignorance. Her nightly visits to the castle after work soon became routine, but although she thought she was maintaining vigilance, she began to get the feeling she was being watched. She would catch the sound of a footfall, but every time she paused to listen, she would hear nothing. The snap of a twig or a sudden flutter of wings would appear to signal someone's presence but could equally be any one of numerous nocturnal creatures on their hunt for food, including a well-known white cat that appeared to live at Mallett's Cottage, the nearby twelfth-century dwelling groaning under its heavy burden of moss-choked thatch. She had seen the feline's eyes glowing in the moonlight, its pale, ghostly form slinking through the bushes in search of its nightly quarry, and although it unnerved her at first, she had felt comforted by its presence.

Making her way quickly through the dark alleys of Orford where every shadow seemed to threaten her mission with discovery, Kate tried to put out of her mind stories of ghosts and ghouls her brother John had oft quoted with gleeful relish, in an attempt to terrorise his gullible siblings. As children they had learned of the Orford Merman, a naked man covered in hair, who, according to local legend, had been caught in a fisherman's net and taken to the castle, where he was kept in the dungeons. Despite being tortured, the man never spoke and would eat nothing but raw fish. Eventually he was allowed to swim in a netted-off enclosure of sea but managed to dive under the nets and escape, never to be seen again. It was said his ghost still haunted the castle and John had delighted in convincing his sister the merman would get her if she ventured out in the dark. Kate wondered where John was now and what he would think of her safeguarding one of the very miscreants whose illicit trade the navy was engaged in preventing.

Ellen's expected explosion came soon enough, but not in the way Kate had imagined. Her mother had had time to calm herself and digest the information in advance. Harry had called on Ellen while Kate was working at the inn and filled her mother in on the battle of Sudbourne, as it had become known. As predicted, new bills were in plentiful supply, ready to be posted far and wide, proclaiming the criminality of various individuals wanted for their crimes. Kate had not been witness to the shock on her mother's face and the rant that followed Harry's revelation. She almost felt sorry for Uncle Harry. He was so enamoured of Joseph's widow, but an incendiary outburst with its accompanying unladylike swear words aimed at her eldest daughter would come as quite a shock to him. He wouldn't expect ladies to know such words. Kate's father had grown used to his wife's outpourings and would laugh and call her a fishwife, wisely keeping his distance until the storm abated, but Harry was new to Ellen's eruptions.

By the time Kate came home from work, Ellen was sitting stony-faced at her sewing, Harry having departed quite some time ago, rather wishing he hadn't come at all.

'Katherine, come here,' called her mother curtly as she opened the door. The use of her full name, as always, preceded trouble. Kate stood waiting for the tirade she expected, but her mother simply laid down her sewing and stared at her.

'You are *never* to see Jack Howell again,' she commanded forcefully. 'He's a smuggler! He's a wanted man!' Ellen's voice cracked. 'One of his kind killed your father! I forbid it!'

Kate said nothing.

'You see him again, my girl, and you are no longer welcome in this house!'

Kate kept silent. There was no point in inviting further fireworks by protesting.

'I'm disgusted with you! Joseph Goldsmith's daughter, a smuggler's harlot!' her mother continued, emotion and fury at her daughter's deception now getting the better of her.

However, this last jibe proved too much for Kate. 'I'm *not* a harlot!' It was Kate's turn to raise her voice at the unjust slur from her mother. 'He's a good man and I love him, but now I won't get the chance to see him again, will I, thanks to you and Uncle Harry…? It's not Jack's fault he got mixed up with the traders. He's known poverty worse than you have, Mama. I don't blame him for trying to better himself!' Kate felt the overwhelming urge to defend her man, despite the hopelessness of his situation, but Ellen ignored her plea.

'You've betrayed your father, all of us, in fact! I'm ashamed of you! Go to bed, Katherine.' Her mother's words reached a crescendo, effectively curtailing any further argument.

Kate obeyed. She knew her mother's anger was in part a result of the shame she would have to bear from the women of the village, who would be smirking smugly behind her back at her daughter's downfall. *Not so proud now, is she?* they would be sure to gloat.

Lying in her lonely bed, her pillow damp with her tears, Kate pictured Jack sleeping on those cold bales in that damp, stone-lined cellar. A fugitive, reliant on others to keep him away from the full force of the law; all his hopes for the future dashed, his destiny in the balance of fortune and for what? A few barrels of cheap liquor, a few pretty trinkets and some fine tobacco? She ached for him, yearned for his touch, the feel of his stubble on her cheek, the taste of salt on his skin, his resonant, soothing voice, his deep blue eyes, his kiss so eager and sentient, his masculinity igniting a fire in her soul that burned so bright it blinded her to any faults. *Oh, Jack, what have you done?* she groaned inwardly. The law offers no medals for bravery, no accolades for skill or enterprise for those who flaunt the rules, no pardons for desperate men driven by nothing more than poverty; only death or banishment from the land of their birth, the land they loved, the land that gave them life, the land that took everything they had and more. Kate took a deep breath of resolve. *I will help you, Jack. I will do whatever it takes – whatever you ask of me, it's yours.* Kate mouthed her vow silently to herself, reflecting on her faith and asking God's forgiveness for what was, after all, simply love. *Surely the good Lord won't punish me for following my heart?*

Downstairs beside the dying embers, her mother's wrath dissolved into silent tears: tears for her departed husband, tears for her brave sons, tears for her youngest child, still naïve and unsullied, tears for her beautiful eighteen-year-old daughter whose only crime was to fall in love.

Chapter Eight

Becky had stayed awake after the first shot rang out. There had been more shots, each closer than the last, the sound of horses whinnying, urgent shouts of men, banging of doors, pounding of feet. She had not dared to look out, regretting now that she had spoken to Uncle Harry. *Supposing he was killed because of me, or even worse, my brother Thomas?* It didn't bear thinking about. She huddled down under the covers and tried to block out the noises, her hands pressed tightly over her ears. She had slept again eventually but was woken once more in the half-light by the sounds of soldiers searching the stables. She heard the house steward's voice, angry and defensive, threatening legal action for the disturbance and violation of his master's property. She heard a wagon being brought in and horses being unhitched. Eventually the sounds died away as the dawn chorus heralded daybreak and the girls rose and readied themselves for another working day. Cook was angry that her stores had been turned upside down during the search and gave the girls the task of clearing up, while the stable lads set to replacing the straw lying bestrewn around the yard.

Gradually news filtered through the gossip channels about the battle with smugglers and excisemen on the banks of the Alde, injuries inflicted on both sides, some of the goods seized, some missing. Becky was relieved to hear that Thomas was not involved, thankfully still learning the rudiments of musket shooting and cutlass wielding. Uncle Harry, she knew, would ensure her brother was well practised and capable before joining the late-night watches. There were rumours that Dick Halesworth's *Sandpiper* was the lugger seen off-loading goods, but none could be sure, although it was certain Jack Howell and old Ben Fosdyke had been captured and identified before the second ambush facilitated their escape.

Becky had not seen Edward at the hall since his last visit, but from what she heard he was actively assisting the customs and excise in their search for Jack Howell. She knew his motive was not purely that of an upstanding citizen who wished to be seen to be assisting the law but also that of a thwarted lover out to seek revenge on the object of Kate's affections. Now he had the perfect justification. Jack was a wanted man with a price on his head and Edward could maintain he would simply be doing his moral duty were his rival to meet with some unfortunate demise! She wished now she hadn't mentioned to Harry about the late-night goings-on at the stables. Since her initial flirtation with the miller's son, Becky had learned of his philandering with more than one local girl and her admiration for him had waned somewhat. Instead, she felt a sense of guilt that unwittingly she had brought her sister into ill repute and at the same time lost Kate the man she loved. *Kate will hate me for this*, she brooded unhappily, and began to wonder how she could atone.

The Revenue men had been busy searching every possible hideout for smugglers and contraband without success. Farms, houses, barns, cellars and even Orford Castle Keep were searched, to the inconvenience of Isaac Smith, who grumbled and cursed at the intrusion, but nothing was found, the trap door remaining undetected. Chapman's boatyard was also a prime target, but an extensive search revealed nothing illegal, much to the frustration of the Service. The free traders seemed to have magically disappeared into thin air, along with their haul. When Becky saw Edward next, he was sitting in the kitchen with Cook discussing the recent confrontation over a mug of ale and a meat pie.

'Good morning, Miss Goldsmith,' he said formally, blatantly studying the teenager's slim figure as Becky walked past.

'Good morning, Mr Sawyer,' Becky answered with polite dispassion, blushing at his scrutiny, but this time any thoughts of encouraging his attentions were replaced by indifference.

She turned away and busied herself in the scullery while he finished his ale and pie, conscious of his occasional glances towards her through the open door. After thanking Cook for the victuals and bidding his farewell, he followed Becky outside as she crossed the yard with a bucket of vegetable peelings for the pig pen. She avoided his gaze and walked away, but he strode over and grabbed her arm.

'Becky, might I have a word?'

Becky stopped and stared at him. 'Yes?' she said coldly, somewhat annoyed that he had addressed her so, all pretence of manners gone.

'Have you seen your sister lately?'

'No.'

'Well, I need to speak to her. She's been seeing that Jack Howell and he's now a wanted man. If she's assisting him, she'll be in trouble with the law.'

'I tell you, I haven't seen her. I don't know what she does,' Becky replied indignantly. *If he thinks I'm going to spy on my sister then he'd better think again*, she thought to herself.

'Find out for me where she goes and I'll make it worth your while,' he cajoled, pulling on her arm and edging closer to her. 'You can't be earning much here and you'll be helping your Uncle Harry. You'll probably get a reward! I'm sure your mother could do with it.'

At the offence to her mother, Becky tried to wrench her arm away crossly. 'I don't want your blood money! Leave my sister out of it, she's done nothing wrong.'

'Shame,' he said icily, letting go of her arm, all pretence of cordiality gone, his mouth twisted into a contemptuous sneer. 'You know, my dear, a pretty maid like you shouldn't go making eyes at those above her station, if she knows what's good for her!' He moved his face closer to hers. 'One day she might get more than she bargained for!' he whispered in her ear, his cheek brushing hers, one hand squeezing her waist, the other pinching her buttock painfully.

Becky stood trembling with anger and mortification at the veiled threat, her eyes stinging with tears. *Pig!* she thought, watching in stupefaction as he abruptly turned and mounted his horse, its hooves slipping and clattering away over the cobbled yard. *So, the fine, upstanding Mr Sawyer is not averse to threatening women!* she reflected speechlessly, her past admiration now superseded by disgust. *What did I ever see in him?* she questioned herself, incredulous at her own callowness and repulsed at the miller's conduct.

The next night as usual, Kate made her way towards Orford Castle Keep, a silent figure in a hooded cloak picking her way along the muddy pathway, her shoes sliding unbidden on a sodden carpet of fallen leaves. Rain had been falling in a persistent drizzle all evening and Kate was soaked through. She smiled to herself. *The things I do for you, Jack!* She stopped suddenly as something like a thump sounded in her ear and the hairs on the back of her neck stood up, visions of the Orford Merman's ghost flashing before her. There it was again! A muffled step, she was sure. After a minute of listening, when all she could hear was the steady hiss of the rain, she dismissed it as a figment of her fertile imagination and hurriedly ran up the steps towards the door of the keep.

She knocked softly, but all at once a dark figure rushed up the stairs behind her, only this was no apparition. The scream she began to utter was stifled by a gloved hand pressed over her mouth and something that felt like a pistol barrel dug into the small of her back. She froze and tried to wriggle free, but the man's grip was too tight. She heard the bolt being released and knew Jack would be ready to pull her inside. She kicked out at the door, hoping the thud would alert him, which it did momentarily, giving him enough time to call out, 'Kate?!' in alarm, but not before the gap had widened enough for her captor to place his bulk in the way and allow a second man to rush in.

If Jack had been any ordinary man he would have been totally unprepared, but years of dangerous living had fine-tuned his senses and taught him to be vigilant, his firearm at once primed and ready. At the sound of Kate's kick to the door he had instinctively reached for his flintlock pistol and jumped behind a bale, cocking his weapon just as Edward's shot discharged above Jack's head, for it was Edward who had come through the entrance while his exciseman friend held Kate in his iron grip. Edward leapt back just as Jack's pistol flashed in response and echoed around the chamber, the ball embedding itself instead in the heavy oak door. The exciseman stepped forward with Kate still in his grip, holding his firearm to her throat.

'One move and she's dead!' he snapped.

'I'm sorry, Jack,' Kate cried despairingly. 'They followed me!'

'It's alright, my dunlin, I've faced worse.'

As Jack hesitated Edward, who had re-entered, cocked his pistol and steadied his aim.

'Edward, no!' cried Kate pleadingly.

Sawyer ignored her.

'Put down your weapon, Jack Howell, or she dies!'

Jack slowly laid down his pistol on the bale, his eyes fixed on the miller's son. For what seemed like an eternity the two men glared at each other, each one sizing up the other, not only as combatants but as rivals in love. Edward felt a pang of envy as he took in Jack's swarthy good looks, so undeniably appealing to the fairer sex, and he could see why Kate was attracted to him. He surmised Jack would be a seasoned fighter and, despite the impasse, sensed he was at a physical disadvantage against this well-built young man, despite he and his friend outnumbering his enemy two to one. However, there was still Kate to consider. His friend's pistol at her throat kept her immobile, but equally it rendered the weapon ineffective against Jack, a fact Edward had not yet deduced.

'So the great Jack Howell has been run to ground!' he boasted. 'Not so clever now, are we?' Edward crowed, pleased to be in a position of advantage.

'Edward Sawyer, I presume?' Jack enquired flatly, taking in the young man's sallow complexion, slim frame and pale, gracile hands, mentally sizing him up and judging his rival distinctly lacking in combative capability.

'The very same.' Edward hesitated. He was unsure what to do next. Gradually the realisation was dawning that he had a desperate and no doubt ruthless man here, who would stop at nothing to escape, and all he himself had was one man to back him up. That man was presently engaged in restraining Kate, who would not hesitate to support her lover given the chance. He cursed inwardly to himself at the folly of coming so woefully prepared. Edward's hesitance was to be his undoing.

All the time that Jack had his eyes fixed on Sawyer, his peripheral vision had picked up a shadow slowly and carefully descending the spiral stairway to his left. He resisted the natural urge to avert his gaze and give the game away, which, together with the curve of the stairwell, meant Edward, from his standpoint, was unaware of a presence on the steps. In an instant a shot rang out and the exciseman dropped to the ground with a cry, releasing his hold on Kate. Edward, too stunned and surprised to react, turned his head to see Isaac Smith standing on the bottom stair, a whiff of smoke still rising from the firearm in his grip. In that split second of distraction, Jack leapt over the bale and seized Edward's pistol, aiming it at the miller's head. Edward swallowed nervously, beads of sweat forming on his brow, a feeling of dread clutching at his stomach with the realisation he had been outmanoeuvred. Kate was standing immobile, dazed by the sudden activity and the proximity of the shot that could so easily have killed her. In that split second of confusion, she had had a fleeting conviction she had died at the hand of the man who was holding a gun to her throat, and it was her ghost, not her living person, who was witnessing the aftermath.

'Kate!' Jack commanded as she stared transfixed. 'Kate!' he shouted again, the urgency in his voice promptly shaking her back to reality. 'Get his firearm!' he urged, nodding his head at the prone figure of the exciseman whose gun was lying on the floor, clutching his arm, where a pool of blood was seeping from his shoulder and into cracks between the stone slabs. Kate did as she was bid, laying down her basket which was still hooked over her arm, her hand trembling, her eyes wide with fear, as Jack took the weapon from her. 'It's alright, dunlin, he'll live,' he said as an agonised groan emanated from the fallen man.

'You won't get away with this, Howell,' Edward growled, 'and you...' he looked over at Isaac, 'you'll be a wanted man for this.'

'For defendin' my Lord's property against thievin' intruders? I don't think so!' Isaac retaliated, a sneer of distaste curling his lip.

'For harbouring fugitives from the law,' Edward countered.

'Know nuthin' about that. Never seen 'im before. Just doin' me job. To me you were just a couple o' thieves after t'Lord's goods.'

Edward realised Isaac had a point. His friend was not in uniform, and to all intents and purposes they could both be taken for miscreants this late at night.

'Secure him, Isaac,' Jack ordered, reaching for a set of manacle chains hanging on a hook beside the fireplace and throwing them to the caretaker, whilst all the while aiming his firearm at the miller's head. Isaac laid hands on Edward, pulled him over to an iron ring set into the wall and proceeded to secure the chain and clamp the restraints around his captive's wrists. He tossed the keys back to Jack, who replaced them on the hook by the hearth. Kate knelt down, concerned for the exciseman.

'He's losing blood, Jack, he needs attention,' she pleaded, unwrapping the food she had brought and using the muslin cloth to staunch the man's wound.

'Ah, the smuggler's whore speaks!' taunted Edward acerbically. He wouldn't admit it, but he was still smarting from her humiliating rebuff.

Kate ignored the slur, brushing it off as nothing more than her spurned suitor's jealousy, but Jack marched across to him, grabbed the manacle chains, wrapped them around Edward's neck and pulled them tight, his face inches away, his intense blue eyes boring into Edward's pallid, arrogant face.

'It weren't so long since you wanted her for yerself, but unfortunately for you, she just couldn't stomach the thought of a spineless milk-sop like you coming anywhere near 'er!' He pulled the chains tighter and whispered into Edward's ear, 'You call her a whore again and I'll make sure I'm not only wanted for tradin' but for murder as well!'

As Jack released his hold, patting the miller's cheek condescendingly, Edward spluttered and coughed, his cheeks scarlet, his eyes watering, but he kept silent. He could tell he was no match for Jack's physical strength so he would have to outwit him by some other means, but clearly Jack was no simpleton either. Still, Edward knew he had the law on his side, which with luck would see his rival at the very least transported, at best hanged. Either way, he smirked, Kate would lose her lover.

'Jack, we have to help this man,' Kate pleaded anxiously, kneeling beside the exciseman.

'Aye, give us a minute, lass. Give him a swig of ale to numb his senses. I need to talk with Isaac.' Jack glanced at the caretaker and inclined his head towards the stairs.

As the pair disappeared into the stairwell and down to the basement below, Kate uncorked the stoneware crock of ale she had brought and took it over to the fallen man. She sat him up carefully and leaned him against the wall, holding the vessel to his lips. He took a draught and coughed, his breath coming in short gasps. She found a rag amongst the bales and began to mop the blood from the stones.

Edward eyed her sullenly. 'So, Katherine, this is the life you chose over me! You've got yourself in a pretty pickle now, my girl, assisting a felon with a price on his head!'

'It's not Jack's fault he got mixed up with the wrong crowd. If you'd known poverty like his you'd have done the same. Just because you've got a rich father it doesn't make you a better person!' Kate replied defensively.

'No? At least I've got prospects, which is more than Howell has now!' he scowled.

Kate didn't answer. She knew he spoke the truth and it touched a nerve. She turned away from him and walked across to the hearth, occupying herself with stoking the remains of the fire in the grate, although she could feel Edward's eyes boring into her disconcertingly. Outside the rain had stopped and a pale moon shone through the narrow casement, as Jack and Isaac appeared again from the stairwell.

'Isaac's going to go for help for your mate. Once he comes back, you'll be freed as soon as we've gone,' Jack informed his prisoner.

'So you're not going to murder me in cold blood then?' Edward taunted.

Jack strode over to his captive and cocked his pistol against Edward's head. 'That can be arranged. May as well be hung for a sheep as a lamb!' he said frostily, Edward's sarcasm hitting a nerve. Jack knew he was putting his life in jeopardy by releasing Edward, but he was not a murderer. He had bade Isaac get word to the Halesworth's, whose threat to life, limb and livelihood would be enough to ensure the miller's silence and that of his exciseman friend. There were enough of the *Sandpiper*'s crew who would not hesitate to exact revenge on an informer, as had already been proved.

Isaac wrapped himself in a greatcoat and pressed a felt tricorn hat over his thinning hair as Jack let him out of the door. 'I will knock only once when I return, be ready,' he said as Jack closed the door behind him and slid the bolt back into its barrel, before turning to Kate. 'You'd better go, my dunlin. You'll be missed.' Seeing Edward eyeing them resentfully, he took her arm and led her round into the small chamber behind the fireplace, out of sight of the miller's scrutiny.

'Oh, Jack, what's going to happen?' she whispered, wide-eyed and fearful, as soon as they were out of sight and earshot.

'Don't fret, my dunlin. It's all in hand. Isaac's going to get a message to Dick Halesworth. They'll deal with Sawyer while I get out of here.'

'Deal with him? They're not going to—' Kate stared in alarm.

'No, of course not,' Jack interrupted, anticipating her question. 'They'll just make sure he knows not to say anythin' and then they'll let him go. They're not murderers – well, not Dick and Nate at any rate!' he qualified, smirking as a sardonic smile played around his lips, before remembering Kate's comment, provoking a frown of envy to crease his brow. 'You're not still struck on him, are you, lass?' He searched her face earnestly.

'No! I never was!' Kate countered indignantly. 'I'm just afeared for *you*, Jack. If anything happens to him it'll be *you* gets the blame. Edward told everyone for whom it was I spurned him.'

Relieved, Jack reassured her, pulling her towards him. 'I'll be alright. There's plenty who'll help me. They'll be watching *you* now, dunlin, so be careful. I'll get word to you somehow, but it may be a while afore you hear.'

A tear trickled down Kate's cheek as she embraced him and held him close. He lifted her chin and kissed her lingeringly before easing her arms away from him.

'Now, go, quickly! Don't come back here.'

Kate avoided Edward's gaze as they re-entered the room and crossed the room to the door.

'Aw, how touching! The smuggler and his doxy having one last grope before you go?!' Edward scoffed mockingly as Jack let Kate out of the door and closed it behind her.

Jack turned, strode over to his prisoner, pulled the manacle chains taut to immobilise his captive's arms, drew a knife from his coat and shoved the blade against the miller's groin. 'You shut your filthy mouth, you lily-livered scum. We've all heard how you've been befouling half the maids in Suffolk! A slip o' my knife and it'll provide a tasty snack for the fishes! Only a snack, mind, judgin' by the rest o' you!'

'Ha ha! Very amusing. You won't kill me, Howell, it's more than your life's worth'.

'I don't need to!' Jack countered. 'One word from me to the traders and the rest of you'll be lyin' at the bottom of the North Sea, and that's more n' you deserve!'

Edward, recognising the truth of his rival's statement, judged it wise to stop goading his captor. Just because Jack wasn't going to kill him here and now, it didn't mean he was safe from the more ruthless amongst the gang. He started to wonder how he had become embroiled in this mess and traced it back to Kate. If he hadn't have gotten mixed up with a smuggler's lass, he would probably have been engaged by now. He began to ruminate on how he could exact his revenge on the cause of his indignity.

After releasing the miller with a scowl, Jack set about packing some essentials into a sack. He took a swig of ale from the jar and sat down on the bales to await Isaac's return, Edward eyeing him sullenly, while the semi-conscious exciseman's head lolled forward onto his chest.

At the King's Head Inn, Michael Barker was interrupted by a thump on the stockroom door as he hauled another keg of beer into the bar, ready for another day's trade. Fifteen minutes later a pony and cart left his stables and made its way quietly to the Castle Keep, its loan sanctioned by the promise of finest duty-free brandy from the landowner's cellar. At the single knock, Jack admitted the caretaker and together they carried the injured man to the cart. As they sat him down Isaac drew a knife from his boot and held it at the groaning man's throat.

'One word o' this and you're dead, understand?' The man nodded his head as the point bit into his skin. Isaac poked a bony finger against the wound. 'You got this chasin' some felons who got clean away, remember?' The soldier nodded again as Isaac squeezed his shattered shoulder, letting out a bellow of agony before he slumped forward and lost consciousness.

'Take him to Doctor Ward in Woodbridge, Isaac, and then do as we agreed,' Jack ordered, as the caretaker took the reins and set the pony off at a slow walk through the darksome streets of Orford.

Jack went inside. Edward was slouched against the wall, snoring softly. Immediately Jack felt a surge of weariness wash over him and, collapsing onto the bales, he too slept, while outside a thin sliver of light lit the eastern horizon over Lanthorn Marshes.

Chapter Nine

Twenty-four hours later, in a sheltered section of the Butley River, a lugger lay moored, her sails furled, her fishing nets piled aft, no lights showing on deck. Below in the cabin a young man sat blindfolded and tied to a chair, his hair unkempt, two-day old reddish-blond stubble delineating his jawline. His knee twitched involuntarily and his breathing was laboured.

'So you thought you'd profit from a bit of smuggler bagging, eh? Betrayin' Jack Howell to the Service?' Dick Halesworth arraigned his captive, casually drawing on his pipe, as he sat on a bale, observing the miller with contempt.

Edward compressed his lips together tightly; there was no point in denying the obvious now that Isaac Smith had brought him on board the free traders' craft and relayed an account of the previous night's events.

'Well, lads?' Dick looked around the cabin at his shipmates. 'How do we ensure this loose-tongued lickspittle keeps his trap shut?'

'A few hauls should do the trick,' grumbled the old sailor with the piercing eyes.

'I don't do keel haulin', Ben, it's barbaric!'

'Mebbe so, but a man'll agree to anything after a

couple of doses o' that medicine. Two hauls and he'll deny the king hisself!'

'I'll think about it. Mebbe if nuthin' else works...'

'Castrate 'im!' another voice piped up. 'He won't be so popular with t' mawthers then!' The voice chuckled to murmurs of approval.

'No!' Edward breathed timidly. 'Please... I won't say anything.'

'Would be a shame if his mill were to burn down one night,' Nate suggested to his father.

'Mmm, could be a useful asset, that mill.' Dick got up and approached the miller, pressing a knife blade against his neck. 'What's in it for us if we let you go, eh? What's it worth to stay alive *and* with all your tackle?'

'Anything you want, take it,' Edward murmured dejectedly, all the enmity gone from his demeanour, attempting to ease his jaw away from the threatening blade.

'A steady supply o' flour and some storage space would be a start.' Dick moved his lips closer to the miller's ear. 'But one word to *anyone*, includin' your father, and some dark night you *will* meet with some unfortunate accident, I can promise you that!'

Edward nodded briskly, perspiration seeping into the cloth tightly covering his eyes, as the knife nicked his skin and a droplet of blood tracked down onto his shirt. He felt like a condemned man who had just been given a reprieve. The death he had fully expected at the hands of these cutthroats suddenly forestalled. His relief was such that he had trouble keeping control of his bowels as he realised the enormity of his lucky escape.

'Tek him home,' Dick commanded, kicking the chair testily.

Ben spat moodily as the miller was manhandled to the deck, silently judging Halesworth as too lenient in allowing the man his freedom quite so readily. He narrowed his eyes and scowled as the blindfolded captive was lowered onto a waiting craft. He would have to keep his eye on Sawyer.

The previous day at the castle keep Jack and his prisoner had slept until well into the next morning. Isaac had returned the cart to the King's Head before bedding down upstairs, leaving Jack to keep watch over Edward, sharing with his captive the remains of his bread, cheese and ale, which was sullenly accepted. The two barely spoke except when the miller needed to relieve himself and was presented with a bucket, which Jack emptied down the castle latrine. When darkness fell again, Isaac climbed the stairs to the roof of the keep and flashed a signal over the marshes towards Havergate Island. His signal answered, Isaac hurried down to help Jack release his prisoner from the manacles and tie his hands together before blindfolding him.

'Where are you taking me?' Edward asked nervously.

'Just goin' for a little ride,' Isaac told him as Jack pressed a pistol into Edward's back.

They lit a lamp, led him outside, locked the door and made their way over mounds and ditches where the old outer walls had mostly been demolished, Edward stumbling his way towards some steps which led down to a door hidden by undergrowth. Isaac unlocked the door to reveal more downward steps into a dank and dark tunnel, which smelt of earth, mould, saltwater, animal waste and foul-smelling mud.

As they progressed through the underground passage, Edward's feet feeling their way clumsily between the two men, it gradually became wetter underfoot until they were ankle-deep in vermin-infested water. At the end of the tunnel the entrance was barred by a heavy metal gate bolted on the inside and padlocked. Isaac sorted through his bunch of keys in the dim, flickering lamplight, trying each in turn until the lock opened and he could slide the bolt over.

They stepped out onto grassy lowland, inhaling deeply to dispel the stench of the shaft, relieved to be breathing the cool, fresh air again. It was a calm night apart from a light breath of wind which whispered through the reed beds bordering the estuary and out across the wide band of the river, flowing in a serene, bright channel against the black marshes. After crossing a wide expanse of rough ground, they came to a muddy bank, where a short landing stage jutted into the water. Jack spotted a small craft with two figures making its way across river, pointing it out to Isaac, who waved his lantern, and soon they were climbing aboard, positioning Edward on the bow seat and joining the two men amidships on the oars. They pushed the craft off from the landing and rowed downriver until the mouth of the Butley River, where they turned upstream towards Butley Ferry and the *Sandpiper* moored close by. Jack helped Edward climb aboard the lugger, to where Dick Halesworth was waiting.

'Tek him below,' he ordered dispassionately, as his crew ushered the miller down into the cabin. Jack called down his thanks to Isaac in the rowing boat before the caretaker turned the craft and rowed off downriver. Dick then turned to Jack and embraced him with a smile of relief.

'Good to see you, Jack! Still in one piece then, well... almost!' He grinned.

'You too, Dick! That were a close thing on the Alde. Best stay away from Sudbourne, now they're watchin' the hall.'

'You can't stop here either, Jack, not now you've been recognised, and Ben'll have to lie low too. Best keep that beard growin', mind – disguise that handsome face!' He patted Jack's cheek affectionately. 'I can mebbe get you out to Minsmere, where you can wait it out until the *Storm Petrel* off-loads at Sizewell next. She'll then tek you to Holland.'

'I'm grateful to you, Dick. When you speak to Mike Chapman, can you ask him somethin' for me? I need my belongings from the boatyard, he'll know where to find them.'

'Mebbe your lass can fetch them from the yard for you?' Dick suggested.

'No! She'll be watched now they know it's me she's been seein'. That's how Sawyer found me, by followin' her to the keep.'

'He won't be sayin' anythin'. We'll see to that.'

'Thank you, Dick, but her Uncle Harry's in the Service. It was he who caught us at Sudbourne before we escaped. He's the one gave me this.' He held up his finger stump. 'He's sweet on Kate's mother too, so she'll be keepin' a close watch on her daughter, if only to please him.' He then remembered something else he wanted to ask. 'Dick, can you reward Isaac Smith for me, somehow? If it weren't for him, I may not be here. He's put himself at great risk to help get me away.'

'Consider it done, Jack.' He patted Jack's shoulder affirmatively. 'Now to deal with Sawyer.' The skipper went below, leaving Jack leaning against the ship's rail, gazing into the murk, listening to the gentle slop of the river against the sides of the lugger, his thoughts turning to his pretty mawther and the uncertainty of the future he had unwittingly consigned to her.

The morning after Kate had said goodbye to Jack at the castle, her mother had quizzed her suspiciously. 'You were late back from the inn last night, Kate. I must have been asleep when you came in. What were you doing all that time?'

'Mr Bird had some stock he wanted unpacked and sorted,' Kate lied. 'He said there'd be a bit extra in my wages this week.'

'I should think so too, my girl. He's taking advantage, and I don't like you out so late. Tell him no next time!'

Kate vowed to herself to do no such thing now she had found a plausible excuse for her late-night excursions. She was worried about Jack and where he would go but also feared Edward might find it hard not to divulge what he'd seen of her involvement, especially now Jack had outwitted him and made him look foolish. Uncle Harry had not visited Ellen since her explosion about Kate, so there was no fresh news about the exciseman. She decided to call on Becky again to see if she had heard anything about the search for Jack, or Edward's intentions.

It was a cold winter's morning when Kate set out for Sudbourne Hall once more. The ground was hard and her toes soon began to feel numb in her lace-up boots, the worn soles letting in water at the seams. Passing the old elm tree, she decided to look to see if there was any message from Jack. She wasn't expecting anything as she knew he was on the run somewhere and probably far from Orford by now, but it was best to be sure. She felt inside for the pouch and was surprised to find it had something in it. She hastily unfolded the note. *The hut, after work tonight*, was all it said. Her heart leapt. So he was still nearby! She decided there was no point in going on to the hall now, so retracing her steps she hurried back to Orford, buoyed up by the prospect of seeing Jack once more.

Custom at the Crown and Castle that evening was plentiful and gossip likewise. Hushed comments were made about Kate being a smuggler's moll and how Jack was now doomed to life as a fugitive but why none would dare betray him for a King's ransom. They all knew payback from the free traders would be worse than any punishment the law could impose for aiding and abetting. Kate kept herself aloof and refrained from being dragged into defending Jack, despite her ears burning and furtive glances coming her way.

Another storm was brewing in the west as Kate left work and made her way down the familiar river path. Strong gusts tugged at her cloak, causing it to flap awkwardly around her legs as she walked. She wrapped it tight around her body against the cold and was glad to reach the shelter of George's hut. There was no light inside when she pushed the door open.

'Jack!' she called softly, expecting at any minute to be swept up in his arms. Instead, she gasped and let out a shriek when a bony hand she had felt before caught her wrist in its iron grip.

'Jack's not 'ere,' Ben announced pragmatically. ''E sent me to tell you 'e's goin' up to Minsmere to await passage at Sizewell. They won't bother lookin' up there in those marshes – never find their way through there!' He chuckled.

'Where is he?' Kate demanded, her disappointment turning to annoyance.

'Can't tell you that, missy, best you don't know.' Ben reached into his greatcoat and pulled out a purse of gold coins. 'This is for you. You're to wait until 'e sends word that 'e's safe in Holland, then you're to get a passage over to join him.'

'Oh!' Kate frowned. 'Can't I see him before he goes?' she pleaded, accepting the purse from him.

'No! Too risky. If you're seen like you were afore, then 'e's done for. They'll mek sure he don't get away this time.'

Kate hung her head. She sensed Ben was blaming her and she felt chastened by the thought that her actions had led to Jack's discovery by Edward and now he was going away. She wanted more than ever to hold her lover close, ask his forgiveness and affirm her undying devotion. For now, though, all she could do was wait for word of his escape.

'Thank you, Ben, and tell Jack thank you and Godspeed.' She looked into the shadow of the old sailor's face, but in the gloom she could not make out his features. 'Are you going to be alright, Ben?'

The old sailor stared at her, nonplussed. It had been many years since anyone had shown the least bit of concern about him, and now here was Joseph Goldsmith's fair daughter, whose father had been on the wrong end of his musket ball, actually concerned for his welfare. If it had been daylight Kate might have detected a flush of colour behind his leathery, sun-browned cheek.

'Y'er mar'nt fret about me, missy, I'll be just fine,' he said self-consciously. 'Watch yersel' now!' was all he could manage in return, and with that he went out into the night, disappearing into the blackness like a phantom.

Kate shivered. There was something about Ben that unnerved her, but at the same time she pitied this compassionless man for whom love had clearly never materialised.

Trudging home, dejected at not having seen Jack, Kate felt the heavy coins in her pocket and her heart sank. How could she go to Holland? Mama would never allow it. It would mean trading her mundane but safe life in Orford for a life on the run, away from everything she had ever known, the places she loved, the people she loved. *If I leave now, how can I ever return?* She agonised. *Oh, Jack, how has it come to this? I love you, but you don't know what you're asking of me!*

Chapter Ten

Jack stirred from his slumber and tugged at a stick of straw poking into his ear. Above him perched under the eaves, beside a narrow opening high on the gable wall, a chalky white barn owl woke from her daytime snooze, preened her silky feathers and prepared for another night's hunting, as a blush of pink suffused the cloud-striated western sky. The top layer of haybales at Gedgrave Hall Farm had made a comfortable bed and Jack wished he could have stayed another night in the pungent warmth of the byre, but he knew he had to get away from the environs of Orford and out to Minsmere, where he would be better concealed. Gedgrave Hall, forming part of the Sudbourne Estate, was only a short sprint from Butley Ferry, where Jack had left the *Sandpiper* and he and Dick had woken the head groom at the stables in the early hours with a request for temporary refuge and means of transport, whereupon the groom had agreed to lend Jack a suitable mount for the journey. Jack would then ride to Sizewell and leave the horse at the Vulcan Arms before making the rest of the way to the mere on foot.

Dick had arranged through a contact at the Vulcan Arms, that 'Mad' Willie Mumford, a gamekeeper, who resided in a shack surrounded on three sides by the watery maze of Minsmere marsh, would give Jack shelter until the *Storm Petrel* could anchor off-shore at Sizewell Gap. Jack had a purse of silver and some fine Virginia tobacco put aside as recompense for the fisherman's inconvenience. 'Mad' Willie, as he was affectionately known, wasn't really mad, just a bit eccentric from living all his life in isolation, having had no education to speak of, eking out an existence from fishing and gaming, but he knew every inch of the wetland and guarded it with a jealous zeal, as if it were his own. No-one dared to fish or go fowling without Willie's permission and he was known to take potshots at anyone invading his territory. He was fond of telling ghostly tales of apparitions appearing on the marsh and monsters lurking in the shallow inlets, which may or may not have been true but which served in its purpose to deter any would-be trespassers.

Wrapped in a long overcoat and wide tricorn hat, climbing down from the top of the hay bale stack, Jack peered out from the barn door across to the stables. All was quiet as he crossed the yard and found a sorrel mare with no markings, harnessed and waiting in her stall. She whinnied softly as he stroked her soft nose and patted her gently, took the reins and led her out, keeping to the shadows cast by the farmhouse, as he mounted the saddle and urged her forward to a trot along the Gedgrave Road.

To avoid Orford, he veered left off towards Broom Cottage, skirting the woods, then turned north, by-passing the town, avoiding Sudbourne Hall and joining the Snape Road. Behind him the River Ore and to his right the shining meanders of the Alde shone out of the gloom, a reassuring indicator of his position. At Snape he crossed the river bridge, turning right after the Crown Inn to go past the Snape Marshes, through Black Heath Wood towards Aldeburgh. He stopped on the open heath beside the wetland to allow the horse to drink from one of the many dykes criss-crossing the common. Dismounting, he took a flask from his knapsack and sat down to quench his thirst.

He must have dozed for a while, jerking back to awareness with a start, as the mare snorted and shied at a sudden disturbance in the dyke and a snipe flew up with a screeching alarm call. *Most likely an otter*, Jack surmised, pulling himself back into the saddle. A pale glow on the eastern horizon told him dawn would not be far behind. He must get on before folk started rising. He sat listening for a moment, then squeezed the horse's flanks, cantering on through the oak woods to the beginnings of the dawn chorus, so delightfully marking that liminal phase between darkness and dawn.

As he approached Aldeburgh from the west, he slowed his mount to a trot, turning off left at the red-brick farmhouse, in order to skirt the town and join the road north to Sizewell. The road then straightened out following the coast, where to his right the flat shingle beach stretched northwards and a barren, treeless heath opened out on his left. Passing Thorpe Mere and approaching Sizewell, the land gradually rose upwards from the shore in sandy cliffs, forming a barrier to the beach, only breached by a depression known as Sizewell Gap. Dawn had broken, but a blanket of thick grey cloud obliterated the sunrise, barely warming the air blowing gustily over Leiston Common, as horse and rider approached the Vulcan Arms. Jack dismounted and knocked on the rear door.

'Who's there?' a disembodied voice called from a window above.

'Dick Halesworth sent me,' Jack replied as the window banged shut, and it was a few moments before the bolt was drawn and the door opened. The landlord, still wearing a nightshirt under his coat, ushered Jack inside before leading the sweating mare to the stables, where he filled a bucket from a water trough and placed it beside her, while he removed her harness.

'You can kip in the storeroom, there's a bunk behind the barrels,' he informed Jack as he re-entered the kitchen. 'Willie'll be along tonight to tek you to Minsmere.' He placed a tankard of ale, some cold meat and bread on the table.

Jack thanked him and drank deeply, aware as he drank that the landlord had noted his injury.

'I'm a carpenter,' Jack offered in explanation, putting down his tankard and cutting a slice of bread.

'It's alright, lad. I know who you are. You're Jack Howell.'

'Bit of a giveaway, isn't it?!' Jack smiled ruefully.

'Don't worry, lad, you're among friends 'ere. Nobody's goin' to squeal on yer. There's no mates o' the Service 'ere. We weeded 'em out long ago!' He chuckled. 'Right, I'm off to mek m'self decent. The missus'll see to your needs. Get yer head down for a few hours, lad. Willie'll be 'ere afore nightfall.'

'Thank you, Mister…?'

'Baxter's the name. Call me Joseph.'

'I'm obliged to you, Joseph.'

Later, having risen from his sleep in the storeroom and having enjoyed a bellyful of Mrs Baxter's mutton stew, generously served with an admiring smile, the landlady remarking gushingly, 'A handsome young lad like you needs to keep his strength up!', Jack had watched from behind the door as the customers arrived.

Sometime later, Mr Baxter inclined his head, indicating Willie's appearance as the fisherman came in, sat down in the corner and laid a brace of mallard on the table in front of him. Even before Jack had been introduced to 'Mad' Willie, he could have pointed him out: a wiry man with milky grey eyes, long untidy grey hair and an unkempt beard, shabbily dressed in a faded blue military-style jacket, long mud-spattered boots and carrying a fowling piece over his shoulder that had seen better days. Aged in his late fifties, he could be taken for ten years older: his back stooped, his bony hands gnarled and curled, his black fingernails like claws, his few remaining teeth stained and crooked. Mr Baxter took the birds gratefully and filled Willie's tankard, leaving him the jug, payment having been made in kind for more than a single pint of ale.

'Come through to the back when you've finished,' he told Willie.

After about an hour of waiting for Willie to enjoy his drink, during which the noise of animated chatter became gradually louder as the liquor took effect on the drinkers, a sudden shout from the door silenced the clamour.

'Bluecoats!' Immediately Willie sprang through the kitchen door, displaying the agility of a much younger man. He was accompanied by three other men, whom Jack did not recognise. The landlord walked out to the front room, closing the kitchen door behind him, just as Harry Goldsmith and half a dozen uniformed Preventive men entered the inn.

‘Custom search!’ Harry announced, Joseph Baxter observing him coolly, arms folded defiantly, as the routine search commenced, his customers regarding the servicemen with glaring hostility.

Meanwhile, in the kitchen, Mrs Baxter, seemingly unperturbed, reached for a lamp, beckoned Jack, Willie and the other men through the stores and over to a door in the corner, which she unlocked with a key hanging on her belt.

‘In here, quick!’ she commanded sotto voce as the men followed, leading them down a set of stone steps into a dark cellar. A stack of capacious beer barrels, crates and kegs were lined up against one wall and an old table with a couple of chairs stood against another, while underneath their feet, the floor was covered in a layer of damp sand. Two of the men moved the table to one side before the landlady knelt down and swept away some sand to reveal a trap door set into the floor. Willie lifted the trap, took the lamp from her and led the way down a wooden ladder into a dark, dank, brick-lined tunnel stretching downwards into a black void. Jack and the three men bent double and followed him, easing themselves along the walls of the narrow passage, now mud-lined, the sloping floor sinking ever downwards as they progressed. As soon as they disappeared, Mrs Baxter closed the trap door behind them, pushed the table back into its place and smoothed the sand back over the floor before returning to the storeroom and locking the cellar door.

Meanwhile, her husband was conversing at the bar with Harry Goldsmith while the servicemen searched the customers and any likely hiding places for contraband.

The delay was enough to ensure that by the time they got around to searching the kitchen and storeroom, Mrs Baxter was calmly washing tankards at the sink. Harry tried the locked cellar door and demanded access. The proprietress deliberately took her time, drying her hands and searching through her bunch of keys, prompting a sergeant to bark at her in exasperation.

'Hurry up, woman, we haven't got all night!' he snapped testily, as she shot him a glance of loathing. The search of the cellar proved fruitless, the sandy floor serving its purpose as suitable camouflage. After a search of the stables proved equally unproductive, the troops departed in the direction of Leiston, leaving the relieved publican and his clientele at the Vulcan Arms to relax into a raucous sing-song.

Chapter Eleven

The tunnel ended abruptly in a small flight of steps, its confining walls giving way into a low-ceilinged cavern, the damp sand on its floor bisected by a water channel flowing through the narrow entrance and out onto the shore at Sizewell Gap, so named for the cleft between the cliffs which formed a useful conduit through which many a haul was conveyed to Leiston Common and beyond. Pushing aside the brushwood disguising the cave entrance, the men stood up and breathed in the salt-laden air, relieved to be able to straighten their backs and fill their lungs with unpolluted ozone. The moon had risen over the sea, bathing the coastline in an eerie glow, and there was no sound apart from the hiss of the shingle as the waves broke, rhythmically, and the faint strains of drunken singing emanating from the inn on the cliff top.

'See ya, Willie,' the three men called, after helping Jack and his new companion replace the brushwood concealing the entrance, before striding off through the gap in the direction of Leiston Common.

Jack grinned at Willie. 'Well, that was a handy trick!'

'Aye, comes in mighty useful when there's a drop. Come on, lad,' he urged, breaking into a jog.

'We've got a bit of a way to go yet. Watch out for the mere phantoms, mind.'

'Mere phantoms?' Jack asked uneasily, staring into the black abyss.

'Aye. Keep up, lad'

Jack deemed it impolite to ask for further explanation from his taciturn companion. 'Call me, Jack,' he offered amicably.

'Lad'll do, son. If they ask no questions, they'll hear no lies. Follow me, lad,' Willie ordered as they traversed the marram grass-covered dunes stretching away to the north before veering off towards Minsmere Marshes, down a track bordered by sea lavender and tightly packed reed beds.

After what seemed like an eternity to Jack following Willie's lantern as it swung along beside him, acres of sighing sedge stretching out on either side – *Just the place for a phantasmic apparition*, Jack thought as he peered into the void – eventually they approached an isolated shack sited on a grassy bank close to the water's edge. An upturned rowing boat served as a roof and the wooden walls supported a couple of old barge windows, while the divided door appeared to have housed a four-legged occupant in its former life.

''Ere we are, lad! Mumford's mansion! What d'ye think?' Willie asked proudly.

'The very height of luxury!' Jack quipped wryly, but then regretted his cynicism as his companion clearly had great pride in his makeshift abode.

'Aye,' Willie agreed contentedly, the sarcasm lost on him. 'Come in, lad.'

They went inside and Jack found it felt surprisingly

cosy, as his host hung up the lantern, revealing a jumble of fishing gear, crates, sacks of straw, a basket of feathers, a pile of rabbit skins, ropes, sail cloths, bottles, a pile of logs, some oars, a small ship's galley stove glowing on a brick hearth in the corner and beside it a black cooking pot containing somewhat unappetising sections of skinned mammal. The abode smelled musty and stale, the pungent atmosphere hardly diminished by the all-pervading odour of Willie's unwashed person, and Jack made a mental note to send him a bar of soap from his next cargo.

'Get some wood on, lad.' Willie pointed to the dying embers. He picked up a sack of straw and laid it down near the stove. 'Then get yer head down here and warm yersel'.'

Jack placed a log into the stove and sat down to remove his rucksack and take his boots off.

'I'll be off early fishin', but no need for you to stir until you want to.' Willie lay down on his bed of straw-filled sacks and was soon snoring deeply, as the large quantity of liquor he had consumed took effect.

Jack extinguished the lamp and lay awake, taking in his new surroundings just visible by the light emanating from the stove, his disorderly thoughts mulling over the night's happenings. *Did Harry Goldsmith simply turn up as a matter of routine, or had he been tipped off about my flight to the Vulcan Arms?* It seemed co-incidental that he had turned up that very night. Either way, the tunnel was a godsend. Jack knew of its existence, as the *Zephyr* had off-loaded at Sizewell on several occasions, but it was the first time he had used it himself. He'd heard there was another tunnel running from Leiston beneath the Common which had oft been used by a large gang of free traders from Hadleigh, notorious for their violence and disregard for human life. Dismissing images of brutishness and bloodshed, so often associated with the more unscrupulous element of society engaged in the smuggling trade, Jack's thoughts turned to Kate, the image of her suffusing his loins with a warm glow of lustful longing. He hoped Ben had got his message to her and given her the purse, which, with any luck, would mean she could soon join him in Holland.

Jack slept fitfully, seeing disturbing images of ghostly figures looming out of the inky blackness of Minsmere Marsh, a slashing blade, a fountain of blood, a hangman's noose; he awoke in a sweat, the ashes in the stove still radiating a slight warmth despite the winter frost outside. There was no sign of Willie as Jack reached for his boots and coat, stepping out onto the rime-iced grass. A watery sun had risen above the reed beds, the frosted seed heads inclined en-masse away from the prevailing wind, shimmering softly, their quivering stalks reflecting soft focussed, in the placid waters of the mere. Breaking the icy crust on a bucket of rainwater and splashing his face generously, Jack cupped his hands for a long draught. As he did so his eye caught a movement in the mere to his right. A dog otter appeared on the mudbank, a large fish held tightly in its paws. Jack watched, stock-still, mesmerised by the sleek, lithe creature, with its keen-eyed, decidedly charming, be-whiskered face, while it ate its fill, seemingly unaware of its captivated audience, before sliding gracefully back into the water.

Jack relaxed and gazed around at the scene before him, marvelling at its ethereal beauty: a blanket of stratocumulus clouds dappling an occasional glimpse of azure sky, reflected like a mirror in the channels and lakes of Minsmere, stretching from Westleton Woods out to the dunes, separating the North Sea shore from the freshwater wetlands. Still awaiting the spring arrival of avocet and tern, the overwintering oyster catchers, curlew, snipe and lapwing gathered on the banks, and somewhere sheltering amongst the brown sausage-like seed heads of great reedmace, resided the shy bittern, not yet ready to utter its familiar booming mating call. Jack's eye followed a marsh harrier gliding overhead unperturbed by a couple of anxious crows, its pin-sharp vision scanning the fenland for a tasty morsel; he watched the coots and moorhens clucking amongst the rushes and a pair of milk-white whooper swans from Iceland, cruising the inlets with imperceptible means of propulsion. Greylag and barnacle geese congregated in pools across the mere; widgeon, pintail, shelduck and divers paddled in the shallows; the air rang with the song of warblers and marsh tits – this was a place of elusive and ever-evolving fascination, the seasons' perpetual journey of timeless repetition, nature living its life unchanged. In spring the birch woods at the edge of the mere sprung from a carpet of blue, and in summer, flowering plants would crowd the sedges: pink fingers of ragged robin punctuating the reeds in a splash of colour; purple loosestrife, yellow ragwort, oxeye daisies, lilac pin-cushions of devil's bit scabious, celandines and water crowfoot spilling over the banks, where the sinister sundew waited patiently for an unsuspecting insect to land on its sticky tendrils. No laws here but the ever-present law of nature, regulating its world in a fine balance of survival, only the strongest and most able chosen to prolong the species, indifferently heedless of man's hopes and fears, loves and hates, wants and needs. No place here for the weak, no concession for sentiment, only the relentless passage of time and evolution marching unyielding to eternity, as each successive generation fought to prevail.

Surrounded by the power of nature, Jack was struck by the insignificance of man and his worldly aspirations. This untouched place, which had evolved over centuries, would survive long after he had gone and nothing he did would be of any consequence to this teeming wetland wilderness of reeds and wildlife. As he gazed about him, Jack thought about his life and the path he had taken to get to this point. He had always known it would come to this sooner or later but was confident that once he got to Holland and profited from a few more runs he would have enough to return to Suffolk and make a new start with a new identity and with Kate beside him as his wife.

His thoughts were interrupted by the return of his host, mooring his small rowing craft on the mudbank beside the hut and presenting Jack with a breakfast of eel, some perch and tench.

The next few days were spent in and around the hut, Jack helping Willie with cleaning his fowling piece, mending broken shelving, patching up holes in the walls, rabbiting on the nearby heath and woodland, chopping wood, fishing and fowling, mending nets and cutting bulrushes, keeping them damp and supple, ready to be plaited into mats or woven into baskets. An accomplished weaver despite his crooked fingers, Willie would earn himself a few pennies by selling his home-crafted wares at Leiston Market along with an assortment of saltwater and freshwater fish. Jack watched, fascinated, as the old man twisted and guided the stalks with expert dexterity, a container or other useful article slowly emerging from the tangle of stems between his leathery fingers. Jack's gift of tobacco was welcomed, along with the occasional jug of ale fetched from the Vulcan Arms. The two would sit by the stove as the sun went down, smoke curling upwards from two clay pipes, regaling each other with smuggling tales and local legends, many of which seemed to Jack to be more akin to Willie's fertile imagination than to reality.

Night-time activities at Sizewell and Thorp continued apace, several successful runs ashore being made during the bad weather, when the excisemen were unlikely to turn out. It was always an ordeal getting goods ashore, with the risk of ships edging ever leeward onto submerged rocks or smashed on the shore by crashing breakers, the exhausted crews struggling to keep the small, heavily laden rowing craft afloat, or from capsizing in the pounding surf. Voices could not be heard over the screech of the wind and men would be wet through, fingers frozen to the bone, and by the time the cargo had been landed and loaded, they were almost too spent to resist, should the excise have appeared.

Jack had seen the lights signalling from the cliff to waiting ships and he hoped his turn would come before too long. Dick Halesworth was in touch with Mike Chapman at the boatyard and would pass on a coded message to Jack when to expect the *Storm Petrel*, via a relay system of messages passed from inn to inn and finally along to the Vulcan Arms. Mr Baxter would then raise a flag on the headland which Jack could see with the aid of Willie's spyglass. The Union flag usually flown would be replaced by the cross of St George when there was a message for him, but so far every time Jack looked there was no change.

Jack was becoming impatient. Life in 'Mad' Willie's shack was at first a novelty and had given him time to take stock and consider his options, but it was cold and cramped, and the meagre rations barely enough to sustain the older man, let alone a young man of Jack's build. Besides, Jack chuckled to himself, a few more weeks of this bohemian existence and his own sanity would be sorely tested, despite the fact that his nostrils had ceased to register the malodourous pungency of his unwashed companion and squalid surroundings. Willie was a man of few words and only spoke when spoken to, as if words were a precious commodity to be stored up and used sparingly, so as not to waste unnecessary energy. The old fisherman had eked out a perfectly adequate life of solitude for himself, needing nothing more to stimulate him, but Jack was bored. There would be time enough for sitting around idly in his twilight years, but for now he was in the prime of life, a young man's passion still coursing through his veins, dreams and aspirations still driving him on. He needed to get back to the sea, to taste the salt-laden spindrift, feel the pull of the wind as it filled the ship's sails, watch the bow slicing through the waves, flinging up spray as it dipped and reared. He longed to feel the cold blast upon his face, the unpolluted air filling his lungs; hear the shouts of his shipmates; feel the constant exhilarating battle between man and the elements. It made him feel alive, and the added lure of the rewards generated by a successful run was a prize worth winning, a risk worth taking.

The *Sandpiper*, the *Zephyr* and the *Storm Petrel* had not been idle in Jack's absence, despite the riding officer patrolling the Orford and Aldeburgh environs and the regular checks of the Customer and Searcher, there had been profitable runs at Shingle Street, Bawdsey, Martlesham Creek and Aldeburgh. A network of inns provided safe storage in stables, cellars, attics and outbuildings until the goods could be distributed. The secret chamber at Orford Castle Keep was in regular use, as was the cellar at the King's Head, where a tunnel led to the underground vault at St Bartholomew's church, stretching underneath the ruined Norman chancel. Accessed via a memorial brass set into the floor of the Nave, the vault was not neglected as a useful repository, the vicar turning a blind eye in return for cheap tea and claret. He persuaded himself it was his philanthropic duty in bettering the lives of those less able to afford punishing taxes imposed by a government who seemed oblivious to the plight of the poorer classes, or, if not oblivious, uncaring of it.

The Preventive Service was severely stretched to cover the extensive network of rivers, creeks and shoreline frequented by the free traders, and the co-operation these bootleggers received from the locals ensured much of their clandestine activities went undetected. A tried-and-tested system of signals from buildings with seaward-facing windows that could not be seen onshore made sure that wherever the excisemen were spotted, a drop could be swiftly relocated to another spot. Despite the regular assistance from detachments of dragoons, the revenue officers were often heavily outnumbered. Even the occasional seizure of contraband by the Service was hampered by gangs of smugglers breaking into the storage cache and brazenly taking back what had been confiscated. They were not averse to fighting pitched battles or resorting to bribery and corruption of officials, persuaded by threats or inducements to collaborate. Many a riding officer had been inveigled to turn a blind eye, or to be occupied elsewhere at an allotted time.

A few interminable weeks later, as the weather calmed and Jack's eye scanned the horizon in the direction of Sizewell, he stopped and reached for his hourglass. *Yes!* The flag was undoubtedly brighter today, the white background with the red cross of St George standing out clearly against the leaden sky. *A message! At last!* Jack enthusiastically collected his belongings from the shack, and before long he and Willie were jogging along the dyke path bordering the mere, before ascending the raised heathland of Goose Hill. Jack sat himself down in a depression behind a large thicket of gorse bushes and sent Willie off to the Vulcan Arms, ostensibly for his regular sup of ale. Sometime later, Willie reappeared with a crock of ale and a couple of Mrs Baxter's meat pasties together with a leather purse, which he thrust into Jack's hand. Inside, in addition to a quantity of silver coinage there was a note. It read simply: *The bird flies to'nite.* Jack knew this could only be the *Storm Petrel* come to take him to Holland. The pair sat down to eat their supper as the sun went down, turning the western sky a deep shade of blood orange before it sank behind the Leiston Abbey ruins. It promised to be a fine night and Jack was itching to feel a heaving deck beneath his feet and the fresh salt air filling his lungs, refreshing his skin, awakening his senses, feeding his soul.

Chapter Twelve

Edward Sawyer had not been seen for some time, either in Orford or at Sudbourne. He kept to his mill and to those who approached him he was sullen and rude. He seemed to have lost interest in the young women who had set their sights on him, preferring to frequent those late-night haunts where ladies of pleasure were known to ply their trade. He had been seen lurching drunkenly outside the Bell Inn at Woodbridge and people who had previously besought his favour now avoided him. Even Ellen Goldsmith, who had thought so highly of him, was forced to admit he was not the man she'd thought, and any ideas of a match with her youngest daughter were abandoned. Edward's exciseman friend had recovered from a recent shoulder wound, allegedly received whilst carrying out his duties, although none had witnessed it, but Harry had confirmed the man had left the Service and was now working as a clerk for a firm of lawyers in Ipswich, having decided an active military career was not for him.

Kate, her mother worried, was unusually quiet and subdued. She knew part of the reason must be the disappearance of her daughter's young man, whose name, amongst others, was now emblazoned across the bills she had posted around Orford for Harry. She was sure, however, that given time Kate would forget Jack Howell and find herself a more socially acceptable suitor. Whenever they were out together Ellen's eldest daughter always attracted admiring glances and it would surely not be long before a new admirer came to woo her.

Kate, on the other hand, far from forsaking her outlaw lover, spent every waking hour waiting for news, fearful for his safety and anxious for his future, for *their* future, yearning for his kiss, aching for him to hold her once again. She thought about the purse of gold coins hidden amongst her belongings and wondered if or when she would be brave enough to use it. Her mother had recently succumbed to a winter chill and Kate had nursed her through the worst of it, but her mother's incapacity had brought home to her Ellen's vulnerability and dependence upon her daughter. The two boys were off forging their military careers and Becky was earning her keep at Sudbourne, leaving Kate to be her mother's sole carer and companion. *How can I leave now?* she agonised, dismally conflicted between duty, devotion for her family and desire for the man she loved.

For now, though, a decision need not be made, and Kate busied herself with her work at the Crown and Castle, hoping that a solution would present itself in time. She was dreading seeing Edward again, since the confrontation in the keep. His humiliation at the hands of his rival in love was hardly likely to endear him to her. She wondered what threats had been made against him to ensure his silence and that of his friend, although she was relieved to hear from Uncle Harry news of the exciseman's recovery.

It wasn't until late in the evening that she saw the man she dreaded. He usually frequented the King's Head, so it was a surprised to see him at the Crown and Castle. She hadn't noticed him come in as she was turned away from the inn door, but when she brought a freshly filled jug of ale to a group of regulars, her heart missed a beat as the newcomer sat down and their eyes met. A self-satisfied sneer tracked across Edward's face as Kate quickly averted her gaze, her cheeks burning. She could tell by his blundering movement and blurry-eyed stare that he had already had a bellyful of ale. She sent Mr Bird to serve him but was aware of her one-time suitor's eyes boring into her while her back was turned. He was still there at lock-up time, slumped over the table, and Mr Bird had to haul him up and push him through the door with the help of another somewhat less inebriated customer.

As the inn closed for the night, Kate set out for home but was concerned to see the miller's horse and trap still tied up outside. There was no sign of Edward and Kate wondered if he had perhaps found a nearby shelter in which to sleep and sober up. She hurried down through the narrow alley towards the river when all of a sudden, a figure sprang out, blocking her way. She turned to go back, but he was upon her, pushing her against the wall of a house, his alcohol-infused breath forcing her to turn her head away.

'So Howell's hussy thinks she's too good for me, eh?' Edward sneered, pushing his torso forcefully against Kate's chest. 'We'll see about that! A trollop like you's clearly not fussy about whom she lifts her skirts for!'

He pawed at her roughly as she struggled to free herself from his grip, but he had one hand constricting her throat while the other one slid up her skirt and squeezed her thigh. As he pushed his face towards hers Kate turned her head away from his fetid breath and sunk her teeth into his ear, causing him to bellow and loosen his grip, his hand grabbing the side of his head, giving her sufficient time to wrestle free and run back up the path. She screamed as he caught up with her, knocking her to the ground. 'You bitch cat! I'll give you something to scream about! Whore!' He knelt down on top of her and started to unloose his breeches.

'No, Edward, no! Please!' she screamed, but he pressed his knee into her stomach, winding her momentarily.

'Please, is it? Can't wait, eh? Not surprised, a slag like you—'

But just as he spoke Kate's hand chanced upon a chunk of brick lying by the path and she smote it with as much force as she could muster into the side of his temple. He cried out as blood streamed from his head, dazing him temporarily. Kate leapt up and ran towards the castle, being the nearest likely place of refuge. She needed a someone to help her and she knew Isaac Smith would still be about judging by the light from the first-floor window.

As she ran, she heard Edward in hot pursuit. He was gaining on her, blood dripping from both ear and head wound, the alcohol in his veins only serving to numb the pain and enrage him further. As she reached the steps of the castle, he caught up with her, slamming her back against the wall and ripping the front of her dress down to her waist.

'Playing hard to get, are we?' he snarled between his teeth, supressing her scream with his hand hard pressed over her mouth, and as he leered forward, his free hand roughly fondling her breast, Kate brought her knee up into his groin. He doubled up with a groan of agony, but just as he did so there came a dull thump; his back arched, his eyes opened wide and he crashed to the ground. Kate, momentarily stunned, stood motionless, staring down at Edward's prostrate form, the sheep's horn handle of a large folding knife protruding from his back, its blade sunk deep between his shoulder blades.

'Havin' a bit o' trouble, missy?' a familiar voice croaked from out of the shadows.

Struck dumb, Kate remained rooted to the spot. It had all happened so quickly. The man who a minute ago was about to violate her, now lay dead at her feet. She stared from her assailant to her liberator and back again, her emotions vacillating between relief at her rescue and horror towards her deliverer: both an angel of mercy and an angel of death, standing but a few feet away.

'Ben!' she breathed in disbelief, clutching at the bodice of her torn dress in an attempt to preserve her modesty.

''E had it comin',' Ben remarked impassively, then, stepping up, he bent down, twisted the knife and pulled it from the corpse, wiping it on the grass, folding it and placing it back inside his coat. 'Are ya hurt, miss?' he asked, with cool objectivity, as if nothing serious had occurred, as Kate turned away from the scene of distaste.

'No.' She shook her head dismissively. Her ordeal was nothing compared to the tableau of murder now set before her.

'Get yerself home then, miss. Me 'n' Smith'll deal wi' this,' Ben announced with the pragmatism of someone dealing with a simple pile of rubbish.

Kate turned and ran homewards, wrapping her cloak around her torn bodice, tears streaming down her cheeks, her heart pounding in her chest. Upon reaching the sanctuary of her room she thrust the door closed, throwing herself on the bed, her body shaking, the horror of what she had just witnessed now eclipsing the earlier nightmare of Edward's assault. She had been witness to murder, seen a man die in front of her. Lying awake, reliving every minute of her ordeal, her mind repeatedly revisiting the sequence of events but always ending with the same inescapable conclusion that Edward now lay dead and the undoubted conviction it was all her fault. She knew now he had deliberately come to the inn to wait for her and exact his revenge for her rejection of him. She couldn't have felt more wretched.

As the glow of dawn gradually invaded the safety of Kate's dark chamber, illuminating her blood and mud-spattered clothing, she roused herself to undress, hiding the torn garments under her mattress for washing and mending later when her mother was out. She felt stiff and sore from the fight with Edward, and no doubt bruises would soon appear. Regarding her dishevelled appearance in her vanity mirror, she noticed a long scratch across her chest, running from her collarbone to her breast, which would have to be concealed. Reaching for a pitcher of water, she poured the contents into the bowl beside the bed, washing her face, chest and arms as best she could before slipping into clean clothes, adjusting her bodice to cover the scratch and tying her hair back neatly.

Ellen was at the stove stirring the porridge pot when Kate appeared downstairs.

'You were late again last night, Kate.'

'Yes, we were busy.' Kate tried to sound casual, but her mother could sense a variance in her daughter's voice.

She glanced round and noted Kate's fresh clothing. 'I thought you had a clean dress yesterday?' Ellen remarked, looking askance at her daughter's flushed face.

'I fell over in the mud on the way home,' Kate lied.

'Bring your washing down then, I'm doing a load this morning.'

'No!' Kate said quickly. 'It's alright, Mama, I'll do it.'

She tried to feign indifference, but Ellen picked up the unguarded tremor in Kate's voice. She studied her daughter's face. 'Are you alright?' she asked quizzically. 'You seem—'

'I'm fine, Mama,' Kate interrupted. 'I'm just tired. I didn't sleep well.'

Ellen thought it best not to pursue the matter but could not help speculating on a possible reason for her doubt. *A man, most likely*, she decided, not realising the truth of her conjecture.

Edward's pony and trap mysteriously turned up at his mill the next morning, the horse unhitched, watered and stabled by the break of day, but there was no sign of Edward Sawyer. His absence went unheeded by the young lads in his employ and no questions were asked until a few days later when nothing had been seen of the miller. The next news they heard was to shock the townsfolk of Woodbridge. A man's body had been washed up on the banks of Martlesham Creek alongside a wrecked rowing boat. Although bloated and discoloured after several days in the water, the body was identified by the clothing he usually wore, his gold pocket watch engraved with his initials and later by his distressed father who came to confirm his son's demise. The undertaker had failed to notice the thin wound on his back, the blood having been washed away and the skin swollen around it. It was assumed the miller had gone out fowling or fishing and had met with some misadventure, it being well known he was lately over-fond of his drink, although it was somewhat odd that teeth marks were visibly puncturing his right ear.

Chapter Thirteen

As darkness fell on Sizewell Gap, Jack and Willie made their way down onto the beach. They had seen the sails of a brig approaching from the south and now the *Storm Petrel* lay less than a mile off in Sizewell Bay, sails luffed, anchor down. A crowd of about sixty men had gathered in the gap, along with twenty ponies and ten carts in readiness for the drop, and on the foreshore, a dozen small rowing craft were beached on the wet sand, each manned by two oarsmen. A lamp flashing twice on the cliff top was echoed by two flashes from the brig as the boats pushed off. Two fishing luggers approached and waited in the shallows, one of them the *Sandpiper*, adding two more rowing boats to the number as they brought their crewmen to the shore.

Nate Halesworth jumped down from the small craft and strode up to the base of the cliff where Jack and Willie stood waiting. Nate grinned, greeting Jack affectionately with a slap on the back. 'Good to see you, Jack.' He smiled, handing Jack a familiar flintlock pistol and cutlass. 'Here's your weapons, mate. Ben retrieved them from Sudbourne Common for ya.'

'Thank you, Nate. I've been feeling naked wi'out 'em!' Jack beamed, tucking the weapons into his belt gratefully. He turned to Willie and shook his hand warmly. 'You'd best be off now, Willie. Thank you for your help and for shelterin' me.'

'No need to thank me, lad, I've enjoyed t' company. Mind how you go now, lad.' Willie gave a kind of salute and dashed off towards the dunes.

'See ya, Willie!' Jack called.

'Not if I see you first!' came the reply as Jack chuckled, watching his eccentric friend striding off without a backwards glance.

'Mad Willie Mumford, I presume?' Nate laughed.

'Aye, but he's not so mad, as it 'appens. Knows a thing or two about these parts. I'd trust 'im with me life.'

'Aye that's what Pa says. They've known each other since boys.' Nate stared out to the brig as the heavily loaded rowing boats began to make their way back to shore. 'Right then, Jack, let's get this drop done and you can be on your way.'

His friend went back to the water's edge and rowed off towards the ship, while Jack joined the line of men forming between the gap and the waterline, ready to pass goods to the carts. It was a good haul. About three hundred half ankers of gin, one hundred casks of spirits and fifty barrels of wine, 500lbs tobacco, 5cwt tea, 200cwt coffee, some crates of soap, bolts of fine silk, French lawn and lace. It took a couple of hours' backbreaking work to load the carts, horses and tub men with as much as they could carry, some of the stronger men with two tubs, one on their back and one on their chest. Some of the haul was taken into the tunnel underneath the Vulcan Arms and the rest trundled off towards Leiston Common.

The last few remaining items were just coming off the boats when a shot rang out, then another and another. A small party of about six dragoons and as many commissioned boatmen appeared, some running through Sizewell Gap and some firing from the dunes. The traders scattered and began to return fire, Jack amongst them. Crouching behind a beached boat, he primed his pistol, aimed and fired, return musket balls whizzing past his head. Both traders and soldiers were pinned down for some time, until a number of tub men and batmen, thugs who had been hired for just such an encounter, turned back from Leiston Common to join those on the beach outnumbering the uniformed men, three to one. Hand-to-hand fighting then ensued with clubs, swords and cutlasses. Jack ran to assist his colleagues, pushing the soldiers back up through the gap as several of them broke and ran. More traders were coming off the boats with pistols freshly loaded and began picking off the servicemen, who then decided to abandon the fight. As Jack ran down through the gap, he saw a young recruit lying on the bank, a musket ball lodged in his ankle. The lad screamed and writhed on the ground as Jack went over to him. He couldn't have been more than seventeen and was clearly terrified, but there was something familiar about his features that stopped Jack in his tracks.

'What's yer name, lad?' Jack asked, kneeling down and peering closer to look at the young serviceman.

'T-Tom... Tom Goldsmith.' The boy breathed erratically, his eyes wide with alarm, panic stricken this swarthy trader was about to finish him off in cold blood. He heard Jack's intake of breath, followed by a blasphemous profanity, but instead of the blow he was expecting, the handsome trader squeezed his shoulder and said quietly, 'Keep your head down, lad,' before he stood up, turned and ran back down the beach.

As he disappeared, a stray shot from a group of smugglers running towards the gap, pursuing the fleeing soldiers, caught the stricken youth on the temple, killing him instantly. Oblivious to this tragedy, Jack was at the water's edge when he saw Nate running back up the beach.

'Get yerself on board, Jack, she's about to weigh anchor!' Nate yelled.

Jack pushed one of the rowing boats into the surf and clambered in, along with two other traders. He swore again as he thought of Kate's young brother, lying injured on the grassy dune between the cliffs. Unaware it was already too late, he reassured himself the boy would soon be rescued by his colleagues. He cursed the Service for sending such a youngster to oppose hardened lawbreakers and wished he could have done something for the lad, but he knew this was his one chance to get away. Hopefully, Tom would recover from his injury and opt for a less dangerous career and Jack would one day come back from Holland a rich man and settle down in comfortable anonymity with young Goldsmith's pretty sister at his side.

Scrambling aboard the *Storm Petrel* Jack was greeted by Captain Hammond. 'Cuttin' it fine, Jack. You nearly missed us! Glad to see you're still in one piece!' He slapped him on the back cordially. 'Come below. Did they get the goods away?' Hammond enquired as they clambered down the ladder.

'Aye, we did. We outnumbered 'em and they gave up,' Jack confirmed cheerlessly, his thoughts still haunted by

Tom Goldsmith's terror-stricken face. Stephen Hammond reunited Jack with his belongings from Chapman's yard and after stowing his property safely below his hammock, Jack went back on deck. He couldn't get the image of the young man's face out of his mind and needed a few moments alone with his thoughts. Leaning over the rail, breathing in the fresh salt air, watching the dark silhouette of the Suffolk coast slide by behind him, instead of delighting in his freedom, he felt a deep sadness and emptiness overwhelm him – Englishmen killing Englishmen and young boys sent to do a man's job! He thought about Kate's reaction when she would learn of her brother's injury and if it would cripple him for life. *Another reason for her family to hate me*, he thought. He realised gloomily it was through his own actions his lover had become embroiled in all this subterfuge against her will. She didn't deserve this. *Would she turn against me? When will I see her again? How long will it be before I'm able to return?* he reflected bleakly, searching for reassurance, while the brig's sails filled above him and the *Storm Petrel*'s bow skimmed over the ink-black water, throwing up plumes of spindrift, as gracefully effortless as the bird whose name she shared.

At River Cottage the following afternoon, Kate was upstairs when Uncle Harry called. She heard him come in, but she could tell by his unusually solemn greeting and hushed tone that something was amiss. After a few moments, a heart-rending scream echoed through the house. Kate rushed downstairs to see what had occurred and found her mother collapsed in Harry's arms, while he looked up, white-faced, shaking his head.

'No, no, noooooo!' Ellen screamed. 'Not Tom, not my baby boy! No, no. No!'

Kate clapped her hand over her mouth, hot tears stinging her eyes. 'Oh my God! No! Is he dead?'

Harry nodded. The very thing she had dreaded now come to pass, but so prematurely, so soon after he had joined the Service.

The lump in Kate's throat reduced her voice to a whisper. 'How? What happened?' she asked, part of her dreading the reply.

'I'm so sorry, my dear. He caught a smuggler's musket ball at Sizewell Gap last night, when our men tried to stop a run.'

'Did you see it happen?' Kate asked tearfully, as her mother sank to the floor, bent double, holding her stomach, rocking to and fro, moaning softly.

'No, I wasn't there,' Harry sighed, 'otherwise I would have stopped him going. They were just on routine patrol at Sizewell when some tub men were spotted making for the Common and then they saw the boats on the shore. They shouldn't have tried to intervene, but the sergeant thought he could prevail until he saw they were outnumbered three to one, by which time it was too late.' He touched Ellen on the shoulder. 'He shouldn't have been there! I'm so sorry, Ellen.'

'He was only seventeen!' Kate exclaimed bitterly, sitting down at the table, leaning her head on her arms, sobbing woefully, recalling the proud and happy grin on her little brother's face as he showed off his new boatman's uniform. She then remembered her sister, who must be told.

'Becky!' she exclaimed, raising her tear-stained face. 'Uncle Harry, please can you fetch Becky from

Sudbourne, and can you get a message through navy channels to John somehow?'

'Of course, m'dear. I will go at once.' Harry got up and let himself out, relieved to have something to occupy him and to leave the women to grieve in private.

Kate put her arm around her mother's shoulders and they sobbed together on the kitchen floor as the sound of the pony and trap faded rapidly into the distance.

Later that evening Harry brought Becky home, red-eyed and shaking. She ran to her mother and the three of them wept in unison for their beloved brother and son who had followed his father to an early grave, both victims of the free trade that permeated this quiet Suffolk coastline and subjugated its population.

Lying in her bed that night, clutching a damp handkerchief, Kate thoughts raced. Her mother's hatred of the free traders would be even more virulent now that they had taken the life of her son as well as her husband. She would need Kate to support her in her grief, and to leave her for a man caught up with the very enemy Ellen loathed, would be like a knife in her mother's heart. *A knife!* She could see it now, embedded deep in Edward's back; she heard again the nauseating sound as the blade was pulled from the flesh and she retched. She thought of Ben and wondered what sort of life had turned his heart to stone that he could be so cold and unfeeling, and yet he had saved her from Edward's assault, so he must have some empathy, she adjudged. She heard his words telling her Jack would be awaiting passage from Sizewell and she sat up with a jolt. *Sizewell! Was Jack there last night? Did he see Tom? Did he witness my brother's last moments? Did he get away, or is he too lying dead on the dunes? No.* She realised almost immediately that could not be the case; his body would have been found and identified, and Harry would know Jack Howell was no longer a wanted man. *No, he must have got away!*

She breathed a deep sigh of relief and sank back down under the bedcover, curling herself into a foetal position, hugging the pillow to her breast. *Oh, Jack!* A fresh tear trickled down her cheek for the handsome man who made her pulse race and her heart flutter, but at the same time the lead weight of guilt twisted in her gut. Here she was worshipping a man who was mixed up with the very perpetrators of her family's distress. She knew once her mother's grief turned to anger, she would be in the firing line. Despite this and despite the sorrow of her brother's untimely death, she knew she could never give up her lover. She wanted Jack more than ever. He was part of her psyche, her soul, her true being, the vital force that gave her life. She heard his voice, the affectionate way he called her 'my little dunlin', that charming little bird of the mudflats, endearing and fragile, vulnerable yet spirited; to him she was all these things, in need of his protection, yet free to fly and spread her wings if she should so desire. He understood her; born of the same Suffolk stock, they were raised under the same sweeping skies, surveyed the same reed-congested mudflats, trod the same barren shingle wastes, breathed the same salt-laden air, felt the same irresistible pull of the land of their birth. No matter what he had done or was involved in, he was her true love, her soulmate. *How could I give him up?*

Chapter Fourteen

John Goldsmith came home on a few days' bereavement leave. He had matured, his body noticeably bulked out, more muscular, his confident bearing of authority boosted by the fact he was now in line for promotion to midshipman in His Majesty's Navy, several engagements with French pirate ships and English smuggling vessels under his belt. Despite a fresh outpouring of grief, Ellen was suitably proud of her one remaining son who was now the head of the family and welcomed his gifts of Bordeaux wine and Normandy lace, plus a quantity of silver coin which he had put by for them. He looked healthy and suntanned in his navy frock coat with gold buttons and cocked hat, and Kate guessed he would not be short of female admirers who would, no doubt, flock to His Majesty's mariners when they enjoyed shore leave. She hugged him and, after a further tearful commiseration with his mother for his lost brother, the two siblings strolled down to the river path to catch up on each other's news.

After expressing their sorrow at Tom's death and recounting some of their happier shared memories of him, Kate asked her brother about life in the Navy. John spoke animatedly of his daily tasks, his rendition of gunnery practice, the strict firing drill with guns ranging from the small twelve-pounder top-deck guns to the heavy thirty-two-pounders on the lower deck, painting a vivid picture of life on a warship. He described learning the various types of shot – round shot, cannister shot, chain shot and grape shot – mastering small arms training, manning the halliards, climbing rigging, reefing sails, casting lead lines and log lines for depth and speed, learning signal flags and navigation, taking sextant readings, deciphering charts; each day adhering to a strict routine, every half hour the ship's bell ringing out monotonously. He reflected on irksome tasks like scrubbing decks, painting the quarterdeck, the boredom of long watches; the diet of salt beef, weevily bread, hard cheese and equally hard ships' biscuits washed down with a daily ration of half a pint of diluted rum; the cramped, stuffy, smelly atmosphere 'tween decks; the seasickness and scurvy. He laughed as Kate's face became a picture of disgust.

'It isn't all bad, though,' he assured her: he had made some good mates; they took pride in their skills and the efficient fighting force they had become, enjoying the camaraderie of men thrust together in a common experience. He described the bracing momentum and beauty of a ship under full sail; the stunning night-time sky over the ocean, as he took the middle watch from midnight to 4am; the excitement of visiting new ports; the thrill of receiving a share of the prize money from captured ships and the prospect of advancement up the ranks.

Kate listened attentively, the impression of naval life her brother depicted vividly implanted in her mind's eye. She could see he enjoyed his new career, proudly admiring the man her irritating big brother had grown into, the image of her father reflected in his face, save for their mother's eyes. Kate congratulated him on his forthcoming promotion and ventured to ask him about any possible lady loves he had encountered on shore leave, upon which he blushed, brushing off her enquiry with a vague allusion to a couple of romantic liaisons which had not led anywhere. Embarrassed, he quickly changed the subject, steering the conversation towards his sister and the happenings at home.

Kate dreaded telling him about Jack, but he would find out anyway and she wanted to give her side of the story before Mother had a chance to colour John's opinion of his sister. She told him about refusing Edward and her reasons for doing so, which led to the subject of Jack. She described his job at the boat builders and how he planned to ask her to marry him when he had finished his apprenticeship. She made light of his involvement with the crew of the *Sandpiper* and how he was just helping an old friend when he got mixed up with the free traders, was then recognised by Uncle Harry during a run and was now a fugitive. Of course, she was not going to tell him about the goings-on at the castle keep, or the fact she knew what had happened to Jack, or Edward, for her brother was on the side of the law and obliged by his commission to impart what he knew to the authorities.

She told John of Edward Sawyer's mysterious death by drowning, which by all accounts was a tragic accident, but she mentioned nothing of his assault on her or the truth of his demise. She told him she knew nothing of

Jack's whereabouts, which, she satisfied herself, was not a lie, in that she had not heard from him. She described her work at the Crown and Castle, Ellen's recent illness, which had left their mother weakened with a hacking cough, and she praised Becky for her diligence in the kitchens at Sudbourne Hall.

John listened, frowning occasionally, uttering a disapproving, 'Oh, Kate!' as she related her story. He was concerned for mother's health but also for his sister's welfare.

'I'm relying on you, Kate, to help Mama,' he charged his sister. 'You are all she's got now, until you find a suitor and marry. No more smugglers, Kate!' he scolded. 'Mother would take it as the ultimate betrayal, now that Tom's gone too. She took it bad enough when Father died, but now...' He stopped walking and gazed across the river, a lump in his throat constricting his words.

Kate's heart sank. She knew he was right. She understood only too well the burden that was now placed upon her and her obligation to her family, but she felt it a little unfair that both John and Becky were free to make their own lives while she was left to bear the heavy load of care without a thought for her own happiness. She didn't need her brother loading on the guilt, expecting her to make the self-sacrifice.

'It's alright for you, John, you're a man!' Kate grumbled resentfully. 'You can go off and live your life as you please.'

'Yes, it may be true to an extent, Kate, but a man has to do what he can to support his family. He *has* to be the breadwinner. Women are the homemakers, that's just the way it is.' He put his arm around her shoulder and squeezed it sympathetically. 'It won't be forever, not with your Goldsmith good looks!' he quipped with a placative smile, attempting to appease his sister. 'You've already had two suitors wanting to marry you, I can't see it being too long before the next one comes calling.'

'Even if they did, how can I leave Mother? You said yourself I'm all she's got,' Kate sighed dismally.

'Yes, for now, but I'm hoping Uncle Harry will ask for her hand one day.'

'Well, I was too, but I'm not sure now. He was shocked at her temper when she found out I was seeing Jack. Perhaps he's decided she's not for him?'

'He still seems to care, Kate, and I know Mother is very fond of him. He's very much like Father, albeit not so good-looking, of course!'

'Of course!' Kate agreed, brightening up.

They laughed together and turned for home. Kate linking her arm through John's in a rare display of affection for her older brother, now the only brother she had. She thought of how he used to tease her when she was a child and how much she had hated him then, but now they were adults she felt proud of him and hoped he would feel the same of her.

After the distressing ordeal of Tom's burial in the graveyard at St Bartholomew's, John and Harry supporting Ellen between them, while the girls wept for their little brother, John left to join his ship at Deptford, where it was berthed for mast repairs. Harry took him to Ipswich, where he boarded a navy gun brig bound for the Thames port.

Becky returned to Sudbourne, leaving Kate and Ellen to carry on as best they could. Becky had also been shocked to hear about Edward's death but not as overly sorry for it as Kate had expected. Talking quietly in bed at night, Becky related to her sister the details of her last encounter with the miller and how he had threatened her, and although it was Kate's turn to be outraged at Edward's behaviour, she was not surprised, given the assault she had experienced at his hands.

The people of Orford were outwardly kind and understanding of the family's second tragic loss, but many viewed Kate with enmity and suspicion, convinced her previous involvement with a free trader had somehow contributed to her brother's death. Kate's own guilt did little to prevent her from agreeing with them, especially as Ellen had angrily expostulated the same opinion.

Another month went by before Kate received the news she had half dreaded, half longed for. A mariner of about Jack's age, whom Kate did not recognise, had come into the Crown and Castle at midday and sat drinking on his own. He was clearly a seaman from the way he was dressed in short brown jacket, loose shirt and wide-legged trousers, his tawny shoulder-length hair gathered in a ponytail at the nape of his neck. Removing his felt hat, he pushed a stray strand of hair back from his sunburned face and sat observing Kate admiringly for some time before beckoning her over. She brought the jug of ale to refill his tankard, but he placed his hand over the rim and leaned towards her.

'I reckon you be Kate Goldsmith?' he asked quietly, fixing her with kindly hazel eyes, as Kate nodded expectantly. From Jack's description of his pretty dark-haired mawther, with her big blue eyes and pale skin, she could not be anyone else. He reached into his jacket pocket and pulled out a crumpled missive, thrusting it into her hand. 'For you,' he whispered, casting about for any unwanted observers, but the few customers patronising the tavern were too busily engaged in animated chatter to notice the exchange.

'Thank you, er, Mr...?' Kate smiled politely, her heart racing at the prospect of hearing from Jack at last.

'Nate Halesworth, miss, from the *Sandpiper.*'

'Thank you, Nate. Do you require a reply?'

'No miss. 'E says he'll be waitin'.'

'Thank you, Nate.' Kate hurried to the kitchen and unfolded the letter, her hand trembling. The ink on the dog-eared paper had run, but she recognised Jack's distinctive scrawl. *Kate, my dunlin, Friday night, eleven o'clock, wait at Orford Quay for the* Sandpiper. *She will take you to the* Zephyr *for passage to Flushing. Bring only essentials. I'll be waiting. Burn this! Jack.* Friday night! That was only two days away! Kate's stomach churned. This was it! She had to make her decision now. There was no more time. She dropped the note into the fire and watched it curl, blacken and disintegrate to ashes.

Chapter Fifteen

Friday came round far too quickly. The day after receiving Jack's letter Kate had walked over to the hall to see Becky. She had no way of knowing when she might next see her little sister and she wanted to make sure there was no cause for worry and to let her know she might not see her for a while. Becky was pleased to see her sister and the pair sat in in Mrs Barrell's kitchen drinking milk and enjoying a piece of fruit cake, chatting amiably about local goings-on. At a suitable break in the conversation Kate took a deep breath. She hoped her nerves would not give her away.

'Becky, I'm going to go away for a while. Great Aunt Agatha in Ipswich is unwell and I've offered to look after her. Mother says she can do without me for a short time and it will give me a break from work.' The lies were so convincing Kate almost believed them herself. 'You will be alright, won't you?'

'Oh, yes, of course! Although I wish I could come too! I would love to visit Ipswich!' Becky's innocently enthusiastic reply assured Kate her sister did not suspect anything amiss.

'I'm sure you will get the chance, Becky, but please call on Mother sometimes to check she is managing on her own. I don't want her to get ill again.'

Yes, I'll go on Sunday week, when I get my day off. You won't be away too long, will you, Kate?'

'Oh no! I will be back before you know it!' The falsehood tripped off Kate's tongue with unexpected ease; she stood up, not wishing to dwell further on her deception, relieved her sister had taken her at her word. 'Now, I must go.' The sisters hugged each other, Kate holding on to Becky just that little bit longer than usual before walking away, waving until she was out of sight, her guilt weighing heavily on her conscience. *No going back now*, she brooded. Kate knew she had just over a week before Becky would go home and reveal her invention about Aunt Agatha, but by then Mother would be well aware of her daughter's late-night flight and Kate safely distanced from the inevitable fallout.

All too soon it was Friday evening and Kate's stomach churned as she nervously cleared the tables, watching the clock on the old inn wall tick relentlessly forward. At last, saying goodnight to Mr Bird as normally as she could, Kate reached for the bundle she had hidden in the pantry, pulled her cloak around her shoulders and stepped out into the night. She had left a note on the windowsill apologising for her actions and wishing her landlord well, figuring he would not see it until the next morning. Her bag held the minimum of belongings: one spare set of clothes, nightgown, hairbrush, a cake of soap, her pearl earrings, the money Jack had given her and a small prayer book. Hurrying through Orford down to the quayside, she was pleased it was a calm, clear night, a full moon casting a spectral radiance over the water, silhouetting the masts of the *Sandpiper*, as she lay moored by the jetty.

Relieving Kate of her bundle, Nate Halesworth helped her aboard, handing her a lantern and ushering her down into the tiny, cramped hold, the crewmen on deck eyeing her up lustfully, a low whistle and a few coarse comments generating the inevitable libidinous snigger as all eyes followed her. Kate was glad the darkness hid her blushes, settling herself down between kegs, bales and crates as the crew cast off and the lugger slipped away from the quay, down the Ore and out towards North Weir Point.

What am I doing? Kate remonstrated with her conscience as she sat dismally reflecting on her actions. Mama would soon find the letter she had left propped up beside her bed. There was no going back now. She pictured Ellen opening it and collapsing on the bed with the shock of her daughter's words.

I'm sorry, Mama, please forgive me, but I have to go. Don't worry about me, I will be alright. I have gone to be with the man I love. He will look after me. I will return once all the fuss has died down. Please don't think too badly of me. My love always, Kate.

Brushing away a tear which had gathered in the corner of her eye and spilled down her cheek, Kate leant against a bale and closed her eyes, slipping into unconsciousness until a change in the motion of the ship woke her. Her stomach churned and she tasted the bile rising in her throat, as the *Sandpiper* emerged from the estuary into Hollesley Bay, where the deep waters of the North Sea swelled underneath her hull. She decided to go up on deck to feel the cool wind upon her face and fresh air in her lungs, which hopefully would dispel the nausea threatening to overwhelm her. The thought of spewing her stomach's contents in front of all these seasoned seamen was just too humiliating a prospect. Already they were eyeing her with some amusement.

'Feeling a little queasy, lass?' Dick Halesworth asked kindly with a knowing grin.

'A little,' Kate admitted shyly.

'It won't be long before we reach the Deben,' he reassured her. 'You'll feel better aboard the *Zephyr*, lass, she's a steadier craft.'

Kate smiled politely, gripping the taffrail tightly, breathing in as much oxygen as she could to keep her biliousness at bay. Thankfully the lugger soon slowed with the lessening swell, approaching the lower reaches of the Deben Estuary, and eased herself round Bawdsey point and into calmer water. As they approached the quay the graceful bulk of the *Zephyr* hove into view, anchored in midstream, and as soon as the *Sandpiper* was spotted a rowing boat launched towards them.

'Thank you, Mr Halesworth.' Kate shook Dick's hand gratefully as she prepared to disembark, relieved she had not embarrassed herself.

'That's a'right, lass. You be careful now. Give Jack our best wishes.' Nate handed over her belongings. Kate fumbled in her purse for a coin to give the seaman, but Dick stopped her. 'There's no need for that, miss. Howell's like a son to me. I don't tek money from family!'

Kate reached up and kissed him on the cheek, much to his surprise. Before the blushing captain could react, Kate climbed down the ladder into the rowing boat, smiling to herself as the sounds of whistling, laughter and bawdy suggestions emanated from his diverted crew.

The *Zephyr* slipped her moorings and filled her sails just as the western sky was lightening with the dawn, the crew busy with their allotted tasks as the nimble brig negotiated the channel through to the open sea. Joe Willis introduced himself and showed Kate below into his small cabin at the stern of the ship. Kate had seen him at Chapman's when she first met Jack but had not so far spoken to him. He was a tanned, middle-aged man with greying hair and an aquiline nose which Kate thought made him look like a bird of prey, his manner curt and matter-of-fact.

'Ye can get yer head down 'ere for a few hours, miss. I'll rouse you when we near Flushing. If ye need anythin' Pip 'ere will get it for ya. Just ring t' bell.' He pointed to a small hand bell and nodded towards the cabin boy stood waiting by the door. The lad was about twelve years old, wiry and solemn, a mass of brown freckles dappling his face, his big eyes staring at Kate as he held the lantern up and hung it from a hook on the beam.

'Away with you now, lad, leave the lady in peace,' Joe Willis commanded as the boy disappeared up to the deck.

'Thank you, Captain Willis. I am obliged to you.'

The door closed and Kate looked around her. The small cabin was dark, with no window, save for a tiny porthole, the lantern's weak flame emitting just enough light to illuminate a bunk bed, a chest, a chair and a table, hidden under a pile of charts and logbooks. In the corner behind the door, Kate noticed a porcelain bucket with a lid and was comforted she had a suitable receptacle in which to relieve her queasiness, which was threatening to return now they were once again in open water. The fully laden brig, her cargo of English wool bound for France, lying stacked to the beams in her hull, was steadier than the *Sandpiper* but the heaving swell still enough to make Kate dizzy and nauseous. She lay down on the bunk and closed her eyes. This was the first time she had left Suffolk – indeed, left England. Mother would soon be reading her letter and all hell would break loose. *At least I'm not there to witness it*, she sighed with relief as she sank under the coarse blanket and offered a quick prayer for her safety, her family and her lover in whose arms she would soon be held. A warm glow of excitement and anticipation enveloped her at the thought. Before the new day was out, she would be reunited with Jack and a new life would begin.

A loud knock on the cabin door woke her with a start, followed by the captain's voice. 'Just comin' into Flushing, miss.'

Bright midday sunlight streamed through the porthole and Kate peeped out at the busy port situated at the mouth of the Scheldt, the dozens of Dutch East India company trading ships, forming a forest of masts, against a backdrop of colourful red-roofed houses. Arranging her clothes and tidying her hair before collecting her belongings, she went on deck. The ship slowly edged towards the quay, the crew climbing the mast, busy furling sails, preparing to weigh anchor, muscle-bound seamen throwing up wool bales from the hold ready to be taken off, the air ringing with shouts and commands. As the *Zephyr* docked Kate watched from the rail, amazed at the spectacle of such a busy port, scanning the dockside for any sign of Jack, but she could not pick him out from the throng of people. The ship's ropes were soon secured to its mooring and a gangplank pushed out. Kate turned back to thank the captain, but as she did so, a tall, bearded figure ran up the ramp and a voice she knew called her name. Her heart missed a beat, and before she could focus, she was swept up in the arms of the man for whom she had given up everything.

'Kate, my dunlin!' Jack breathed, almost taking her breath away with the vigour of his embrace, planting a long kiss of desire on her lips, his full beard shocking her with its unfamiliarity.

'Oh, Jack!' she sighed when she could breathe again. She stood back from him, gazing into his deep blue eyes, scanning his handsome face, her body trembling with emotion as she tried to fight the tears welling in her eyes. 'No wonder I couldn't see you!' She smiled, stroking his beard affectionately before her self-control buckled under his gaze and she wept.

'Don't cry, my dunlin.' He smiled tenderly, 'You're here now. Thank you for comin', I was afeared you would not.'

Kate didn't tell him it had taken every ounce of her courage and resolve not to stay in the familiar safety of home, as she nestled her head into his chest and wept fresh tears. As she clung to him, the gamut of emotions she had struggled to hold back for too long now swept over her in a tidal wave of relief at being in the arms of her lover once more, someone to whom she could pour her heart out without censure.

'Tom's dead,' she cried, and Jack swore under his breath.

'Oh, I'm *so* sorry, my dunlin,' he said with genuine sorrow. 'I thought he'd be alright. It wer' just a leg wound!'

'What?!' Kate looked up at him, aghast, blinking away her tears. 'Did you see him? Were you there? It wasn't you, was it? Oh, Jack, tell me!' She clutched at his arm.

Jack sighed, recalling the scene, relating what he knew. 'There was a run at Sizewell Gap the night I left. Some soldiers and Revenue men spotted us and decided to engage despite being outnumbered. There was a gun fight and they ran off. I found Tom lying in the gap, his ankle shattered by a musket ball and...' He held Kate's face between his hands and fixed her with a measured gaze. 'No, it wasn't me, my dunlin. I told him to keep his head down. He should have been alright!' he said with exasperation.

'He was shot in the temple,' Kate said glumly, closing her eyes, as if to shut out an image too horrific to visualise.

Jack swore again. 'It must 'ave happened after I left. I didn't know, Kate, I'm *so* sorry. Poor lad.'

'He was only seventeen!' Kate sobbed again, burying her head in Jack's chest.

'I *had* to go, Kate. If I'd stayed, they would have taken me! I thought he'd be alright!' he reiterated heavy-heartedly, feeling partly responsible. 'Must'a been a stray shot. Our men don't shoot someone who's down, especially not someone so young.'

'Uncle Harry said he should never have been there. He said the army sergeant was wrong to try to intercept the run with so few of them.' Kate sniffed.

'Madness!' Jack fumed. 'I'm surprised you came after that, my dunlin.' Jack stroked her hair gently, kissing the top of her head affectionately.

‘I thought about it,’ Kate admitted, ‘but I wanted to see you again, Jack. Tom dying wasn’t going to change how I feel about *us*.’

‘Thank you, my dunlin, that’s good to hear.’ He kissed her again. ‘I don’t deserve you, Kate,’ he sighed, embracing her once more. ‘I will make it up to you, I promise. Now come on, let me show your new home… for now anyway.’ He took her bundle and called over to Joe Willis to thank him, pressing some coins into his palm. They spoke for a moment and then he led Kate down the gangplank, away from the hustle and bustle of the crowded quayside and into the unfamiliar town.

Chapter Sixteen

Jack found Kate some lodgings close to where he was staying. He was determined not to tarnish her reputation by cohabiting until they could marry. He continued to work for Mike Chapman's merchants in Flushing, sailing regularly on the *Zephyr* and *Storm Petrel*, off-loading goods along the East Anglian coast but not venturing ashore himself. He was able to procure spirits, wines, tea, tobacco, coffee, soap, cloth and luxury goods, some of it legitimate for export to Ipswich and Felixstowe but much of it bound for the free trade distribution so prevalent on the Suffolk coast.

To ensure he wasn't reported to the authorities as a known smuggler, Jack now went by the name Will Pallant, after an uncle of his from Aldeburgh who had died some years ago. In effect, Jack Howell had disappeared off the scene, except to the crews of those ships with whom he had spent many years, his shipmates and friends who would never think to betray him. To the Dutch, he was just another English merchantman of no particular notoriety but upon whom they could rely for a steady and lucrative trading relationship. Who he was and what he did with the goods he bought once they had left their waters, was no concern of theirs.

The couple's first few days together were blissful. Jack's ardour for his young Suffolk beauty had not diminished; in fact, he was hard pressed to control his natural urges as they embraced, their kisses hot and erotic, having been starved of physical contact for what seemed like an eternity. Kate realised how much she had missed her eye-catching sailor and delighted in the fact they could be openly seen together without censure. Anonymity was a new sensation to Kate, having lived all her life in the close confines of a rural village, and she enjoyed the freedom it afforded. They both longed to consummate their partnership in marriage, but a licence had to be procured and a church found where no questions would be asked. At least they were both over eighteen, which meant they could marry without parental consent.

They had a lot to catch up on: Jack describing to Kate his adventures since they parted that night at Orford Castle, his flight to Minsmere, his time at 'Mad' Willie's shack, that last night on the shore at Sizewell before his escape. Kate listened with interest and shared with him the circumstances around Edward's death. Jack paced the floor angrily, swearing when he learned of the miller's assault on Kate, his wrath tempering somewhat with the news of Ben's timely intervention. He was on the point of remarking that Edward had got what he deserved, but picturing Kate on her own, defenceless and vulnerable, witnessing a scene that must have shocked her to the core, such a remark seemed flippant and indifferent to her ordeal. Instead, he held her close, tight-lipped, guilt-ridden and self-reproachful, for not being there and for the situation now forced upon an innocent girl. He determined to make amends for the trauma she had suffered on his behalf and reward her with the life he had promised.

For Kate, once the euphoria of her reunion with her handsome sailor had mellowed into happy contentment and the novelty of her new surroundings had waned, she found herself at a loss for something to do. Not speaking the language, she could not make friends, nor find gainful employment of the sort her husband would approve, although she did help out her kindly landlady with cleaning the boarding house and collecting groceries from the local market. Grada, as the affable host liked to be addressed, had a smattering of English words, so with that and a comical combination of sign language the two women managed to communicate sufficiently to understand each other.

Jack was busy working, sometimes away for days at a time, but often on a Sunday they would stroll around the town, sitting by the canals, watching the ships coming in and out of the busy harbour, dreaming of settling down together. Jack always had a pocket full of money and he thrilled Kate with gifts of a new set of clothes and shoes, which, although pretty enough, left her feeling as if she were living some kind of dream, a bubble which was soon to burst and plunge her back into the reality of the working life to which she was more accustomed.

For now, though, she was fascinated by the comings and goings in this Dutch port, the vivid colours of the costumes, the pretty houses and the ubiquitous blue and white Delftware pottery, its intricate designs adorning everything from practical dinnerware to tiles and ornamental vases. She bought herself a small sketchbook and amused herself with copying tile designs, costumes or architectural features, which to her surprise were quite accomplished and elicited admiring glances from passers-by. She felt a certain pride in herself for displaying that natural talent which hadn't revealed itself to an audience since childhood, and encouraged by Grada, she managed to sell a few sketches at the local market. Jack was proud of his gifted and personable girl, and liked to show her off to his Dutch and Flemish colleagues at every opportunity. He had picked up a smattering of the language to make himself understood and Kate was equally proud of her man as she watched him interact with these merchantmen in their own tongue, though their English was considerably more proficient than his Dutch.

As winter turned into spring Jack hired a pony and trap to show Kate the delights of the Dutch countryside, the windmills, dykes and vast fields of bright tulips, once highly prized for their colourful blooms. The landscape featured very few trees, but with miles of white sand beaches backed by rows of windmills catching the breeze as it raced across the lowland. They would sit in the sunshine, Kate sketching the scene, while Jack enjoyed a slice of Grada's apple cake, washed down with a jug of local beer. Somehow, though, Kate mused, as she surveyed the colourful vistas, all this gaudy prettiness was a world away from the soft, muted tones of Suffolk, the big skies, empty shingle beaches and windswept marshes she loved, yet they were still there, not just in her memory but tantalisingly close, just over the sea, a day's sail away. Kate thought about her mother, the burden of guilt weighing heavily on her conscience. *Surely, once her anger's subsided, she will understand I'm in love?*

Love so all-consuming, so undeniable, it banished all reason, all sensibility.

Strolling along the dyke wall towards the prominent windmill standing sentinel over the North Sea, its sails pointed in the direction of England, the couple stopped one fine April evening to watch sunset's dazzling orb sinking into the western horizon in a blaze of colour. They stood spellbound by the spectacle of the scarlet and gold cloud-banded sky until the light faded and a fresh breeze caught their hair, whipping it across their faces. A shiver ran down Kate's back as Jack embraced her and held her close, kissing her hair while she leant against his chest.

'Are you cold, my dunlin?'

'No, not really.' She heaved a long sigh. 'Jack... I... I'm homesick. I want to go home.'

'I know,' Jack admitted gloomily. 'I feel it too, but I've got our marriage licence now.' He brightened, pulling a paper from his pocket. 'We can get married here and go back as Mr and Mrs Will Pallant.'

'Oh, Jack, I *do* want to marry you *so* much, but can't we do it in England?' Kate gazed up into his eyes. 'I don't feel right doing it here.'

Jack took a lingering breath of disappointment. 'Well, if that's what you want, my dunlin, but it can't be at Orford. I'll be recognised.'

'Anywhere, Jack, I don't mind, just as long as it's in England.'

'Alright, sweetheart. I'll arrange passage for us,' Jack conceded, crestfallen at yet another delay to their long-awaited nuptials. It was a risk to go back to Suffolk, but if he searched his innermost feelings, he felt exactly the same, and with any luck Jack Howell would be a distant memory in the minds of local folk, who would surely by now have a new focus for their enmity.

By the middle of May, the *Storm Petrel* departed Flushing at dawn with her usual cargo of luxury goods plus two passengers, Mr Will Pallant and his intended Miss Katherine Goldsmith. No longer known fugitives, the smartly dressed couple were, to all appearances, a well-respected merchant and his betrothed, on their way to England to marry. Jack was now clean-shaven, his hair neatly tied at the nape of the neck with a black ribbon, and Kate wore her long dark hair fashionably ringleted underneath a lace-edged bonnet, her bodice-hugging jacket and checked skirt completing a co-ordinated outfit, allowing her to feel proud and pretty. *Quite the respectable lady*. She smiled to herself at the thought of Becky's envy. She was unashamedly proud of her man and their new-found prosperity, although she had could not quite relax into complacence, knowing their identity was based upon a lie, the nagging doubt of which always played on her mind beneath an outwards show of confidence. The couple stood on deck watching the coast of Holland diminish into the haze, both eager to feel the rich earth of Suffolk once more beneath their feet and excited at the prospect of their new life as man and wife.

After a calm crossing, the brig anchored off Southwold harbour at the mouth of the Blyth, where a shingle spit prevented safe passage for larger craft. Captain Hammond wished his passengers well while they waited for a rowing boat to be lowered to take them ashore. It was a fine evening:

gulls wheeling and screeching around the fishing boats at anchor in the Blyth and across the river, the bell tolling from the tall tower of St Andrew's in Walberswick summoning the righteous to evensong. Along the mudbanks black and white avocets swept the shallows with their upturned beaks, a flight of black-tailed godwit busily probed the muddied river margins, and somewhere upriver, the liquid notes of a woodlark echoed across the salt marsh. Alighting at the quay between the many tightly packed herring busses, Jack and Kate paused to take in the comforting sights and sounds of home. The estuary was serene and peaceful, in marked contrast to the hubbub of Flushing, and Kate's heart swelled with delight as she surveyed the scene and she couldn't help a breaking into a smile.

'Happy now, my dunlin?' Jack asked, squeezing Kate's hand lovingly.

'Oh, *yes*, Jack, thank you,' Kate confirmed happily as they embraced before turning northwards along the track to Southwold. They walked the half-mile pathway through the water meadows into the town, keeping the marshes to their left and on their right the dunes, their luggage loaded onto a small handcart borrowed from one of the many local fishermen.

They lodged at the Red Lion coaching inn, where Jack enquired after renting a small property nearby. He spoke with the vicar at the fifteenth-century church of St Edmund, procured a marriage licence and a month later Jack and Kate were married, a handful of locals witnessing the ceremony, congratulating this handsome young merchantman and his fetching bride who had recently settled in the town. Kate wore a silk dress of soft cornflower blue, with lace inserts around the cuffs and neckline, and Jack cut a fine figure in a new navy-blue military-style coat and matching breeches. Mr and Mrs Will Pallant were now official and nobody had any reason to doubt this attractive couple were not all as they seemed.

Kate's joy at finally being wed to the man she loved was tinged with sadness for her absent family. She knew they would have thrilled to see her wed, but if they had married locally, Uncle Harry was sure to have attended the ceremony and would immediately recognise Jack. As it was, Jack's missing finger would mark him out as a possible suspect, even by those who did not know his face. However, sharing the quaint rented cottage atop the bluff overlooking Southwold's sandy foreshore with the man she adored was all Kate hoped it would be, the euphoria of their physical union deepening her love until she thought she could burst with happiness. She revelled in the intimacy of marriage to this desirable man, whose touch made her heart race and her pulse quicken, whose kisses set her on fire and whose body aroused feelings she didn't know she had. For Jack, his pride in his beautiful wife who turned heads and charmed all who met her was clear for all to see, their wedded bliss the envy of many who endured less than ideal partnerships.

With Jack frequently away on his trips to and from the Dutch coast, Kate immersed herself in domesticity at their tiny cottage, and when her chores were done, she would explore the town and enjoy the wide expanse of inviting sandy beach. She had offered to take in sewing as her mother had taught her, but Jack would have none of it. 'I wouldn't be much of a trader if my wife had to work to supplement my income!' he had declared emphatically. Though it would take Kate a while to adjust to her new status, the need to work having been drummed into her since her mother had become widowed.

Wandering along Southwold's golden shoreline, her shoes clutched in one hand, the hem of her skirt held up by the other, cool saltwater and wet yellow sand oozing up between her toes, Kate could not have been happier. She had her man, they had money, she found herself almost forgetting the lie she was living, with the ease of acting out the fantasy, until something reminded her and settled in the pit of her stomach like a lead weight. There was only one thing missing that would have made her life perfect. Gazing southwards along the coastline, she longed to be back in familiar surroundings and reunited with her family.

Only a few miles further down, past Minsmere, Sizewell Gap and Aldeburgh, where deep drifts of shingle triumphed over sand, lay the River Ore and the sleepy town she called home. She wondered what her mother was doing and whether her anger had turned to acceptance and forgiveness. Hoping for the latter, Kate decided she would write. Ellen would be sure to rejoice in the fact her daughter was now the wife of a respectable trader and happily enjoying her union. Kate hoped to alleviate any fears her mother might harbour for her welfare and safety, the guilt of her night-time flight still weighing heavily on her conscience.

Dear Mama, she wrote, *I hope this finds you well. I have some joyful news which I hope will please you. I am now wed to a successful merchantman, a Mr Will Pallant, by whose means I am comfortably supported. We are very happy and are returned to Suffolk. I hope to visit you when I am able, but until then, please be assured of my well-being. Yours most affectionately, your loving daughter, Kate.*

Chapter Seventeen

Ellen's shock at her daughter's disappearance had been as traumatising as Kate had feared. With the pain of her son's tragic death still raw, the fact her daughter had chosen to desert her family for a man mixed up in the very trade responsible for her young son's untimely demise was a double hammer blow. 'Oh, Kate, how could you?!' Ellen had wailed upon finding Kate's farewell note, her knees giving way as she slumped onto the bed, the crumpled letter shaking in her hand.

A couple of days later Uncle Harry had made his usual call to find Ellen had taken to her bed in a state of collapse and mental torment, the kitchen table displaying an assortment of unwashed crockery and left-over food, piles of clothes awaiting washing, her sewing still lying untouched on the chair. Ellen passed him Kate's note, which he read with shock and anger at his niece's actions, a few choice swear words spilling unapologetically from his lips. He called for Doctor Ward to check on Ellen's health, his sister-in-law's hacking cough, listless posture and pallid appearance a concern, before riding over to Sudbourne to arrange for Becky to have leave to come home to help her mother.

After the initial shock, Becky's anger at her sister's actions matched her uncle's, with the added humiliation of realising Kate had lied to her, using Aunt Agatha as a cover story, clearly knowing full well her little sister's naivete could be exploited. She felt humiliated and let down that Kate felt she could not share the truth of what she was about to do, and to do it just after Tom's death, knowing what that would do to mother, was unforgiveable. Not only that; the burden of care for Ellen now fell upon her own shoulders, and while she was away from the hall, no wages would be forthcoming.

Resentful of her sister's actions, Becky did her best to care for her mother through the winter months, and Harry's frequent visits, cheerful disposition and gifts of foodstuffs were a welcome tonic to both mother and daughter. With the onset of spring, Ellen's health had improved enough for Becky to return to Sudbourne and the arrival of Kate's latest missive had been a much-needed fillip, lifting her mother's spirits and alleviating her concerns. Nevertheless, it was not without a pang of disappointment that Ellen learned her daughter had wed without the support of her family.

'I would have loved her to marry at St Bartholomew's like her father and I,' Ellen complained to Harry, showing him Kate's letter. 'I wonder who he is and what business he's in? Oh, why couldn't she bring her bridegroom back to Orford, so we could meet him?!' she bemoaned.

'Perhaps it was *his* choice?' Harry reasoned. 'Will Pallant. Hmm, I think there was a fisherman by the name of Pallant in Aldeburgh, but he would be dead by now. Perhaps he had a son? I will make enquiries. They probably wed at his local church.'

'Well, Aldeburgh's not far from here. I would have thought she could have visited and introduced him! Still, at least she's seen sense and got rid of that smuggler she was involved with,' Ellen satisfied herself.

'Hmmm,' Harry mused doubtfully. 'It's not right she's put you through all that worry, though, Ellen.' He examined the note again. 'There's no return address either. They could be anywhere.' Harry frowned, nagging misgivings forming in his mind as to the lack of information volunteered by his errant niece. Kate's brief note had clearly been nothing more than a calculated measure to stop her mother worrying, which had to some extent succeeded but which left more unanswered than answered. For now, though, he would say nothing as Ellen appeared markedly cheered by the news that her daughter was safe and happy. He would, however, make discreet enquiries into this Mr Will Pallant. Since the disappearance of Jack Howell there had been no let-up in smuggling activity along this stretch of coastline and for all he knew this Pallant may be involved as well. He certainly thought it strange that his niece, who had been so enamoured by Howell, to the extent of running away, could have suddenly transferred her affections so readily and wed another man in the space of six months.

There was always the possibility that Howell had met an ignominious end during the course of his illicit activities, but Harry deemed it unlikely the local gossip-mongers would not have picked this up. The general population held a fascination with these lawbreakers, and a young man of Howell's charisma and presence would not be forgotten in a hurry. Even Harry had to admit to a pang of envy towards the handsome young man who had so defiantly confronted him: the confidence of youth, the arrogance of a man in his prime, unconsciously winning the admiration of lesser men and the enduring desire of women, imbued with the conviction that the world owed them a living and fuelled by the reckless courage to make it happen. He remembered the fearlessness and determination of his own youth when, twenty years before, he had followed his brother into the Service, naive and callow, untried and untested, his new uniform bestowing such a delusory air of self-importance and invincibility on the virgin recruit.

Harry sighed to himself. He had vowed to bring his brother's killers to justice, but the stray shot that had killed Joseph Goldsmith that night ten long years ago could have been fired by any number of men. It was a risk accepted and understood by the dragoons and excisemen who patrolled these cheerless coasts, and all he could do was to act as a deterrent to the determined men willing to risk all. He would uphold the law for as long as he was physically able, hopefully until retirement, when he would accept his pension gratefully for his years of service to the Crown, taking pride in his law-abiding citizenship as a respected member of the community.

Deep down, though, he understood what drove desperate men to desperate deeds. Punishing taxes on goods, low wages, grinding poverty, the hopelessness of those slaving all hours in the workhouses, hand-to-mouth living with little prospect of relief until you were laid to rest; who could blame those wishing to alleviate their allotted time on this earth by a little night-time enterprise? Even those outwardly upholding the law were not averse to benefitting from the odd bounty of seized goods, or a sweetener for turning a blind eye, and so long as an apparent semblance of respectability was maintained, who really cared what went on under cover of darkness? The merchantmen plying the channel, kept the cogs of commerce turning and the country's coffers filled. The rich were always going to be monied and the poor impoverished, so if a few indulgences filtered down to the bedrock of society, why should anyone begrudge them a little joy in their wretched lives?

Harry's beef was not so much with the contraband that went astray but with the violence that went with its procurement. As with any illicit activity, it was always going to attract the more hardened and ruthless miscreant to whom brutality was a part of life, and it was this element he wished to stamp out. His young nephew's untimely death on the dunes of Sizewell Gap drove home to Harry just what a fine line separated life from eternal darkness. *How fickle is destiny and how precious and fleeting our existence. Saint or sinner, benefactor or miscreant, death makes no distinction, offers no mitigation, when our time is up.*

Musing on this, he finally resolved to make the most of the years he may still have and at the same time lessen the burden of livelihood upon his sister-in-law, with his long-withheld proposal of marriage. No longer in the first flush of youth, they were far from love's young dream, but both craved companionship and now Ellen's remaining children had flown the nest, there seemed no barrier to a union of two lonely adults. Ellen accepted Harry's proposal without hesitation, having of late expected as much and besides, it would mean a welcome relief from her financial struggles as a single parent. Not only that, it put paid to several unwelcome advances made by unattached tradesmen in Woodbridge who had for some time had their eye on Goldsmith's handsome widow. She was, however, very fond of her late husband's brother, who, although not quite as attractive as Joseph, was kind, caring and understanding of her moods.

Chapter Eighteen

As content as he was to be wed to his beloved Kate, it was not in Jack's nature to be satisfied with a humdrum life of domesticity at their small Southwold cottage, no matter how blissful their union. He now had a wife to support and nurture, no longer opportunistically fulfilling his own needs and desires but mindful of hers and the vows they made to each other. He wanted to do the best for her, to make her proud, no longer fearful and afraid for their future. At the same time, though, he was not quite willing to resist the intoxicating lure of the felonious lifestyle that had so far seduced him. He was young, healthy and in his prime, so why not make the most of his talents and at the same time get rich?

He dreamed of owning his own ship, a fast, sleek schooner of the latest design, capable of outrunning any other craft of its class, maybe even a fleet of ships, plying the North Sea ports from Holland down to Calais, bringing luxury goods across and profiting from both legitimate and illicit traffic, outwardly respectable but at the same time making his fortune from the lucrative free trade to be had along these windswept coasts. He knew every inch of these waters well, from the exposed shores, where the surf smashed onto the shingle spits, to the quiet river inlets with their combination of deep channels and shallow reed-bordered creeks. He craved excitement, the exhilaration of a swift vessel in full sail crashing through the waves, the thrill of the chase, the battle with the elements, the wind in his hair, the salt spray on his face. He would train a crew of skilled and loyal mariners, men who would be dependable and steadfast, brave and trusted, friends and shipmates whom he would trust with his life. He would bring his winsome wife beautiful trinkets, fine clothes, the best French wines; he would live with her in a grand house, raise sons to carry on the family business and daughters to marry well. He already had a tidy sum put away, enough for a medium-sized craft but with a few more runs he could have a ship of which he could be justly proud.

Sailing with Captain Hammond on the *Storm Petrel*, pursuing its trade from Lowestoft down to Ipswich and across to the Dutch ports, Jack was well placed to facilitate the free trading activities of the many smuggling gangs proliferating around eastern Suffolk, and while they could still operate mostly undetected, it was a risk well worth taking.

Frequenting the inns of Southwold and nearby Walberswick, Will Pallant, Chapman's dashing merchantman, was soon to gain the trust of local businessmen, fishermen and traders, his outward propriety the perfect cover for extracurricular enterprise. He would habituate the inns and coffee houses, where local businessmen gathered to discuss deals, gamble, play cards or socialise, although Jack seldom participated in wagering, mindful of holding on to his hard-won profits and unwilling to attract undue attention. Most just saw him as another marketeer, plying his trade between England, Flanders and Holland. Some of the locals patronising the Bell Inn and Blue Anchor thought they recognised Jack, but loyalty to their common cause and the unspoken code of honour amongst free traders ensured their silence and indeed drew some admiration for their charismatic colleague.

One evening, as the early autumn nights drew in, Jack was drinking with some Walberswick fishermen at the Bell Inn when he clearly heard the name Goldsmith, the name instantly alerting him, engaging his focussed attention over the hubbub of conversation. A farrier from the King's Head was relaying the local Orford gossip.

'I 'eard, Goldsmith's widow is getting yoked to 'er brother-in-law, the exciseman. The banns were said last Sunday,' the voice declared. '...be that even legal?' the man asked his companion.

'Aye, I think it is, Jez, as long as 'er first husband's dead.'

'Huh, I wouldn't want my wife marryin' *my* brother if I snuffed it!'

'No, nor me, but she's a bonny mawther, for all her years, and she took it hard when her boy died. I expect she wants the company.'

'She could ha' asked me! I'd give 'er company!' a third voice piped up.

'Yeah, I bet you would, you horny old dog! Give me the daughter any day!'

'Which one? The one that ran away or the young 'un?'

'Either, I'm not fussy! Breast or rump, both fine cuts o' young meat!'

Ribald laughter ensued before the conversation turned to other folk.

'I 'eard the vicar at St Bart's got caught with a haul in his vault! 'E denied it, of course! Said 'e had no idea it wer ther! Lyin' old devil!'

Jack turned his ear away. His initial instinct was to clout the man who had insulted his wife, but he resisted the urge. No point in giving himself away so carelessly. Instead, he drained his tankard, took leave of his colleagues and hurried down to the jetty, rowing himself across river, eager to tell Kate the news of her mother's impending wedding.

Kate was delighted at the news and asked Jack to find out the date of the nuptials. She decided it would be a surprise for her mother if she turned up at the wedding, giving her the chance of reconciliation and forgiveness. She knew Jack could not attend but was hopeful she could maintain the guise of being Mrs Will Pallant, whose husband's business kept him conveniently absent for long periods.

Having been advised of the date of his mother-in-law's marriage ceremony, Jack considered Kate's travel arrangements. He would take her in the pony and trap as far as Snape, which was as near his home turf as he thought it wise to be seen in daylight. He then arranged with the landlord of the King's Head in Orford, Michael Barker, to have a horse ready and waiting at the Crown in Snape for Kate to ride on the final leg of her journey. From there it would just be a short five-mile ride for Kate to Orford. Kate was excited to be going home, as she sat beside Jack in the trap on their way to Snape. She had packed in a saddlebag, gifts for her family: some fine

French lace and a pair of Delftware candlesticks for her mother, some enamelled earrings and matching bracelet for Becky, an elaborately carved Dutch clay pipe for Uncle Harry, and a Delft tankard to be kept for John when on his next leave.

At the Crown Inn stables, Jack helped Kate load up the waiting mare with her baggage before embracing her warmly. His kiss, as always heartfelt and passionate, was enough to make Kate's head spin and her heart swell with pride for her handsome spouse.

'Oh, Jack, I wish I could take you with me!' she sighed wistfully, pressing her head into his shoulder as he stroked her hair.

'I know, my dunlin. Maybe one day, when Jack Howell has been long forgotten. Convey Will Pallant's best wishes to the happy couple, but remember, don't be too free with your enthusiasm for me. I don't want Harry gettin' too suspicious. He'd recognise me straight off if he saw me!'

'It's just his job, Jack. He suspects everyone.'

'At least I know he won't be at the drop tomorrow! He'll be too busy drinking your ma's health at the weddin' feast!'

'You've got a drop tomorrow?' Kate was anxious. Every time she heard those words her heart sank and her stomach churned.

'Aye, just up from Aldeburgh. It's not a big one, though, so no need to fret, my dunlin.'

'Oh, Jack, do be careful!'

'Nuthin' to worry about, sweetheart,' Jack assured her as he helped Kate onto her mount. 'I'll be right.' He winked comfortingly. 'See you back here Sunday afternoon with the trap. If you get any unwanted attention, just flash that weddin' ring, my dunlin – you're mine now!' He grinned, patting Kate possessively on the backside.

Kate laughed, leaned down and kissed him before urging her horse into a trot. She loved the fact he was covetous of her and jealous of unwanted attention she was sure to receive.

Passing the Sudbourne Hall turning, Kate had half a mind to call on Becky but surmised, correctly, as it turned out, that she would most likely be in Orford helping Mother with preparations for the morrow. Approaching the familiar streets of her childhood town, Kate felt a lump rise in her throat at the calming and heart-warming sense of belonging that rose in her breast. This was her home, the place that had nurtured and protected her, memories of her happy childhood flooding back, but now she saw it through the eyes of a fully grown woman, a wife, and one who had left and returned with the objectivity of a stranger. It was as if she could see her well-loved surroundings with a new appreciation, a new attention to detail that before she had taken for granted. Making a mental note to bring her sketchbook the next time she visited, she left her mount at the King's Head stables, informing the groom she would need it again on Sunday.

'Very good, Miss Goldsmith,' he replied.

'It's Mrs Pallant now,' Kate informed him proudly, still finding the new appellation somewhat alien but nevertheless enjoying the novelty and the sense of esteem it gave her. She would rather have been known as Mrs Jack Howell, but for now any anonym would do, so long as she was wed to the man she adored.

'Beggin' your pardon, ma'am,' the lad replied, his cheeks colouring.

Kate wandered down past the church, where tomorrow her mother would be wed, the autumn leaves fluttering down in anticipation of the rice and petals that would soon be thrown; past the towering mass of Orford Castle, its pale stone walls warming in the late afternoon glow, Kate forcefully shutting out a dark memory before it had time to materialise; past the rows of brick terraced houses towards River Cottage, where the road sloped down towards the quayside overlooking Lanthorn Marshes. She held her breath as she nervously knocked on the door of her mother's cottage, fearful of the reception she might get and deeming it impolite to just walk in unannounced.

Becky lifted the latch and peered out. 'Kate!' she squealed happily. 'Mama! Come quickly, it's Kate!' she called as the sisters embraced.

Hurried footsteps descended the stairs before Ellen pulled her daughter to her and held her tightly as tears progressed down her cheek. 'Katherine! Oh, Katherine!' was all she could say.

'Forgive me, Mama,' Kate cried as all three women held hands and gazed at each other.

'You look very well! Marriage is clearly suiting you!' Ellen managed, after a few moments of tears and shared handkerchiefs, Kate observing afresh her mother's new-found glow of happiness and her sister's burgeoning beauty as they sat down at the kitchen table to exchange news.

'I can't deny your leaving was a great shock to me, Kate. To disappear in the middle of the night like that—'

'I'm so sorry, Mama. I know it was foolish and rash. Can we put it behind us now?' Kate implored, hoping the subject could be dropped.

Ellen ignored the request, not quite ready to fully absolve her daughter of her wrongdoing. She would forgive her in time, but for now it would not hurt to let the guilt imbue. 'You caused me great heartache and you lied to Becky.' Ellen blew into her handkerchief, looking up at her daughter suspiciously. 'I thought you were in love with that free trader? Is he dead?' she asked, causing Kate stomach to churn.

'No!' Kate snapped, immediately realising her response was too quick. 'Well, I don't know, perhaps he is,' she qualified. 'It didn't work out.' She looked away, embarrassed by her untruth, but to her relief Becky, who had been admiring her clothes, offered the perfect diversion.

'Look at you! Kate! All grown up and married! Look at your riding dress!' Becky exclaimed, enviously fingering the quality of her sister's apparel, all thoughts of remonstration for her sister's duplicity forgotten. 'Are you rich?'

Kate laughed. 'No, Becky, but Ja... my husband provides well for us, we are comfortable.' Kate checked herself quickly at very nearly uttering Jack's name, but thankfully her slip was not heeded.

'I can see that, my dear, I am pleased for you,' Ellen applauded, taking in her daughter's healthy complexion and shapely figure, clearly accepting Kate's explanation without further enquiry. 'When are we going to meet your husband? Will, is it?'

'Yes, but he's away at the moment. He's over in Holland trading goods.'

'Where are you living? Aldeburgh?'

'No, Mama. We're in Southwold.'

'Southwold?!' Ellen exclaimed, surprised. 'How did you get here?'

'I came by pony and trap as far as Snape then I rode.' Seeing her mother's quizzical expression, Kate quickly added, 'Will arranged a mount for me at the King's Head. Will knows Michael Barker.'

'Oh.' Ellen frowned. Kate could tell her mother still harboured doubts about Will, but now was not the time to address her concerns. The excitement of opening Kate's gifts soon dispelled any misgivings, and the three women busied themselves in eager anticipation of the day to come.

In the morning Kate and Becky took the dozen or so sweet and savoury pies Ellen had prepared for the wedding breakfast round to the Market Hall and helped to set out the tables. Kate found the women of Orford more gracious towards her, now she was apparently the wife of a respectable trader, and she was warmly welcomed by Mr Bird of the Crown and Castle, who complained bitterly how much she had been missed, not only by himself but by the regulars. They had a new barmaid, of course, but the girl was sullen and loud-mouthed, not shy of uttering an occasional expletive, her frizzy shock of red hair redolent of her quick temper and abrasive wit. She had no problem silencing customers with a cutting retort, and they missed Kate's quiet demeanour and fetching smile.

Kate and Becky helped dress Ellen in a new cream-coloured gown of fine cotton lawn, printed with a dainty floral motif, bought for her by Uncle Harry at great expense, from the Woodbridge drapers. The girls then pinned and curled their mother's hair with fabric flowers, coloured to match her those adorning her dress. It was a cool, breezy day and the wind whipped up the leaves around their feet as they made their way round to the church. Harry grinned as Ellen walked up the aisle towards him while his nieces, soon also to be his stepdaughters, watched from the pews. Despite no longer being in the first flush of youth, the bride and groom made a handsome couple: Harry resplendent in his exciseman's dress uniform, beaming elatedly at his new bride. Kate and Becky were pleased to see their mother looking happy for once, though at the same time sorrowful that Tom was not with them, as he ought to have been. Kate thought back to her own quiet wedding and wished it could have been equally candid and open, surrounded by people who knew and loved her. The wedding breakfast was jolly and relaxed before the couple were waved off in their decorated trap to Harry's home in Woodbridge. During the meal, Kate had managed to steer Uncle Harry away from discussing her husband in any detail, and Harry, after several tankards of ale, ceased to care, his thoughts more inclined to the prospect of his wedding night with the woman he had long admired, rather than worrying about his niece's itinerant spouse.

River Cottage was due to be sold, as it was no longer needed now that the Goldsmiths had all gone their separate ways. Kate and Becky spent a last night in their bedroom, packing up the rest of their belongings, reliving old times and recounting childhood memories, both sad and joyful. Kate apologised to Becky for her deception, and to her relief, Becky admitted she would have done the same in her place. During the evening they heard the sound of guns reverberating out in the bay. No doubt the Preventive Service cutter was in action against a smuggling craft. Kate hoped her husband wasn't involved and was relieved when the sounds faded and ceased.

The next morning Kate was up early. She decided to take a pre-breakfast stroll down the river path that held so many precious memories. Dawn was breaking over Lanthorn Marshes, where the two Orford light towers formed a pair of black silhouettes against a spellbinding backdrop of green, then orange as the sun rose, fading to delicate pink, the salt marshes reflecting the sky in a blaze of colour. Flocks of sanderlings, redshank and pretty ringed plovers crowded the mudflats while over them the fresh breeze brushed the reed beds before it, the fronds shimmering golden in the oblique morning light. She walked down to the quayside, along the track beside the oyster beds and out in the direction of old George's hut, as fingers of mist curled and evaporated intermittently in swirling pockets of water vapour. The hut looked sad and neglected, no longer the illicit lover's rendezvous so fondly cherished, simply a derelict building, no longer holding any promise. Kate smiled at the memories it prompted but did not proceed any further. It had served its purpose and would not be needed now she and Jack were husband and wife, but she was grateful for the shelter and cover it had once afforded a young man and his sweetheart.

Offering a silent prayer of thanks, she turned back for home, although at the back of her mind was a nagging doubt. Her monthly flux had not arrived and this morning she had woken with feelings of nausea. She did not feel fully prepared to be a mother yet, so, dismissing the thought as nothing but over-active imagination, she retraced her steps to River Cottage, where Becky had prepared a pan of fresh porridge for their breakfast. Not wishing to disappoint her sister, she forced down a few mouthfuls, claiming she had no appetite after yesterday's wedding feast. They cleared the dishes, washed the pans in the sink and packed away Mother's last remaining possessions in chests waiting to be collected by Harry in a few days.

Gathering up their belongings and leaving the cottage, the sisters walked back to the church to visit the graves of their father and newly buried brother, say their farewells and make their way to Sudbourne, Kate mounted on the mare she had hired from the King's Head and Becky walking beside her. They parted at the gates of the hall, Kate apologising once more for her deception and promising to visit more often. Her annoying little sister was maturing into womanhood and showing signs of becoming quite a beauty, no doubt catching the eye of many of the young lads working on the estate, and Kate knew it would not be long before she would be courting.

Dismounting at the Crown Inn at Snape, Kate was surprised to find Jack was nowhere to be seen. The landlord showed her into a small parlour, where there was a fire lit and a comfortable window seat to sit on while she waited. In the main bar, Kate noticed a couple of off-duty dragoons enjoying a drink. They were stationed at the inn to guard the bridge and watch for any signs of illegal traffic, although, unbeknown to them, the inn had a secret windowless room, accessed by a trap door, where goods could be secreted. A lamp placed in the small dormer window upstairs would signal the coast clear while the soldiers were otherwise occupied. The locals would laugh at the absurdity of two lone servicemen sent to deter or hamper the large gangs of miscreants so frequently engaged in illegal activities right under their noses, the unfortunate recruits frequently plied with drink by their hosts, rendering them completely unable to carry out their duties.

A couple of hours ticked by interminably while Kate sat fidgeting and occasionally pacing the floor. *Where's Jack?* She remembered the sounds of gunfire last night. Jack had told her he would be at Thorpe Bay so presumably not engaged in the sea battle. At last, she heard the sound of a trap pulling into the yard and hurried out, expecting to be gathered up in her husband's arms with a heartfelt apology. However, it was not Jack. A young lad climbed down from the seat and strode over to her. Her heart sank.

'Mrs Pallant?'

'Yes?' Kate replied, unable to disguise the annoyance in her voice. 'Where's my husband?'

'He's been delayed, madam. I'm to tek you home.'

'Oh!' Kate exclaimed crossly as the youth helped her climb onto the seat before stowing her baggage behind them. Glancing at his profile as he sat beside her and urged the horse forward, she sat sullenly, trying to remember where she had seen the lad before. It soon came to her, although Pip appeared older and more mature than when she had first seen the cabin boy on the *Zephyr*, the night of her flight to Holland, that night which seemed so distant now. Pip had grown tall, his freckles faded into an all-over tan and his voice deepened with puberty. She wondered what he was doing ashore and where Jack was, but it was not something she was going to discuss with the lad, thereby admitting she was in ignorance of her husband's whereabouts.

Chapter Nineteen

When Jack had waved his wife goodbye as she trotted off from Snape, instead of returning to Southwold, he made his way down to Aldeburgh, where he lodged for the night with the second mate from the *Zephyr*. The brig was expected the following night with a cargo to be unloaded at Thorpe Bay and then transported to Saxmundham via Leiston. Jack was to act as lander, organising the packhorses, tub men and temporary hiding places for the goods. They had made sure the customer and searcher, who patrolled the coastal towns, was over in Orford and Jack knew Harry Goldsmith was safely off duty, busy getting wed to Kate's mother. He smiled to himself that the couple were now his in-laws, unbeknown to them, and would no doubt be horrified at the prospect of being related by marriage to a wanted free trader.

The wedding breakfast in Orford had been well underway by the time the sun set and the *Zephyr* had made good headway up the coast until she was two miles out from Aldeburgh, whereupon a Preventive Service cutter which had been shadowing her for some hours aimed a cannon shot across her bows and gave chase, firing as she approached. The *Zephyr* replied in kind, attempting to slow the cutter, but her mainsail was holed, her bowsprit sheered and soon her pursuer was abreast of her starboard side. Meanwhile, over on the *Zephyr*'s larboard side, her crew were busily dumping the last barrels of spirit, roped together to float just under the surface, along with oilskin-wrapped bales of tobacco and tea, a fisherman's buoy marking their position for later collection, as the cry from a loudhailer came across: 'Hove to, in the King's name!' Much of the illicit cargo had already been transferred to fishing smacks waiting in the vicinity before the cutter engaged and the rest of the brig's crew were now making their escape in rowing boats, hastily lowered on the ship's blind side along with some tubs of spirit and smaller packets of contraband. Before being boarded the *Zephyr*'s crew had managed to alert Jack and the waiting tub men onshore by shining a red light towards Thorpe Beach as a warning not to approach.

Jack, however, mounted and keenly patrolling the shoreline between Aldeburgh and Thorpe Bay, already alerted by the distant gunfire, had been watching the pursuit through his spyglass. He instructed the waiting men to lay low and await the arrival of the smaller craft, while the Service cutter was engaged in preparing to board and commandeer the *Zephyr*. The *Zephyr* might be lost, but with any luck part of the haul would still be salvageable. The waiting fishing vessels moved out towards the rowing boats and escaping seamen while Jack stood by to assist those who made it ashore. Pip was among them as they leapt into the shallows and they and the remainder of the smuggled goods were soon disappearing towards Aldeburgh and Leiston, distributed between the waiting tub men and carts.

Off-shore a lugger stood by at a safe distance to collect the floated goods once the Service cutter had left with its prize of the *Zephyr*. It was most likely the *Sandpiper*, and Jack guessed it would not be long before Mike Chapman would learn of the night's events and would be making plans to regain possession of his appropriated vessel, by force if necessary. This game of cat and mouse, possession and re-possession, was a constant battle of wills between the hard-pressed Preventive Force and the determined free traders, who in many cases outgunned, outnumbered and outwitted their pursuers.

Pip gratefully jumped up behind Jack as his horse trotted off behind the carts, trundling their way along the exposed track bordering the shoreline. As they rode, a misty moon peeped out behind a veil of pewter cloud, illuminating a shaft of bright water before the stretch of wet sand exposed by the low tide disappeared under the dark mass of shingle. Jack could see the silhouetted sails of the brig and cutter against the luminous sky and further north the fishing smacks making for Southwold with their heavy load. To the south along the coastline, the outline of the lugger, its sails furled awaiting its chance to retrieve the rest of the run from where the marker buoys had been placed. It might be the *Sandpiper*, although Jack could not be certain.

He was just starting to relax in the knowledge that the run had been mostly successful, although the loss of the *Zephyr* was a stroke of bad luck, when his thoughts were interrupted by the crack of a musket shot and a ball whizzed past his shoulder. His horse shied and bucked as another shot narrowly missed its head, the affrighted animal unsaddling both its riders, who slid down its back and landed heavily on the grass verge. A party of dragoons was approaching from Aldeburgh, but already the smuggling outriders had dismounted and readied their weapons in response, the carts hurrying off towards Leiston while the rest of the men returned fire.

'You alright, lad?' Jack asked Pip, cursing and breathing heavily from the sudden fall.

'Aye,' the boy responded nervously as Jack thrust a pistol and powder pouch into his hand.

'Know how to use this?' he asked as Pip nodded.

The dragoons quickly dismounted and a gun battle ensued, keeping both parties at bay long enough for the tub men to disperse into the shadows with their burdens, the nearby marshland to the west being an ideal place to conceal their goods until they could return to retrieve them. A smell of strong liquor permeated the air as a barrel was holed and dropped by its carrier, the contents gushing out across the road. Jack cursed at the waste of fine spirit as it seeped away down into the dyke. He strained his eyes in the gloom and tried to make out how many soldiers they were up against. A low mist was creeping up from the shore but had not yet reached them, and they were still in clear view of the soldiers.

'Can you count t'horses for me, lad?' he whispered to his young companion. 'Go along the ditch and keep your head down.'

If, as he suspected, the smugglers outnumbered the military men by more than two to one, they may be able to overwhelm the soldiers and force them to retreat. Pip nodded and was soon back at Jack's side. Holding up his hand, he indicated the number five.

'We're more than four to one! Good. Go and tell the men to get ready to charge them when I give the signal.'

Pip did as he was bid, and as the dragoons paused to reload their pistols, Jack raised his cutlass and the smugglers rushed forwards in a mob of flashing blades and shouts of murderous intent. Faced with this onslaught, the young recruits turned and fled back towards Aldeburgh amidst the cheers and jeers of their victorious adversaries. The sergeant in charge, however, was able to turn in the saddle and carefully aim one further shot before cantering after his comrades.

Jack never heard the shot. It could have been minutes or hours later when he came to. He had no idea how long he had been unconscious. Opening his eyes and adjusting his focus, he put his hand on the shadowed figure slumped beside him, who awoke with a start. 'Pip, what happened... how long have I...?' Jack tried to sit up, but his head throbbed and a wave of nausea overcame him as bile rose in his throat. He put his hand to his head and it felt sticky, his hair adhering to his skin in a congealed clump.

Pip described how the trooper's last shot had grazed Jack's temple but by a stroke of luck had fallen short of penetrating his skull. Jack sank back into the ditch where Pip had dragged him, his blurred vision registering an eerie lightening of the eastern sky, the dawn of the new day not far behind. The tide was in, the mist slowly clearing, waves tumbling onto the shingle in a steady, respiration-like rhythm as the surf slapped and sighed over the stones. On the horizon a fleet of herring smacks were busy hauling in their catch and a heavy-laden coal collier was making its laborious way down from

Newcastle, but the graceful brig and cutter of last night's encounter were long gone.

'Help me up, Pip.' Jack raised his arm to his young companion, pulling himself up and cursing as his head spun. 'My horse?' Jack narrowed his eyes to focus his vision along the roadway. Pip pointed to the animal standing several hundred yards away, contentedly grazing on a patch of red clover at the edge of the ditch. 'Right, I'll get him. Go and find my hat, will you, lad? It'll be over where we were unhorsed last night. 'Good boy.' Jack patted his mount gratefully, as he approached, stumbling drunkenly as his head wound throbbed, hauling himself up into the saddle.

Pip ran up, hat in hand, and Jack pulled him up to sit behind him. 'Thank you, Pip.' He gingerly pressed his hat over his bloodied crown with a grimace before urging his steed forward. 'We'll go to the Vulcan at Sizewell. I can get cleaned up there.'

As they progressed along the headland, the ground gently rising, the sea on their right dropping away where the cliffs rose under them, Jack remembered Kate, who would soon be waiting at Snape. 'I'll need you to help me, lad. I'll make it worth your while. Then you can get back to your folks.'

'Yes, sir.' Pip nodded while Jack passed him a handful of coins, instructing him to make his way to the White Horse at Leiston, where he could hire a trap to take him to Snape.

'Go to the trades entrance, ask for Mrs Gildersleeves, she'll help you, but watch out for the dragoons who are stationed there. If they question you, tell them you're to go to Snape to pick up Mrs Will Pallant from Southwold to tek her home.' As Pip accepted his errand, Jack thought about Kate's reaction. 'Tell my wife I've been delayed, nuthin' more. I don't want her worryin'.'

Dismounting at the Vulcan Arms, Jack watched his companion trot off in the direction of Leiston before knocking quietly on the kitchen door. Mrs Baxter was already about, busily clearing the ashes from the grate, but upon opening the door she recognised Jack and ushered him quickly inside.

'We thought you'd had it,' she exclaimed calmly, tutting with concern as he removed his hat to reveal a mess of congealed blood and matted hair. 'Sit ye down. I'll get you cleaned up. We can't have you goin' about like that!'

'Did they get the goods away?' Jack asked as the landlady poured him a mug of ale and set about washing the blood from his temple with a clean rag and cool boiled water.

'Most of it, aye, but they're comin' back tonight for the rest of it. Now, sit still while I clean this mess up,' she ordered tersely. 'Lucky escape there, my lad, another inch and you'd ha' been done for!'

Chapter Twenty

After a wash, clean shirt and a belly full of Mrs Baxter's game pie, Jack paid his hosts and left the Vulcan Arms to make his way home to Southwold. By this time Kate would be back and he dreaded the inevitable but justifiable rebuke his pretty wife would deliver when she heard news of last night's run. At least, he knew he was safe from recognition, a close-quarter's fight not having been necessary, and Will Pallant could carry on his outwardly respectable business with impunity. Jack Howell was assumed long gone and the latest bills posted were focussed on other miscreants now wanted for crimes against His Majesty's Services.

His temple wound still stung and his head ached uncomfortably, feelings of nausea still lingering threateningly every time he bent down, his ears ringing with an intrusive high-pitched drone. Jack pulled his hat down as low as he could to hide the strip of cloth Mrs Baxter had used to bind his wound and hoped he could make it back without encountering anyone who knew him or might suspect he had been involved in the night's activity. Upon reaching the cottage unchallenged, Kate ran to his arms, her initial relief at his return rapidly changing to fretful concern as he removed his hat to reveal the bloodied cloth covering his head wound.

She immediately bade him lie down while she bathed the fresh blood from the lesion, demanding a full explanation of the night's events, all thoughts of relaying the news of her mother's nuptials now seeming trivial by comparison. Kate listened tight-lipped to Jack's account, realising guiltily she had not thanked Pip for his part in her husband's escape and that Mrs Baxter also deserved thanks for her care and discretion. Later she watched her husband soundly sleeping and thanked God the musket ball had not penetrated his skull, shuddering at the image of widowhood that had oft been her fear and that so nearly came to pass.

'Please be careful, Jack, I can't lose you!' she entreated a few days later, as her husband recovered sufficiently to resume his employ and sail for Holland, Mr Baxter's shirt freshly washed and ironed, ready to return. Kate knew her pleas would make no difference to her husband's resolve, but she felt it had to be said, so that whenever he thought of her he would remember her words.

'Don't you fret, my dunlin. I know what I'm doin'.' He kissed her palliatively. 'I'm lookin' at a new schooner in Flushing and maybe the next time I'm home I will be my own master! I can get you anythin' you want, my dunlin, you name it, it's yours!'

'Jack, I want nothing! Don't you see? No amount of trinkets and luxuries could replace *you*!' Kate was going to refrain from telling Jack her news until she was certain, but this latest brush with death had forced her hand. *What if he were killed on the next run?* she had agonised; he would never know he might be a father. *No, I have to tell him*, she concluded.

'Jack... I think I'm with child.'

'Kate!' A huge grin spread over Jack's face, forcing him to put his hand to his scabbed temple still throbbing painfully, before grabbing her round the waist and planting a passionate kiss on her warm lips. He let go of her more gently this time, caressing her face and holding her away from him to look at her figure. Nothing showed as yet on his wife's slim form, but he ran his hand over her abdomen tenderly and whispered, 'It will be a boy! I know it!'

Kate grinned and rolled her eyes. 'It could just as likely be a girl! Would you mind?' She searched his face.

'Of course not, my dunlin! She will be every bit as beautiful as her mother! ...and if not, we can always dress her up as a boy!' he quipped jovially as they both descended into giggles before embracing ardently, each acutely aware that now they were more than a couple and the responsibility for another human being would soon add a new dimension and purpose to life. *Perhaps it will make Jack more careful*, Kate thought wistfully to herself as she waved him goodbye, but as always, the leaden weight forming in her gut confirmed the futility of such a wish.

Jack whistled happily to himself as he made his way past the water meadows and down to the harbour, his face lit up with a satisfied grin as he contemplated fatherhood. He was picturing in his mind how he would sail with his son, teaching him the ropes, watching him grow into a fine seaman, following in his father's footsteps. The sun was setting behind Southwold, bathing everything in a soft golden glow as two crewmen from the *Storm Petrel* cast off their small craft from the jetty to ferry Jack out to the waiting brig. She had just arrived from Lowestoft, her hold crammed with sacks of wool bound for the cloth makers of northern Europe.

As he climbed aboard, Stephen Hammond greeted him warmly. 'Good to see you, Jack! Pip told us of your close shave at Aldeburgh!'

'Aye. He's a good lad. Dunno what I'd ha' done without his help.'

'Aye, he's one of us alright, a proper seadog now. Right, come below, Jack, we've got a big drop to organise now what with the *Zephyr* gone.'

'I hear she's to be requisitioned for the Navy after a re-fit. Chapman won't be happy!' Jack chuckled as they descended the steps into the cabin.

'Na, but he's got a few tricks up his sleeve.' Hammond winked.

Jack raised his eyebrows as the pair sat down and uncorked a bottle of Jamaican rum.

'Is he gonna tek her back?' he asked, surprised.

'Mebbe, but he's watchin' her progress. She's moored down near Bawdsey at present. Once she's sailed for Harwich it'll be too late.'

A week later the *Storm Petrel* sailed from Flushing, her hold stacked to the gunwales with a mixed cargo of luxury goods, on the majority of which, Captain Hammond had no intention of paying full excise duty and which would be off-loaded at several strategic points along the Suffolk coastline. There was, however, a legitimate cargo of 5cwt of tea stacked in the brig which was bound for Ipswich. The government had recently slashed the duty on this commodity, in order to discourage the illicit trade, but its conveyance at lower profit still afforded good cover for the spirits, wines, tobacco, silks and other European-sourced luxuries that kept the smugglers in business.

A winter squall was threatening to blow in from the west as the ship approached Hollesley Bay. Mike Chapman, who was aboard his ship, having agreed a new trade deal with Dutch merchants, had organised for several smaller luggers, including the *Sandpiper*, to meet the *Storm Petrel* at anchor a mile off-shore. The local riding officer based at Orford was known to be off duty for the next couple of days and that stretch of coastline would be unguarded. In actual fact, the officer had been 'persuaded' by a tempting offer of free goods and a veiled threat if he did not comply, to be otherwise engaged in procuring a new horse – his meagre salary not sufficient compensation to outweigh the rewards proffered. Besides it was a filthy night and not many folk would be keen to venture out, he would assure his employers if questions were asked.

Accordingly, the drop went as planned and the waiting luggers soon dispersed to their various destinations, stacked with the contents of the *Storm Petrel*'s hold. The dark night and strong winds made it slow going for the smaller boats making for the calmer estuaries and secluded creeks before unloading, many a load dumped in ditches by their jaded crews, hurriedly concealed until they could be retrieved later, the Swan Inn at Alderton being a favoured dropping-off point. A tunnel from the inn to the nearby church had been in use since the Civil War as an escape route for Catholic monks, where the altar cloth now served to conceal contraband, although the passageway was reputed to be haunted. The Sorrel Horse Inn at Shottisham served as another smuggling bolthole and could be accessed from the Deben, via Shottisham Creek. Indeed, hiding places along this sparsely populated coastline were so numerous as to make detection of many of them impossible for the over-stretched Preventive Service, who relied heavily on tip-offs and guesswork.

Aboard the brig, sails shortened and luffed, the *Storm Petrel* eased round Bawdsey Point towards the leeward shore of the Deben, where she weighed anchor. The crew could make out the masts of the *Zephyr* in the gloom and quickly and silently lowered their boats into the river and rowed across to her. Their oars were muffled, but no sound could be heard above the wind. There were but a couple of sentries patrolling the deck, due to the forethought of Chapman, who had arranged an evening's entertainment at the Ferry Boat Inn on the Felixstowe side, for the excise officers, who were only too pleased to be inside on this inclement night. Jack's crew swiftly boarded the familiar craft, bound and gagged the surprised sailors before putting them ashore with threats for their lives should they attempt to raise the alarm. Before long the *Zephyr* was inching away from her moorings, her remaining sails soon filling once more, her rigging creaking and straining, her progress eased by an empty hold as she followed her sister ship out of the estuary and into the choppy waters of the North Sea once more.

On board the *Storm Petrel* Mike Chapman laughed at the thought of the officers staggering from the inn to find their captured craft nowhere to be seen. He flashed an acknowledgement to the *Zephyr* before heading south along the coast to the Orwell and his destination at Ipswich. 'Gotcha, my beauty!' He chuckled to himself. Jack responded from the repossessed craft with a return signal and set course on a slow tack for Holland.

'Well done, lads.' Jack congratulated his men on board the *Zephyr*. 'There'll be a bonus for y'all when we get across. Good night's work, lads!' He went below to inspect the ship's empty hold, his echoing footsteps on the ladder accompanied by ominous groans and cracks from the tired vessel. *Let's hope she holds up in this sea*, he thought to himself, measuring the water sloshing in the hull with a yardstick and calling for the bilge pump.

Two months later a re-fitted brig, remarkably similar in shape and size to the *Zephyr*, put out to sea from Flushing, the name *Mascarade* freshly painted on her side, the French spelling designed to deflect from her origin, the Preventive Service assuming she was just another captured French privateer. Her new mainsail gleaming white in the sunshine, a new bowsprit, her hull strengthened with new bulkheads, a fresh cargo of tobacco and gin safely stacked below in watertight bales and casks, she quickly resumed her former activities. Michael Chapman stood on deck beside his ship's new captain Will Pallant, who had offered to command the *Mascarade* until his own new schooner was ready. The *Lady Katherine*, as he would call his ship, was nearing completion in the Dutch port, a fast craft, gaff-rigged, built for speed and agility, soon to be plying her trade across the familiar waters of the North Sea to the windswept coastline of Suffolk, so dear to her owner's heart.

'Well, Jack,' Chapman patted his companion's shoulder affably, 'we'll soon be competing for business, you and I.'

'Huh.' Jack chuckled. 'Aye, I guess we will, Mike, but t'will be a friendly rivalry and we can help each other out on occasion.'

'Aye, you've done well for yourself, lad, I'm pleased for you.' They watched as the busy port retreated to the horizon, Chapman drawing on a handsomely carved clay pipe and Jack staring down at the surging water, lost in thought. 'How's that pretty lass of yours?' Chapman broke his reverie.

'She's expectin', Mike. I'm going to be a father.' Jack grinned, his cheeks reddening at the disclosure.

'Congratulations, my boy! A good enough excuse for a celebration, I'll be bound! I reckon that crate of fine French brandy'll need samplin'.' Chapman grinned, slapping Jack on the back again as they went below, accompanied by the shouts of the crew as they trimmed the sails to the nor'easterly that was ruffling the wave tops and set course for England.

Chapter Twenty-One

Despite posters offering a reward for the recapture of the *Zephyr*, there were no further sightings, and rumours she had sunk in the recent storms battering the eastern coastline were accepted without question by the gossip-mongers frequenting the seaside taverns. Mike Chapman had ostensibly acquired another serviceable brig, the *Mascarade*, whose provenance was unknown, and by spring there were reports of another sleek new schooner, the *Lady Katherine*, plying its trade from Southwold to Ipswich. Captain Will Pallant's elegant craft, the envy of many, was noted by the customs house officers as a possible lawbreaker but so far had not been found with illicit goods and any challenger at sea was soon shown a clean pair of heels by this fast, ably manned vessel.

As spring warmed into summer, Mr and Mrs Will Pallant became the proud parents of a strapping baby boy, baptised Christopher but affectionately dubbed Kit by his doting mother, who would hold him on her lap, gazing into his big blue eyes, and wonder at this perfect little man, so innocent and so full of promise. Jack was as proud as a father could be, a new resolve to become a respectable trader now his goal, the building of a profitable business a priority, which would ensure his son's future and the family's prosperity. His pride at his new son, however, was tinged with regret for the name he had had to forsake to keep himself and his family safe. He would have loved to give his son the family name the boy should have inherited, but he could not risk alerting the authorities to the inevitable question of kinship that would arise should a Howell resurface. Already too many folk knew of Jack Howell's continued existence and it seemed only a matter of time before Will Pallant's true identity was unmasked, intentionally or otherwise.

Kate travelled to Woodbridge in the trap with Kit, eager to introduce her firstborn to his grandmother, who was suitably delighted and enchanted by her first grandchild, commenting on his big blue eyes and shock of dark hair. 'Is he like your husband?' Ellen enquired, curious.

'Yes, he is,' Kate answered proudly, glancing up at Uncle Harry, who had just come in.

He strode over to Kate and beamed down at his great-nephew, now cradled in Ellen's arms. 'A fine-looking boy, my dear, congratulations! When are we going to meet his father, Kate?'

Kate had involuntarily thought to answer, *Jack is away a lot*, but managed to stop herself and turn it into, 'J... ust as soon as he can, Uncle Harry. Will is away a lot on business – he's doing really well,' she added, hastily attempting to deflect attention from her near mistake. She still found it hard to use her husband's assumed name.

Harry stared more closely at Kit, taking in his colouring and trying to recall of whom the child reminded him. He glanced sideways at his niece, who averted her gaze quickly, her cheeks colouring slightly at the deception she knew she was acting out. Harry turned away and reached for a flagon of Port wine.

'Well, my dear, we must toast the new arrival,' he offered as Ellen handed Kit back to his mother and went to fetch some glasses.

Kate, glad of the diversion, laid her son down on a cushion and went to help her mother. 'How's Becky?' she enquired.

'She's found herself a new beau, Sebastian. He's a groom at the stables. They rode over to see us last Sunday. He's a pleasant enough lad.'

'Oh, I'm so glad. I hope he treats her well.' Kate placed three glasses on a tray and took them through to Harry, who was standing over Kit, his finger tightly clasped in the infant's hand.

'She seems happy enough,' Ellen affirmed.

'And how about John, have you heard from him?' Kate began a new topic of conversation as she glanced at Harry, attempting to distract him from her child, and to her relief he extricated his finger and moved away.

'Yes, he's doing well. He's a midshipman now,' Ellen said proudly. 'Now, tell us your news, Kate.'

Kate sat down and proceeded to describe her life in Southwold and how Will had purchased a new ship and was building a steady business. Harry was silent as he sipped his port, allowing the women to chat together amiably. Kate glanced his way a few times and he smiled back politely, a nagging suspicion infiltrating his thoughts as he watched his pretty niece, noting her modish dress and well-groomed appearance. *Mmm, business is clearly good!* he thought. He decided not to say anything to Ellen yet, but he would make further enquiries about Will Pallant and his trading exploits.

When the time came to depart, Kate kissed her mother and uncle affectionately on the cheek and promised to call again soon, placing her sleeping babe carefully into his bassinet and mounting the front seat of the trap.

'Don't forget to bring that elusive husband of yours next time, Kate!' her mother called after her. Kate nodded and waved, a sinking feeling weighing in her stomach. *How am I ever going to do that?* she agonised. *Harry's bound to recognise Jack! No!* she decided. *They must never meet!*

Passing the turning to Sudbourne Hall, Kate elected to make the brief detour to see her sister, the long summer day still affording plenty of time for the diversion, and besides, Kit was grizzling for a feed. The old hall was obscured by scaffolding and builders were working on demolishing large sections of the building. Becky was delighted to meet her new nephew and cooed over him. She ushered Kate into a back parlour where Kate could feed her baby in privacy and they sat down together, as Kate held Kit against her breast.

'I can't believe I am an aunt!' Becky exclaimed. 'Aunt Rebecca! Makes me sound so old!' She grimaced at the thought. 'What was it like, Kate, the birth?'

'I can't pretend it wasn't an ordeal, Becky, but it was worth it in the end. The midwife was very firm with me. At one stage I said I thought I would die, but she told me not to be so foolish.' Kate laughed at the memory of her own fearfulness and thought it best to change the subject. 'I hear you've found yourself a sweetheart?'

Becky blushed. 'Yes, he's called Seb. He's a groom, he takes me riding with him on Sundays.'

'Can I meet him?'

'No, he's not here at the moment. He's out with young Lord Seymour.'

'Is he handsome?'

'Lord Seymour?'

'No, silly... Sebastian?' Kate affirmed, the girls giggling happily together.

'Yes, *I* think he is. What about *your* husband Kate? Is he...?'

'Of course he is! That's why I married him! You would *love* him,' Kate enthused, unable to contain her pride.

'When are we going to see him then?' Becky said, echoing Ellen's words.

'One day, I'm sure. He's away for long periods, Becky, it's his business.' Again steering the topic of conversation away from her husband, Kate asked about the building works she had seen being carried out on the house, which were clearly quite substantial.

'Oh, they're demolishing part of the hall and re-building it. A celebrated architect is re-designing it in the modern style. We're going to be sent to Gedgrave Hall instead soon,' Becky told her. 'Seb's pleased about it, he's going to be promoted to head groom there!' she boasted proudly. Kate wondered if the free traders' midnight manoeuvres would also be transferred to Gedgrave along with the staff, but she thought it best not to bring up the subject again, especially if her sister's new beau might be involved.

On the way back to Southwold Kate's mind was in turmoil. *How long can I keep up this pretence? How many excuses can I keep making for Jack's non-appearance?* She was longing to show off her charismatic husband, the man she adored with her all heart and soul, but the very act of revealing him would put him in danger and expose her own deceit. This was almost worse than her mother finding out she was courting a free trader, as now she had married him and he had changed his identity; it was not only herself who would pay the price.

It was a profitable summer for the *Lady Katherine.* Jack took great pride in his new schooner and was before long known as a reputable trader in fine cloth and other luxury items from Holland and France. In return he conveyed wool and fine worsted yarn, made in Suffolk, to Harwich for export to the continent and the profits were rolling in. He had asked Nate Halesworth to join him as first mate, to which Nate had agreed with enthusiasm, bringing with him several time-served seamen, who were only too pleased to sail a sleek new craft and to whom Jack had become something of a hero figure. His true identity was well known amongst the free-trading fraternity, but being one of their own, his anonymity was assured. However, there was always the possibility that a slip of the tongue from an inebriated sailor might inadvertently give him away.

Since frequenting the inns around Southwold, Jack had become acquainted with men from several smuggling gangs who operated locally and who had agreed to share proceeds in exchange for man and horsepower and the use of a number of hiding places for contraband not yet discovered by the authorities. He had struck up a friendship with one Patrick Harvey, who was a nephew of John Harvey from the notorious Hadleigh gang, who had been sentenced to seven years' transportation and whose gang had terrorised the local population and caused many a problem for the excisemen some forty-odd years ago. Riding officers had had many a run-in with these men, but the sheer weight of numbers of felons riding in large groups meant that they were unable to enforce their authority, when faced with as many as one hundred carts, three hundred horses and 150 men, all armed with clubs and pistols and not afraid to use them. The Hadleigh gang, who often worked in collusion with groups from Yarmouth and Norwich, were more elusive now, but many a son had followed in his father's footsteps, continuing to ply their trade with a resolve and fervour that had not diminished.

Pat Harvey had agreed to assist Jack when he needed more men and Jack had in turn agreed to ship goods for Pat on the *Lady Katherine*. Pat's local drinking house was the fifteenth-century inn the Queen's Head at Blyford, whose previous landlord John Key had made his fortune in the free trade. A trap door beside the inglenook fireplace led into a tunnel which emerged into All Saint's Church across the road, a convenient hiding place for contraband. Pat and Jack were of similar age and outlook, swapping tales, jests and aspirations over many a pint of ale, meeting halfway at the White Hart Inn, overlooking Blythburgh Water, and had built up a mutual trust and alliance, enabling Jack to reveal to his friend his true identity. He was surprised when Pat had admitted he already knew who Jack was from men who had crewed for Michael Chapman in the past. 'I wondered how long it would take you admit it,' he had joked with Jack, who laughed sheepishly at his own futile subterfuge.

Pat, fair-haired and blue-eyed, fearless and strong, had Norse origins, and Jack could well imagine him as a close-helmeted Viking, long-handled axe in hand, leaping from his longboat, intent on plunder and pillage. The pair would sit at the back of the inn discussing the next shipment and where it was to be landed; above them, the tiny attic window facing out over the lagoon afforded an ideal lookout and signalling post for the 'starlight traders' activities. When the light shone the coast was clear for cargo landed at Dunwich to proceed upriver to be stored at the Queen's Head, Blyford, where kegs were placed in a recess above the fireplace and in the church opposite. In addition, three miles to the north, the twin thatched roofs of St Andrew's Church, Westhall, provided a handy space for contraband, hidden high up out of sight between the two roof ridges.

Pat regaled Jack with stories his father had told him. One in particular had gone down in local folklore and of which Jack had heard the rumours. About six years or so ago, three hundred tubs of gin had been landed at Sizewell and conveyed to Leiston Common Farm and hidden in a barn. The cache had been discovered by one 'Clumpy' Bowles, a club-footed man who reported his find to the revenue men. The dragoons at the local White Horse were drunk, so two more were sought at Eastbridge. However, the enterprising landlady at the second inn had also plied the soldiers with drink, so by the time the excisemen arrived at the barn with reinforcements summoned from further afield, the smugglers had locked the barn doors and begun passing the tubs out through the loft into the adjoining barn and loading it onto carts. The smugglers guarding the door then let in the Preventive men and locked them inside whilst the goods made their way to Coldfair Green unhindered. There the tubs were stored in an underground vault, which was then covered by a dung heap, after which a flock of sheep were herded over the resultant footprints. Unfortunately, when the smugglers returned some while later to open the trap door, the eager first-comers were overcome by the fumes, two of the men dying as a result. Despite the haul having been moved yet again, it was eventually discovered at the Parrot and Punchbowl at Aldringham and confiscated, the exhausted smugglers by this time too spent to retaliate. However, they took their revenge on the hapless informant Clumpy Bowles, who was kidnapped, gagged and whipped, then thrown over a hedge, with a beer barrel bung wedged firmly in his mouth, as a lesson to other would-be whistle-blowers. Clumpy survived his ordeal, but unluckily for the smugglers, the bung was recognised by its owner's markings, which led back to several of the kidnappers being identified and arrested. Now Pat and Jack laughed at the witlessness of the smugglers who had failed to grasp the dangers of the resulting methane, ammonia and hydrogen sulphide mix produced by the stored manure, something that had been a valuable lesson to those later attempting to conceal contraband amidst animal waste.

As autumn approached, Kate, busy at home with caring for her young son, expressed a desire to move nearer to her mother. Jack, at first doubtful of the wisdom of moving nearer to old haunts, decided that it would do no harm to move to Aldeburgh and set about searching for a suitable property for his young family. From there it would be a shorter trip to Woodbridge for Kate to visit her mother yet still far enough not to be on her doorstep. He would keep the cottage in Southwold as a convenient lodging for when he needed a bolthole further up the coast. Jack Howell was but a distant memory, assumed dead by many in the Service, as nothing had been heard of him, and as far as he knew, nobody was actively seeking him, so he felt safe in his obfuscation.

He determined to keep his new purchase as a surprise for Kate for the new year and before long was signing the deeds of a larger brick townhouse in the main street at Aldeburgh, sheltered behind the seafront cottages facing the shore. The house faced directly onto the street where Kate would be able to watch the toing and froing of folk going about their business and not feel quite so isolated as she did in Southwold. Although she liked the pretty town raised on its headland, with its sandy foreshore, it had never felt like home and Kate would oft gaze southwards in homesick longing for the winding waters of the Alde and Ore and the memories they held. She wanted her son to grow up in the same childhood haunts, experience the same carefree days of youth in the places she held dear. Jack, conscious that his misdemeanours had forced Kate away from the life she knew, determined to do what he could to make it up to her and keep her happy, his long days away at sea always intensifying the guilt he felt.

Jack was therefore feeling pleased with himself at his new purchase when he arrived home for the Christmas period laden with luxuries for his wife and child. Kate had decorated the cottage with holly, ivy and mistletoe and as a gift for Jack had drawn a portrait of him, which she had coloured in with some new watercolour blocks he had purchased for her. She also employed the skills she learned from her mother to hand-sew a white silk shirt adorned with lace cuffs. 'Only to be worn on Sundays and special occasions!' she instructed him firmly.

'Aye, aye, Captain!' He laughed, saluting her, pulling her towards him and searing her lips with a burning kiss of possessive passion.

Kate had lost none of her youthful beauty and indeed had blossomed with the curves of new motherhood. Jack was fiercely covetous of his desirable wife who patiently awaited his return from long days at sea and was aware of his good fortune in such a faithful partner who would not be tempted by the attentions of local admirers. He brought Pat Harvey home with him one evening and he could see Kate was attracted to his friend's Viking looks and that Pat was equally enamoured with Kate and a pang of jealousy arose in Jack's breast. Kate, well aware of her husband's pique, enjoyed impishly teasing him, using every opportunity to play on his insecurity with praise for his handsome friend. She meant none of it, but the satisfaction it gave her was hard to resist. Pat could see Jack's annoyance and played along with Kate, winking at her as they smiled together at her husband's disgruntlement.

Although she knew they discussed mutually advantageous business, Kate knew that when they lowered their voices and retreated behind closed doors, there was more to it than a simple trade deal. She had heard the gossip about the Hadleigh gang and the involvement of Jack's new friend, and she knew Jack was only trying to protect her by keeping her in ignorance of their clandestine activities. If Jack began to elaborate on the details, she would put her finger to his lips and shake her head. 'Don't tell me, Jack. I don't need to know, neither do I wish to. It's better that way.' She hated the fact that he was so involved with the free traders but could not deny the profits had greatly enriched their lives. Jack would always be a smuggler and it was better she knew the truth, despite the outward lie they were living and her aversion to it. Lately she had bade him make her a solemn promise. 'Don't put our son in danger, Jack, that's all I ask.'

'Never, my dunlin,' he had sworn with heartfelt sincerity, to which Kate had to be content but all the time knowing it was unlikely, despite Jack's resolve. Life had a habit of re-shaping the best-laid plans in the most unexpected ways, as they both well knew.

New Year storms pounded the Suffolk coastline, several fishing smacks went down and a Preventive Service cutter was lost in a particularly ferocious gale, claiming the lives of many of its crew, reminding both law abiders and law breakers that nature favours neither the good nor bad when it comes to its awesome power. Wreckage had strewn the beaches, amongst which the bodies of those who perished had washed up on shore. Jack had been cautious and kept the *Lady Katherine* at her berth in Flushing for nearly two weeks, unwilling to allow his new craft to be buffeted by high seas, but the warehouse had been filling up, orders needed to be filled and the surfeit of luxury commodities needed to be gone before questions were asked. Hidden in liquor barrels between the tin lining and the outer cask, a quantity of fine Cuban cigars had been secreted, procured from the Dutch West Indian traders, which would bring him a good profit along with 150 tubs of high-quality Jamaican rum and coffee from Martinique.

Jack was eager to surprise Kate with his recent purchase of their new more spacious home in Aldeburgh, especially now she was expecting their second child. She had imparted her news to him on the eve before he left, prompted by her constant nagging fear that one day he may not return and would either be rotting in some felon's cell at His Majesty's pleasure or worse, feeding the fishes at the bottom of the North Sea. After a warm embrace of unexpected joy at Kate's revelation, Jack hinted at the surprise he was keeping from her, chuckling at her frustration at not knowing and smiling smugly to himself, imagining her delight at the news when he returned, pockets bulging and with their financial future assured.

Kate had watched the schooner sail towards the horizon, standing on Southwold cliff top, holding little Kit in her arms, as a flight of swans passed gracefully overhead in perfect V formation, their long white necks lit up starkly against the grey storm-filled clouds, making their way down to Minsmere before nightfall. As the birds' mournful trumpeting echoed across the shore, receding gradually in volume as they passed, an unbidden feeling of dread settled in Kate's stomach, the doleful sound somehow discomfiting her; she knew not why. Dismissing the cold shudder running down her spine, she turned for home, wrapping her child tightly in the folds of her cloak against the salt-laden blast coming off the sea. *Come back to me soon Jack*, she prayed.

Chapter Twenty-Two

Harry Goldsmith had been making enquiries about the Captain of the *Lady Katherine* amongst his business acquaintances but so far had drawn a blank. However, drinking in the Cross Keys at Aldeburgh one evening, he struck up a conversation with an old regular, Josh... who, at the mention of Will Pallant, confirmed he had known the man but that he had died many a long year back.

'Did he have any children?' Harry enquired.

'No, 'e never married, but his sister had a son of whom he was quite fond. He used to visit 'em regular, in Woodbridge, until 'er husband died. After she died soon after, the son went rogue and got mixed up wi' them starlight traders.'

Harry stiffened, the noise around him suddenly muted as his thoughts raced. He already knew the answer to his next question. 'What was her husband's name?'

'Howell,' came the expected reply.

Harry took a measured draught of ale to quieten the heartbeat thumping loudly in his ears. He almost dreaded the reply to what he knew he had to ask. 'Was the son named Jack by any chance?'

'Aye, that's right... well, John, but he was always known as Jack, Jack Howell,' Josh confirmed.

Harry's stomach churned and settled like a lead weight, as the realisation hit him. 'Christ! I knew it' he exclaimed, slamming down his tankard, his outburst causing several heads to turn in his direction.

Josh chattered on but Harry was not listening. Anger rose in his breast. Now he knew Kate's secret. His niece had deceived him, deceived them all! She had gone ahead and married Jack Howell, her smuggler lover, and they had returned with a new name, conveniently borrowed from his deceased relative. *How am I going to tell Ellen? How can I tell her that her cherished grandson is the son of a wanted smuggler?* It all began to fall into place: Kate's disappearance, their private marriage away from friends and family, her reluctance to introduce her husband, her smart new clothes, her child's shock of dark hair and deep blue eyes! *Yes, of course! The child is a Howell, not a Pallant, and now Howell is the master of the* Lady Katherine *and it's odds-on she will be plying her illicit trade right under their noses!* Harry left the inn shortly afterwards; he needed time to think, to digest this bombshell, and was about to untether his horse when he felt a tap on his shoulder.

'Lieutenant Goldsmith?'

Harry spun round with a start, his thoughts still racing with the knowledge Jack Howell was alive and well and no doubt laughing at him as he continued his clandestine activities unhampered.

'Yes?' he said curtly, in no mood for an unwanted distraction until he had fully absorbed this new revelation.

A man of about sixty with greying hair and a pale pinched face stared at him in the gloom. 'Sorry for disturbing you, sir, but I couldn't help overhearing your conversation in there.' The man inclined his head towards the open door of the inn. 'My name's Sawyer, Charles Sawyer, my son Edward... he died...'

'Yes, I know who you are, I am sorry for your loss, Mr Sawyer. How can I help you?'

'I heard a mention of Jack Howell. Is he returned hereabouts?'

Harry could not be sure of Sawyer's intentions and as yet could not confirm one way or the other if his hunch was correct. *Best not say too much*, he cautioned himself.

'Mebbe,' he swerved, 'it's just a rumour. Why do you ask?'

'I reckon it was his lot that killed my Edward – those free traders. Got no proof, but Ed told me he was looking for Howell and was going to turn him in and the next thing I find my son wound up dead in Martlesham Creek. Of course, it wer' deemed an accident, but Ed was no fool and he said Howell had threatened him. They were rivals in love, you know.'

'Yes, I know,' Harry said flatly, although he wasn't going to admit his niece's involvement to Sawyer.

'Aye, well, I swore to find those responsible for my Edward's death. If ever Howell turns up, I want to be there when you apprehend him.' Sawyer clutched Harry's arm earnestly, fixing him with a determined stare.

'Look, I'm sorry, but we can't get civilians involved, Mister Sawyer. It's too dangerous. These men are armed and ruthless. I can let you know if we arrest Howell if that would help, but you could endanger our operations if we let you know beforehand. I'm sorry.'

Harry turned away and mounted his horse, trotting off down the main street. He was still trying to take in the information about Howell and for all he knew Sawyer could be spying for the traders to let them know the militia's next move. He did actually feel some sympathy for the man who had lost his only son, for whom the miller had built up his business. He knew Edward Sawyer's death was questionable, but like so many deaths along this bleak coastline, there was no way of proving it given the fear of retribution from the tight-lipped community. Besides, despite Jack Howell's reputation, Harry did not think him open to murder in cold blood; there were others amongst the *Sandpiper*'s crew more dangerous and less discerning.

Harry was still trying to ingest this latest intelligence. He was incandescent with rage at Kate, whom he saw as flagrantly flaunting her errant husband under his nose, no doubt laughing at her uncle's naivete and congratulating herself on her dissemblance. He had to admit, however, to a certain admiration for the cunning and enterprise of the young man who had evaded capture and returned as a successful marketeer right under their noses. He held no wish to deprive his niece of her beloved husband and render her child fatherless, but he felt an obligation to his dead brother and to Ellen, who had lost both husband and son in the fight against the free trade, and besides, it was the job he was paid for.

Charles Sawyer stood watching the exciseman disappear down the main street, a sour sneer curling his lips. 'Don't you worry, Edward, my lad,' he muttered to himself. 'Goldsmith won't stop me. I swear I'll catch up with Howell before he does, if it's the last thing I do!'

Harry relayed his newly gleaned information about Will Pallant's real identity to his superiors, who advised him to keep it to himself until they could catch Pallant in the act of smuggling and establish him as Howell. There was no point in alerting locals with the absolute certainty it would get back to Howell, allowing him once more to run to ground. Enquiries into the trading activities of the *Lady Katherine* had so far revealed no unlawful irregularities. The schooner had been transporting legitimate merchant's goods at a competitive rate for some time and routine customs searches had revealed nothing untoward. No, Harry realised, they would have to apprehend the *Lady Katherine*'s master and crew in the act of landing an illicit haul to stand any chance of preferring charges against them.

Harry also deemed it wise to keep this information from Ellen for the time being, who would be unable to hide her distress and anger at her daughter's deception from the scandal-mongers of Woodbridge. Ellen was acquainted with several ladies from social groups in the town and Harry considered it prudent to refrain from discussing his work with his gregarious wife. He trusted her to be discreet, of course, but there was no point in risking a misplaced remark that might endanger a covert undertaking. He would tell Ellen when the time was right and he was better prepared for the inevitable anguish and outrage his revelation would precipitate. He would think about the repercussions later; for now, though, he must focus on his first objective, to catch Howell red-handed.

Chapter Twenty-Three

As the *Lady Katherine* set course for Southwold on a fine bright morning, her hold laden with goods packed to the gunwales, Jack stood at the helm guiding his graceful craft out of Flushing and into the North Sea, proudly surveying the deck, breathing in the fresh salt spray as the schooner eagerly thrust her bows into the deepening water, lurching forward as her sails filled, cleaving her way through the surf.

Watching Nate Halesworth barking orders to the crew busy setting the billowing sheets of canvas to catch the prevailing wind, before his first mate went below to check the stability of the cargo, Jack felt on top of the world. His dream of owning his own ship had been realised, he had married his sweetheart, his family was growing, his pockets well lined, their future secured. There was only one nagging doubt still eating away at his conscience – as much as he wanted to be Will Pallant, he was not; he was Jack Howell, and Jack Howell was wanted by the law, well known by those who knew him and easily identified by his missing digit. He looked down at the unsightly stump where his index finger should have been and cast his thoughts back to that night on the Alde, when at least one exciseman had been killed along with two of his own men who had later succumbed to their injuries. He swore under his breath, but what was done, was done. This was the life he had chosen and he would live it to the full while he could. He owed that to Kate. His thoughts were interrupted by Nate, who came back on deck to review the plan for tonight's drop, and Jack readily pushed his misgivings to the back of his mind.

Before Jack left Southwold, he and Pat Harvey had discussed the landing in detail. They would anchor off Dunwich, Pat's men waiting in small craft to disburse the haul at various dropping-off points along the River Blyth and up towards Blythburgh, while Jack's men would make temporary use of the cellars at the Ship Inn and the crypt of the abandoned All Saint's Church, now perched precariously on its ever-diminishing headland, before making the run across Westleton Common when the coast was clear. They were confident of a successful run, Pat being acquainted with the riding officer at Sizewell who, for the right inducement, agreed to be 'coincidentally' engaged elsewhere on the night in question. The officer had clashed with the Hadleigh gang before and as a result deemed it preferable to stay alive for the remainder of his career, collect his pension and retire in peace. The prospect of a single man intercepting a large gang of uncompromising men armed to the teeth and well used to violence, was not a pleasant nor a prudent one, neither was the temptation of informing on them to the militia, with the inevitable repercussions such an act would provoke. Instead, the exciseman would trot off in the direction of Aldeburgh with a pocketful of cash and the promise of a half anker of premium brandy sitting on his doorstep, awaiting his return.

Approaching the low shadowed outline of the familiar Suffolk coastline, silhouetted against the orange glow of a cloud-striated sunset, the *Lady Katherine* veered northwards, following the known landmarks that served to determine her position, Jack watching for the lantern signal from the abandoned tower of All Saint's Church on Dunwich cliff. As they passed the marshes of Minsmere, he pictured mad Willie Mumford making his inebriated way home from the Vulcan Arms, settling down for the night in his ramshackle abode, cooking himself a supper of freshly caught fish and falling asleep by the light of the stove. *There's something to be said for a simple existence, beholden to no-one, free to do as one pleased.* Jack chuckled to himself. However, comparing it to his life with Kate – his lovely wife, his precious son, his newly purchased house, his fine ship, the excitement of his trade, the salt spindrift blowing in his face that made him feel alive – Jack knew he had everything he craved. He felt sad that his parents, who had given him life, had not lived to see their only son make his fortune, but he hoped they were looking down on him with pride for his enterprise. The expected beacon of light from on shore duly came and then another, snapping him out of his reverie, and as his crew returned the signal, he hurried below to begin the night's endeavour.

As darkness fell, a freshening breeze soughed over the marram grass on the headland bordering Dunwich Heath, whipping the quivering fronds around Pat's ankles. He took a swig of brandy from his hip flask and raised his spyglass to the horizon just as the sails of the *Lady Katherine* hove into view, silhouetted against the darkening sky of receding twilight. A lantern flashed twice from the church tower and was echoed a few moments later from the schooner, as she approached as near as she dare, on the high tide, and furled her sails. The landers manning the ponies and carts assembling on Westleton Heath, the fishing smacks setting out from their anchorage on the River Blyth, and a row of four-oared craft lined up on Dunwich foreshore, oars muffled, their crews readied for the drop; all waited in silence while the sailors lined up on the *Lady Katherine*'s deck, passing barrels and bundles along from the schooner's hold.

Harry Goldsmith, meanwhile, had been busy ascertaining the whereabouts of the *Lady Katherine* and its master, using his network of paid informers who frequented the ale houses along the Suffolk coast, and he knew Will Pallant's ship was expected shortly from Flushing. He had also reasoned that a drop would most likely take place a little further up the coast, now that Jack Howell was living in Southwold, the same patch where the Hadleigh mob operated, and with any luck, two groups of felons might be apprehended for the price of one. Harry had accordingly stationed his Preventive men at Sizewell, along with a squad of dragoons, but for over a week there had been no evidence of night-time activities, the wild weather having made it unappealing to the smuggling fraternity, so the excisemen had moved up to Dunwich, where they were billeted in the Downing's jail house, converted from the ruins of the Franciscan Priory.

Again, their watch proved fruitless and they were planning to leave, but Harry, convinced a drop was still imminent, delayed their departure one more night. He had made sure the locals drinking at the Ship Inn would overhear their loudly vocalised agenda to move down to Aldeburgh, surmising correctly that the smuggler's spies would relay the news to the landers that Dunwich would be clear of militia. Instead, his men, accompanied by the dragoons, made their way quietly back around the old priory walls to await the drop he fully expected on this moonless windy night. They would wait until the goods had been landed and loaded. There was no point in fighting a pitched battle on the open foreshore before the cargo was fully beached and where there was no cover. The horses with their heavily laden carts would have to use the roads where Harry's men would be waiting for them. Harry knew from experience, many of the traders would just melt into the darkness, but if he could relieve them of their booty and apprehend Jack Howell once and for all, he would be satisfied; his job would be done.

As Harry left the inn, he failed to notice a shadowed figure quietly tracking his movements as he approached the priory ruins. Charles Sawyer had not fallen for the charade at the Ship. He had been tailing the Revenue men for some days, determined to be present at any confrontation with Jack Howell, his brace of flintlocks primed and ready for the payback he had lately visualised. He would avenge his son, come what may, and if he died in the attempt then so be it. He had no other family to whom to bequeath his business, his wife having died many a long year back when Edward was but a few months old. Edward had been his pride and joy, his hope for the future of Sawyer & Son, and the profitable expansion of his growing collection of mills had all been for nothing. Sawyer, plagued by a persistent cough, his lungs weakened by a debilitating chest complaint brought on by years of inhaling flour dust, felt old and wearied. The son who should have been stepping into his shoes was gone. Now his resolve was channelled into one concluding ultimate goal, one irreversible purpose, one unrelenting mission, regardless of consequence. Nothing else mattered. Edward would be avenged, and if his father went down for murder he cared not. *An eye for an eye and a tooth for a tooth*, Sawyer obdurately appeased his conscience.

Out in the bay, Jack sprang down the rope ladder on the schooner's starboard side, jumping into the waiting jolly boat to take his seat at the oars, his shipmates pushing the heavy-laden craft clear and pointing the bow landwards. He could see the line of torches snaking up the beach where a procession of landers was already engaged in silently handing over kegs and bales along the line, up the steep cliff path to the waiting horses and tub men. Several fishing smacks were making their way back to Walberswick and the River Blyth, with a share of the heaviest ankers of Geneva and brandy, which would be sailed upriver to various setting-off points along the banks of the widening inland lagoons of Blythburgh Water. Here Pat Harvey's men would be waiting on the watersides, keeping watch for the all-clear lantern signal from the White Hart before disbursing the goods to a multiplicity of hiding places.

Atop Walberswick bluff, the dark mass of All Saint's long-abandoned church tower loomed above them as Jacks' craft beached and they jumped ashore to off-load their cargo. Already the first loaded horses and carts were leaving in the direction of Westleton, the tub men disbursing into the darkness, the barrels slung front and back over their strong shoulders. Jack waited on the beach until the last of the bundles were run, when suddenly a voice whispered behind him. 'Jack!'

Jack's instinct when he was startled was to grasp his pistol, and he swung round sharply to see Pat holding a lantern up to his face.

'Whoa!' His friend chuckled. 'It's only me, mate!'

'Christ, Pat, you made me jump,' Jack breathed with relief. He wouldn't admit it, but he was on edge tonight; he didn't know why. He didn't consider himself psychic, but always when he felt this feeling of anxiety, something would inevitably go wrong. Tonight, however, had been a good haul, and he dismissed his qualms. They had the use of forty horses, thirty-five carts and fifty of Pat's men. They had got all the goods off the beach or upriver: five hundred tubs of Geneva, one hundred casks of spirit, seventy barrels of wine, 600lbs of tobacco compacted and wrapped in oilskin bales, bolts of silk, calico and lawn, starch, sugar, soap and coffee, nutmeg, cloves, and a nice collection of silver snuff boxes. Jack was particularly pleased with a ruby and pearl gold filigree necklace he had bought from a French jeweller as a surprise for Kate, tucked into his inside coat pocket. Now she was expecting his second child, he wanted to reward her for giving him the family he had always longer for, the sons or daughters who would carry his genes down the generations, if not his name.

Upon reaching the cliff top he and Pat mounted their waiting horses and trotted off behind the batmen, who were ready with clubs and pistols to defend the cavalcade of contraband making its way over Westleton Heath. Some of the cache had already been stored in the ruined church tower and some buried on the dunes for collection later, while some was making its way into the cellars of the Ship Inn. Over at Blythburgh water, ankers of gin were being transported upriver and off loaded to several well-used underground pits. The local spies had told them the excisemen had left for Aldeburgh along with the riding officer who had been bribed, and they were feeling confident of an undisturbed run.

As the cavalcade snaked past the shadowed ruins of the priory to their left, Jack thought he saw a flash of light reflecting off something metal. He gestured to Pat and put his finger to his lips. They reined in their horses and stood in silence listening for a few moments, Jack straining his eyes for shapes in the gloom, but all he could hear was his heart thumping in his chest, the sigh of the wind through the archways and the whirr of bats darting to and fro above their heads. Jack took his pistol from his belt and fingered the reassuring hilt of his cutlass, senses alert, adrenaline pumping. He was ready for a fight, but he was sure from the information they had been given that the area was clear of militia, so he squeezed his horse's flanks and trotted on.

They hadn't progressed a hundred yards before a flash lit up the road and a volley of shots pierced the stillness. Jack's horse whinnied and reared, his rider sliding off hurriedly. Pat jumped down and ran for cover, as angry shouts from both soldiers and smugglers rang out. Two of the landers went down and one of the packhorses fell, tipping its wagon-load onto the ground, while the men scrambled for cover, or ran in all directions, the tub men relieving themselves of their burdens where they could, the batmen readying themselves for a pitched battle, crouching down, pistols primed, clubs and cutlasses drawn, itching for hand-to-hand combat.

Jack swore. He couldn't make out how many servicemen they were up against, but it seemed a good number. A party of dragoons were blocking the road ahead, using the abandoned carts as cover. The only thing for it was to retreat back the way they had come before the militia could surround them. Jack crawled over to Pat as musket balls whizzed over their heads. 'Pat, tell the lads to leave the goods and run. We can always take 'em back later. We'll give 'em cover while they get away. Go!' Pat ran off, bent double to avoid the volley of gunfire, and gradually the free traders disbursed into the night. Some of the terrified horses had bolted, their loads trundling clumsily behind them, unnerving them even more, and were soon making their unbidden way home across Westleton Heath.

Jack lay on the edge of the ditch at the side of the road, taking careful aim at the boatmen darting amidst the crumbling priory walls. He was reaching for his gunpowder when, without warning, the point of a bayonet blade jabbed between his shoulder blades.

'I wouldn't if I were you,' a gruff voice barked. 'Hands up!'

Jack's hand automatically felt for his cutlass hilt, but two dragoons were on him, wrenching his arms back and kneeling on his back before he could stand up. He cursed at his carelessness and looked around for Pat, but his mate had gone. The soldiers and excisemen were rounding up the smugglers who hadn't been able to get away when Jack recognised Harry Goldsmith striding towards him. He cursed vehemently the realisation that the game was up hitting him like a brick wall, as a bright lantern was thrust into his face, forcing him to look away, the image of the flame imprinting on his retina, temporarily blinding him.

'Well, if it isn't Will Pallant, captain of the *Lady Katherine*, or rather should I say Jack Howell?!' Harry announced triumphantly, without waiting for an answer. 'Back from the dead, are we? You won't be getting away this time, lad, I can assure you.' He smirked as the two dragoons on either side of Jack stood him up, relieved him of his weapons and clapped him in irons.

Jack stared impassively at his wife's uncle. He knew there was no use pretending. His heart sank and all he could think of was Kate and Kit. Kate, his beautiful wife who had stood by him, and Kit, his treasured son for whom he had such hopes. Still, he reasoned to himself, a few years in gaol and he would be a free man again, at liberty to resume life as a merchant trader. It was almost a relief. No more masquerading as Will Pallant, looking over his shoulder acting out a fantasy and expecting Kate to do the same. Of course, there was always the option of a new life in His Majesty's Service with an offer of the king's pardon, which, although less appealing and a lot less lucrative, was the choice of many a convicted felon. By the Act of Oblivion recently passed, if a smuggler could find two soldiers and two sailors from amongst his comrades to serve in the Navy, as well as avoiding the £500 fine, he could go free. To Jack, however, that was never an option. *If the Navy expect me to do likewise, they will be disappointed*, Jack resolved. Nothing would induce him to inveigle his mates into a life of service to the Crown and walk free himself. The idea was preposterous and he wondered who on earth could have devised such a contemptible plan. They obviously knew nothing of human nature and the bond of loyalty amongst those struggling for survival, who would fight together and die together if needs be. Intruding upon his thoughts, his captor's words brought him rudely back to the present.

'So you thought you'd get away with a new name, eh, Howell? Bad choice, that lad. Sooner or later someone would twig. Folk round here are too well known,' Harry gloated, unable to hide a smile of self-satisfaction.

'Oh, yeah?' Jack retorted scathingly. 'What took you so long then?' he sneered before the soldiers pushed him forwards.

They led Jack and several of the traders who had been apprehended round to the temporary prison attached to the priory, to await transfer in the morning, first to Woodbridge gaol for holding, then to Ipswich for trial. Harry stared after Jack, his initial euphoria at apprehending this fearless young trader subsiding rapidly to anti-climax. He almost envied the audacity and bravado of this skilled and charismatic young mariner who had become embroiled in the activities of the nefarious moonlighters, evaded capture and made fools of the Service right under their noses: an infamous felon to some, a dashing hero to others. He knew Kate would never forgive him for snatching her husband away, leaving her to manage on her own with a young son to raise, but the law was the law and it was his job to uphold it.

As the abandoned goods were collected up and conveyed to the priory for the night, the exciseman failed to notice a figure watching from the shadows who had witnessed Jack's arrest, Harry's words helpfully confirming the identity of the man Charles Sawyer had sworn to confront. His perseverance in following the soldiers as they moved from place to place had paid off. He could now identify Howell and there was still time to carry out his plan. He hadn't been the first to catch up with the smuggler as he had hoped, but another opportunity would no doubt soon present itself. He crept back to the ruins of All Saint's, where he bedded down beneath the old bell tower, hidden from the smugglers who used it to signal from the topmost window opening. He left them alone. He wasn't going to inform on them; they meant nothing to him – no, he had bigger fish to fry.

Chapter Twenty-Four

Jack dozed fitfully; the old cell felt dank and cold, chilling him to the bone. His companions were noisy sleepers, snoring, coughing, expectorating, cursing and banging around, using the slop bucket to relieve themselves or speaking in lowered tones about the night's activities.

'That jolter head at the Ship!' a seasoned sailor was complaining bitterly, expelling phlegm in disgust. 'If I get 'old of 'im I'll wring his bloody neck. It's no good takin' the excise at their word, 'e should have made sure they'd left Dun'ich before givin' the all-clear!'

'Abe and Jesse thought they'd left too; they sent the signal. It's not *just* Ed's fault, George,' Jack commented broodily, blaming himself for his choice of drop and having led his men directly into a trap. His thoughts were full of his wife and son, and his prized schooner sailing down to Ipswich with Nate at the helm, her remaining legitimate cargo ready for the merchants' bulging warehouses. She would be leaving again in several days, stocked with wool and the finest Suffolk butter, before waiting to pick him up off Aldeburgh after some welcome shore leave at home with Kate. He cursed quietly to himself, wondering how Harry had seen through his guise, if someone had given him away or if he had himself somehow been careless. As he speculated, casting his mind over recent events but coming to no conclusion, he watched a rat scuttle out through the bars of the cell. *Even lowly vermin have more freedom than me at this moment!* he mused dejectedly. His thoughts turned to Pat and the men who had got away. He knew the first thing Pat would do would be to tell Kate, who would no doubt be making plans to travel to Woodbridge once the initial shock of his capture had given way to rationality.

A sudden thought struck him as he pictured Kate. *The necklace!* He felt in his inside coat pocket and yes, it was still there in its velvet pouch, but what to do with it?! Although the dragoon's peremptory search had missed it, Jack knew they would be stripped and searched again tomorrow at Woodbridge gaol, and any possessions secreted inside clothing would be confiscated, his pistol and cutlass already having been wrested from him. Despite the fact the trinket had been purchased legitimately, it had been bought with ill-gotten gains and would be seen as hot goods, no duty having been paid. He wasn't going to let some greedy exciseman get his hands on it. He had chosen it for Kate and she must have it, he settled. *I must get rid of it somewhere.*

Casting his eye around the cell, he noticed that although the side walls were of newer brick, the back wall was formed by the original stone of the old priory. He had already spotted that a few small stones had dislodged, providing rat-sized escape holes for resourceful rodents. He sat back against the wall and felt the stones where they rested along the floor. His luck was in: one of them was loose! He waited until his comrades' breathing slowed into the steady rhythm of slumber, before easing the insecure stone from its placement. It took a while to fully extricate, Jack stopping every now and then to check the scraping noise had not alerted his comrades, until the stone was out. Carefully placing the pouch at the back of the cavity, he replaced the block in the aperture, spitting on the disturbed sand particles before pressing them back into position.

He sat back satisfied, settling on a plan to somehow get a message to Pat, who could retrieve the necklace later when the building was empty. He immediately felt better. Kate could sell it if she needed to, although the money he had in the bank at Southwold would be sufficient for a good few years. He smiled as he envisioned her face when his solicitor would call upon her to deliver the keys and deeds of their new house in Aldeburgh. She would be waiting there for him when he had served his time and they could resume their life together once more. He had it all worked out, and as fatigue set in, he relaxed for the first time that day. Soon he slept soundly despite the cold floor, his departure from Flushing now seeming like a distant flight of fancy, relative to his present predicament.

Kate awoke with a start. Kit was whimpering for his morning feed. She sat up and looked round, half expecting to see Jack sleeping beside her. However, no Jack! *Where is he? Surely he should have been back home by now?* The sombre nebulous light of the new day filtered through the cottage window as she cradled Kit in her arms and held him to her breast. A short while later there was a tap on the door. She hurriedly placed Kit in his cot and ran down the stairs, grabbing her robe around her. Her stomach did a somersault. It was young Pip. *Something must have happened to Jack.* 'Come in, Pip.' She ushered him into the kitchen. He looked exhausted, his hair was unkempt and there was mud on his clothes. 'What's happened? Tell me! Is he my husband hurt?' she demanded urgently, her eyes wide with fear as he sat down in the chair she offered, Pip removing his headgear respectfully.

'No, he's not hurt, ma'am,'

Kate sighed with relief.

'He's been nabbed, er... sorry, ma'am.' Pip corrected his slang. 'Arrested – and they know who 'e is.'

Kate put her hand over her mouth, tears springing into her eyes, her body trembling as she sat down opposite the lad, her legs suddenly like jelly. Her dread had been realised, the game was up, there would be no more pretending.

'I'm so sorry, ma'am.' Pip fingered his hat nervously while she composed herself.

'Tell me what happened, Pip,' she urged, resting her head on her hands as he described last night's events.

When he had finished, Kate raised her head. 'How did they know?' she asked.

'Dunno, ma'am, but Officer Goldsmith confronted your husband with 'is real name. He didn't deny it.'

'Uncle Harry!' Kate exclaimed. 'I knew he suspected us from the start,' she said, as much to herself as to Pip. 'He must have found proof. Oh no, poor Jack!'

'Nobody would have squealed on 'im, ma'am. Goldsmith must ha' guessed some'ow.'

'It was bound to happen sooner or later.' Kate spoke her thoughts out loud. 'We've lived in constant fear of it. What's going to happen now, I wonder?' she sighed, not really expecting an answer, as the question was more of a statement about her life than any immediate outcome, but Pip took her literally.

'Mister Harvey says they'll be taken to Woodbridge, then to Ipswich gaol to await trial.'

Kate smiled at the lad's precise interpretation of her words. *Better stick to the facts.* 'So Pat got away then?' she asked.

'Aye, and quite a few of his men.'

'How many got caught?'

'About a dozen, ma'am.'

'I'm glad some of you got away.' Kate's tension soothed as she felt a sense of relief flowing through her, now that she need no longer keep up the pretence of being Mrs Will Pallant.

In the short silence that followed, Pip's stomach growled. Kate broke into a smile and stood up to fetch a mug of ale, as he grabbed his midriff and looked away, embarrassed. 'You must be starving. I'll make you some breakfast.'

Pip grinned sheepishly. 'Ooh, thank you, ma'am, that'd be prime!'

Kate chuckled at the teenager's unrestrained relish at the prospect of food, memories of her own brothers' voracious appetite visualising in her mind's eye, before her thoughts again turned to her husband and the uncertainty of their immediate future.

Pat Harvey had been busy catching up with his scattered gang, last night's haul having been divided up and secreted in a variety of locations, cellars, churches and pits, ready for distribution. Most of the horses had made their own way home, although some had been rounded up grazing on Dunwich Heath, casks and bundles still strapped to their backs. It had been a long night and Pat was exhausted, but he knew the captured smugglers would be moved from their temporary cell in the morning and conveyed towards the Woodbridge road, then down to the town gaol. There was only one chance of ambush, he decided, and that was at Westleton Heath.

He sent a messenger to his gang's various hideouts before deciding to grab himself a couple of hours' sleep at the Eel's Foot at Eastbridge, easily accessed via the well-used smugglers' trail, linking the village to the sea. As he jogged his way through the darkness, he rather hoped he would not be in danger of encountering the ghost of Black Toby, who was said to haunt the environs of Blythburgh Common. The negro drummer of the Preventive Service had been hanged there in 1750 for rape and murder, crimes of which he was later found to be innocent, and Pat had no wish to encounter Toby's vengeful spirit as he hurried by, his tired eyes unwittingly fancying more than was actually there. As dawn broke a thick roke had descended along the coast overnight, reaching inland for about ten miles, just the setting for a spectral phantasm but at the same time fortuitously providing perfect cover for Pat's plan. A comforting blanket of fog was always a welcome bonus for the smugglers, despite its somewhat unnerving ability to disguise both friend and foe. One could never quite know what was going to materialise out of the swirling vapour.

Jack awoke to the sounds of clanging metal and jangling keys as the priory cell was opened and soldiers roughly manacled the prisoners together, pushing them outside towards the waiting carts.

Harry strode towards Jack. 'I'll take care of this 'un,' he told the sergeant, once more clapping handcuffs around Jack's wrists. 'I want you where I can keep an eye on you, young man. Can't have you scuttlin' off again, can we?!'

Jack smirked silently at his father-in-law, as he was pulled to his feet, led out of the prison and thrust towards a waiting horse.

The mist billowing around them felt cold and clammy. Jack looked around in the murk, listening for any sound that might signal a rescue party. *Perfect conditions for an ambush*, he thought optimistically, wondering if Pat had had the same idea. He was helped up into the saddle, the animal being tethered between two Preventive officers, one of whom was Harry. Goldsmith mounted his horse beside him and they rode off ahead of the wagons bearing the prisoners and the captured contraband, dragoons trotting noisily on either side, harness and weapons jangling as the mist curled silently about them. As they approached Westleton Heath, Jack thought he spied a lone figure moving quickly through the fog to one side of them, but whether it was friend or foe he could not tell, and as the troupe soon put distance between them, it seemed irrelevant.

All at once the cavalcade halted. Ahead of them a large log was lying across the road, where the ditch on either side rendered skirting it with loaded carts impossible. Harry swore, but Jack smiled to himself. *Well done, Pat!* Several soldiers were commanded to dismount and remove the obstruction, the rest aiming their muskets in readiness for an attack, which duly came. A volley of shots rang out from the churning mist as Jack ducked down against his horse's neck before being pulled to the ground by two boatmen, his hands still manacled behind him. Two of the dragoons fell wounded as a bellowing mob of dangerous and fearless men emerged charging out of the gloom, cutlasses and clubs wielded with murderous intent. A hand-to-hand battle ensued, but the militia, clearly outnumbered three to one, judged it better not to fight to the death over a few cartloads of contraband and, after resisting for as long as possible, wisely surrendered their weapons. Jack, lying prone in the ditch beside the road, calmly watched Harry and his men taking measured aim at the smugglers, felling at least three of them, when two figures crept up behind the exciseman, one of them holding a pistol against his head. Harry felt the cold metal digging into his scalp and heard the click as the firearm was cocked. Jack held his breath.

'Drop your weapon, Goldsmith,' a familiar gruff throaty voice commanded, as the second masked man wrenched the musket from Harry's hands.

Jack grinned. 'Ben!' he exclaimed with relief.

'This is gettin' to be a habit, lad, savin' your bacon!' the old sailor quipped dryly, his pistol still aimed at Harry's head, as his companion wrenched the keys from the exciseman's belt and unlocked Jack's manacles, clapping them instead onto Harry's wrists. Jack turned to thank his liberator and grinned, as Pat Harvey winked, briefly tugging his neckerchief away from his face.

'We saw you'd been nabbed! Wasn't gonna leave you to rot in t' clink, mate.' He chuckled as he pulled his friend to his feet.

Jack clapped Pat gratefully on the back, mindful not to call him by name for Harry to identify.

'You won't get away with this, Howell,' Harry snapped crossly before glancing sideways at Ben, 'and you've got a price on your head as well, Fosdyke.'

Ben grabbed the exciseman's collar tightly and thrust his steely-grey eyes into his face, drawing his cutlass and laying it against Harry's throat. Harry could feel the keenness of its sharp edge, a hair's breadth from puncturing his skin, and held his breath.

'Yeah? Well, I got nuthin' to lose then, 'ave I?!' the sailor rasped.

Harry resisted the urge to reply. He knew it wasn't an empty threat. This old seadog's reputation for gratuitous violence preceded him and he wasn't about to put him to the test.

'Leave 'im, Ben! Come on!' Pat tugged at Ben's arm insistently as the sailor grudgingly withdrew his blade, uttering a menacing hiss through his teeth as he did so.

Harry shuddered, exhaling a sigh of relief, an unwelcome image of a slit throat forming in his mind. He clutched his neck for reassurance and cursed to himself angrily, as the smugglers melted into the fog. Howell and his gang had got away for a second time! This was not good, despite in their haste having abandoned much of their booty in favour of their captured colleagues but with an assortment of British Army weaponry to add to their cache.

'We'll get 'em next time, boys, they won't get far,' he assured his men as they removed his manacles, helped the wounded men back on their mounts and gathered up the corpses of the three smugglers who had been shot dead.

Chapter Twenty-Five

The three friends jogged away through the fog, Jack elated at his escape, his companions equally buoyed up by their success.

'Thank Christ for this roke!' Jack exclaimed. 'I owe you fellas!'

'Aye, the debt's mountin' up, lad!' Ben remarked drolly. 'Reckon you owe me a lifetime o' rum so far!'

'I reckon I do, mate,' Jack agreed. 'Where've ya been all this time, Ben?'

''Ere and ther', lad. Spent a bit o' time at Minsmer' wi' Mad Willie 'til me trotters got wet rot. I wer bored out o' me mind, so I thought I'd come up and join Pat's lads. They don't know me so well up at Halesw'th, besides... any longer wi' Mumford and I'd have been as dicked in the 'ead as 'e is!'

Jack recalled his sojourn on the mere and the thought of Willie and Ben together, two taciturn old men for whom conversation was a waste of breath, curved his lips into a smile and chuckled at the notion as they lumbered on. Fighting fatigue and hunger, following the Dunwich River as it snaked up to Walberswick, flowing parallel with the dunes bordering the beach, they jogged on in silence. A couple of times Ben stopped in mid-stride, his finger pressed to his lip, listening for footfall. He could not shake off the unsettling sensation they were being watched. The mist was starting to dissipate, patches of sunlight breaking through, lighting up the sandhills to their right, revealing glimpses of the tranquil shoreline, where the placid water sparkled in a golden haze, with the promise of a fine day.

As they approached the village, Jack announced his intention. 'I'm gonna leave you here, fellas. Gonna mek my way home across to Southwold and see Kate, she'll be worryin'.'

'Be that wise, Jack?' questioned Pat. 'The excise'll be looking for ya and that's the first place they'll look, now they know you're Will Pallant!'

Jack swore. *Yes, of course!* He was so at ease with his cover that the realisation he could no longer hide behind it hit him like a thunderbolt. He knew the *Lady Katherine* would be waiting to pick him up in a few days' time on her way back to Holland. He would have to wait for her here. However, first he determined to see Kate. He must get a message to her.

'Bloody women!' exclaimed Ben irritably. 'They're more trouble than they're worth!'

'You speak for yerself, Ben,' Pat interjected. 'Nothin' better than a pretty mawther to warm me bed and cook me vittles!'

'Hear, hear!' agreed Jack. 'Ye dunno what you're missin, Ben.'

'Hmph! It's aright for you young 'uns! Who's gonna shack up wi' an old fogram like me?'

Jack couldn't resist the retort that immediately sprang to mind. 'Oh, I dunno, Ben, I've 'eard that light-heeled wench at the King's 'ead ain't too fussy! She'd give a good mawtherin' to anythin' wi' half a pulse!'

As the sound of ribald laughter echoed over the marram grass, it was heard by more than just the weary trio, and as they crossed the road towards the Blue Anchor Inn, a shadowed figure followed in their footsteps as they entered the hostelry. The three comrades were ushered downstairs to a warm cellar, already stacked with bales and barrels from last night's haul. The proprietress, Ann Maggs, brought welcome bowls of steaming mutton broth and freshly baked bread to fill their grumbling stomachs and after a mug full of ale the three fugitives slept soundly.

In the bar upstairs an elderly man sat himself down and ordered a drink. He wasn't a regular and he too looked as though he hadn't slept for hours. As Mrs Maggs brought his drink and he reached for it, his coat fell open and she noticed a brace of pistols tucked into his belt, but she said nothing. He saw her looking and pulled his greatcoat across, averting his gaze as he placed his coins on the table. She adjudged him well dressed, so not ostensibly a felon, perhaps an officer of the law in plain clothes, although he was unshaven. He had several days' growth adorning his jawline and his hands appeared strangely white, vestiges of something resembling flour outlining his fingernails. His breath came in short gasps punctuated by the occasional guttural cough as he cleared his chest. Anne made a mental note to alert his presence to her guests in the cellar when they awoke.

It was late afternoon when Jack awoke and roused his comrades. After refreshing themselves with victuals from the inn's kitchen and learning of the stranger who had come into the bar but had now gone, they decided to split up and make their separate ways, judging it wise not to chance it through the village in case the inn was being watched. None of them made the connection between the owner of Sawyer's mills and the pale-skinned stranger, however, dismissing his presence as irrelevant. After generously compensating Anne Maggs for her hospitality, Pat and Ben made use of the short tunnel dug underneath the cellar which emerged alongside Walberswick creek. While Ben doubled back towards Minsmere, Pat made his way towards the harbour to procure a rowing boat for passage upstream. Jack, meanwhile, stayed behind, having written a note to Kate and given it to Pat, who pressed it into the hands of a fisherman bound for the Southwold bank. After accepting a small fee and instructions for delivery, the fisherman was able to satisfy him of its safe conveyance by one of his crew.

'Not for pryin' eyes now!' Pat censured, to which the fisherman grinned wryly.

'Don't you worry, lad, none of us can read anyways!'

Jack remained at the inn while he waited for Kate, his safehouse assured for now. If the excise came calling, he would be able to make his escape via the underground tunnel, through which the remainder of last night's cache was soon to be transported upriver.

Earlier that morning, Kate had thanked Pip and sent him on his way, his belly full of Ellen Goldsmith's special recipe for porridge, a message for Pat Harvey to call on Kate as soon as he was able dutifully recorded in his mind. Kate paced the floor, her mind full of uncertainties and misgivings. She was only just beginning to realise the repercussions Jack's arrest would have on her life. The man she loved would be stuck in a felon's prison for years, or worse, transported halfway across the world to a distant penal colony. Kate would be left to bring up his children alone, his young son bereft of a father figure to encourage and instruct him in the ways of men. She knew Harry would waste no time in telling Ellen the news about her errant son-in-law and her mother would at last realise the enormity of Kate's deception. She would know that against all advice, her devious daughter had gone ahead and married her smuggler lover – the likes of his kind being responsible for the death of both her mother's husband and son, her own father and brother. Not only that, Kate had then presented her mother with a cherished grandson, withholding the truth of his paternity and masquerading as the wife of a respectable trader. Despite the dread of her mother's reaction, Kate felt relief at her exposure, as though a weight had been lifted. *It's done, no more lies*, she sighed stoically. *What will be will be.*

Kate busied herself with her chores in an absent-minded daze, tending to Kit's every need, all the while speculating on Jack's whereabouts and situation. It had been more than twenty-four hours since Jack's capture and arrest, and there was no sign of Pat calling to allay her fears.

As the sun sank low in the west, there was another rap on the door. Kate rushed to open it, expecting to see Pat Harvey, and it took a few moments to realise the figure outside was a stranger. 'Yes?' she snapped frowning, unable to hide her disappointment.

A youth in grubby sailor's garb, smelling distinctly of fish, stood holding a missive. 'Mrs Pallant?' he enquired as Kate nodded. 'For you, ma'am,' he announced, handing her the note before turning to go, relieved he had completed his mission.

'Wait!' Kate commanded. 'Who sent you?'

'Dunno, ma'am, the skipper just told me to deliver it to ya.'

'Alright, thank you.' Kate closed the door and sat down in the kitchen, unfolding the note with trembling hands. Kate recognised her husband's scrawling hand. *Come to Blue Anchor, W'wick tonight. Bring money. J*, was all it said. Kate was nonplussed. She sat and stared at the note. *Is Jack not in custody? Has he escaped? What is he doing in Walberswick?* Her heart was thumping in her chest, as she cast the note into the fire, took the money from the pot over the hearth and packed a generous chunk of freshly baked fruit cake into her skirt pocket, which she had intended for Jack's homecoming. She took Kit to her friend Sarah, a young mother who lived two doors down and who was always willing to mind another child, along with her own unruly brood of under-fives.

Donning a thick cloak and boots, lighting a lantern, Kate set off down the path to the harbour. It was still light enough to make out the way and ahead of her the river stood out in a wide, bright swathe, the placid waters reflecting the fading hues of sunset. A fresh breeze coming off the sea stung her skin and Kate wrapped her cloak around her body tightly, trying to calm her nerves and racing thoughts, as she mulled over what might have occurred with Jack. The old ferryman at the harbour grudgingly agreed to take her over for a little extra than the standard fee. He was settling down for the night and looking forward to his mug of ale at the Fishing Buss Inn on the quay, but a pretty face to ogle at and a hefty tip to spend made it worth his while.

Kate alighted on the opposite shore, thanked the ferryman and hurried up towards the Blue Anchor. 'I'm meeting my husband here,' she told the landlady, who ushered her into a back parlour. A moment later the door swung open and she was swept up in her husband's arms. 'Oh, Jack, Jack!' she gasped between hot kisses. 'What happened? Tell me! I thought you'd been arrested?'

'I was, my dunlin, and we were on our way to Woodbridge gaol, but Pat's lads rushed us as we were being transported along Westle'n Heath, so we got away. Your Uncle Harry knows me now, though, so I've gotta lie low again. I'm sorry, my dunlin.'

'Oh, Jack, not again! I can't bear it! What are we going to do?'

Jack sighed and sat down on the settle, pulling Kate down beside him, reassuringly clasping both her hands in his. 'You'll have to stay here, my dunlin. Look after Kit while I go back to Holland. They'll be watchin' your every move, but you'll be safe. It's not you they're after. I'll figure somethin' out, don't you fret.'

Kate clung to him in an ardent embrace, leaning her head against his shoulder. 'Oh, Jack...' she sighed as tears spilled down her cheek.

He kissed the top of her head gently while they sat in silence, each contemplating their uncertain future. 'The *Lady Katherine*'s due here at the end of the week to pick me up, my dunlin, but they'll be watchin' her an all, so I've gotta be careful. Pat's gonna get word to Nate before 'e leaves Woodbridge. He'll tell 'im to go straight to Flushing, then he'll arrange for the *Sandpiper* to come for me instead on Friday night. I'm gonna see if one of the fishin' smacks can ferry me out to wait for her, rather than her comin' into harbour. It'll be quicker that way, especially if the Service are hangin' around. Stay wi' me tonight, my dunlin, but you must get back first light.'

Kate nodded, laying herself down on the settle with her head on her husband's knee. 'Tell me what happened, Jack,' she asked, picturing the previous night's activities vividly in her mind as he related his story, before fatigue overcame them both and they slept, Kate feeling like she was living in some sort of repeating scenario from which she would one day awake and find it to be just a dream.

However, daylight confirmed it wasn't a dream, and after rising early, thanking Mrs Maggs and saying a tearful goodbye to Jack, Kate found herself trudging forlornly homewards as the sun rose over the sea and the fishermen of Southwold prepared their craft for the day's catch. *Here we go again*, she thought dismally. *Jack on the run once more*. The settled life to which she was just getting accustomed, now thrown into confusion and uncertainty. She felt bad for thinking it but judged it was almost preferable for Jack to be safely interned in Ipswich prison serving his sentence, rather than living a precarious life as an absconder for a second time and simply delaying the inevitable consequence of his felonious life in the fair trade.

Chapter Twenty-Six

A lantern flashed briefly from the cliff top then disappeared. *That's strange*, Jack thought, frowning uncertainly, as he approached the bluff, *the fishing smack must be further down the beach*. He picked his way along the dunes as the land rose upwards and the beach fell away to his left. The sea was calm and the moon peeped out from between striations of purple cloud, outlining the edges in ripples of silver, casting its ghostly glow onto the shimmering waves below, a ribbon of light dancing on the surface in a swathe of diamond spangles reaching to the horizon. Jack stopped to gaze at the ethereal beauty of this deserted coastline, the rhythmic slosh of the tide calming his nerves, the light breeze whispering through the marram grass in a comforting susurration. Despite his peaceful surroundings, that feeling of dread was with him again, churning in his gut, telling him something wasn't right. He raised his spyglass to the skyline, searching for the familiar outline of Dick Halesworth's lugger. *Where is she?* It was Friday night; he hadn't mistaken the day! He moved closer to the edge of the cliff and peered down onto the shingle for the fishing smack he expected to see waiting near the shore, but the beach was deserted.

There was no sign of the lantern bearer either, which seemed odd. He knew he hadn't imagined it.

Something like a twig snapped some distance away and he swung round at the slight sound, holding his breath, listening, peering round in the darkness. 'Who's there?' he called, his senses on high alert, wishing fervently he had his pistol tucked reassuringly into his belt but no, he was unarmed. Minutes later, staring towards the cliff path he heard the distinctive thudding of a galloping horse approaching, compelling him to duck down behind a tussock of sea grass. To his surprise he recognised his own horse and its female rider, who could only be his pretty wife, her long dark hair flowing out behind her like ribbons of kelp swaying in the tide.

'Kate!' he exclaimed, jumping up, as she appeared out of the gloom, reined in her mount and slid to the ground breathlessly, before encircling her arms around her husband in an emotional embrace. 'My dunlin, what are you doing here? Why did you come back? You shouldn't be out here alone at night,' Jack admonished her, his apprehension now doubled by added fear for his wife's safety.

'I wanted to see you, Jack, to say a final goodbye. I don't know when I will see you again.'

'Thank you, my sweet, but please go home. It's not safe here. Have you ridden all the way round from Southwold?

'Yes, although I hadn't realised quite how far it was!' Kate admitted. 'I couldn't be sure the harbour wasn't being watched, so I thought it best to ride round.'

'It m'ebbe was. You'd better stay at the Bell tonight, my dunlin, they've got stables. I don't want you out in the dark. Here…' Jack felt in his coat pocket and thrust some coins into her hand. 'Where's Kit?'

'He's at Sarah's. He's safe.' Kate scanned the coastline. 'Where's your ship?'

'It'll be here soon, my dunlin, don't worry.' Jack tried to sound unconcerned, but Kate could tell he was unsettled. The kiss he gave her was abstracted and brief. There was a nervousness in her husband's demeanour that was unlike him.

'What's the matter, Jack?' she enquired anxiously.

Jack sighed and held her to him. 'I dunno, Kate,' he admitted truthfully. 'I feel unnerved tonight. That fishing smack should have been here by now. Did you see anyone on the cliff path?'

'No, should I have?' Kate stood back, surveying the headland uneasily.

'No, that's just it. I saw a lantern flash, but there was nobody here and I could 'ave sworn I wer' bein' followed.'

'There's no-one about, Jack,' she reassured him.

Had she but known it, her belief was unfounded. Harry Goldsmith had not been idle since the smugglers' escape. He felt humiliated that for a second time he had been outwitted by Howell and his gang, their numbers swelled by collaboration with Hadleigh men and he stepped up searches of local hostelries, placing watches on all possible escape routes. Some of the hastily hidden contraband had been recovered and a few careless felons arrested when they attempted to retrieve their goods, but it was Howell Harry was after. *He won't get away again*, he vowed. He figured Jack would make his escape by sea as he had done before, the *Lady Katherine* in all likelihood picking him up on her outward journey. Again, his hunch that Jack was still at Dunwich had paid off and he felt confident tonight as he positioned his men along the dunes and waited, their presence almost revealed when one of his men carelessly flashed a lantern along the cliff top. 'Put that light out!' he had barked in a frustrated whisper, cursing crossly as they took their positions.

They watched, and as predicted, Jack appeared making his way up the path, followed shortly by Kate. Harry felt pleased with himself that he had been proved correct and once more exonerated in the eyes of his men, after the debacle of the ambush. Although he did not wish to put his niece in danger, her propitious appearance served to distract Jack, who was clearly unnerved and alert to any sudden noise. Harry signalled to his men to lay low and wait for the most opportune moment. Had he known it, he was not the only one watching the couple's rendezvous on the cliff edge that night.

'Have the excise been to the cottage?' Jack was asking his wife as he put her arm around her.

'No. There were a couple of them guarding the lookout on the cliff, but they didn't see me leave. Sarah took the children down to the sand to play and they were watching her, when I slipped away.'

'Good. They'll be lookin' for the *Lady Katherine*, no doubt, but she's not comin'.'

'I wish you didn't have to go, Jack,' Kate sighed, returning her husband's embrace, revelling in his body warmth as she clung to him.

'Me too, my dunlin, but you'll be a'right, don't you fret,' he reassured, kissing his wife's head affectionately.

As he did so Kate's horse snorted and they both looked round sharply to see a rabbit running over the dune. They held their breath before exhaling in relief. 'Bloody rabbits!' Jack chuckled, but just then his gaze caught the distinctive outline of a fishing boat approaching out of the gloom from the direction of the river. Reaching eagerly for his spyglass, he declared exultantly, as the small craft hove into view, 'Fishin' smack's here!' Scanning the horizon, he could also just make out the familiar outline of Halesworth's lugger. *Yes! At last!* A ribbon of cloud obscured the moon briefly, casting the cliff top into shadow, while the wind whipped around the bold young seaman and his alluring wife, susurrating around the couple with a doleful lament, echoing Kate's mood as she shivered in Jack's arms. Her heart sank and a lead weight settled in her gut. In a moment they would be parted for who knows how long. 'Time to go!' Jack announced. 'Farewell, my dunlin, get y'erself home now.' Pulling her to him with an impassioned kiss, Jack patted his wife's rump tenderly, as the moonlight broke through once more, silhouetting the couple against the sky, Kate's hair wafting around her shoulders.

The excisemen were out of earshot of the couple's conversation, but as the luminescence outlined them against the shining sea, Harry saw Jack raise his spyglass before turning to impart his final kiss. Another minute and Howell would be gone. He almost hated to shatter this tender moment of farewell, but this was his only opportunity. He was not going to suffer the ignominy of losing his charge again. 'Now!' he shouted to his men.

As the sudden cry went up, Kate's horse, already uneasy from the encounter with the rabbit, shied and whinnied, before galloping away down the dunes. Kate uttered a shriek of surprise as Jack wheeled round to the sound of a dozen firearms being cocked. 'Kate, run!' he yelled, pushing her from him forcefully.

'Hands up, Howell! You're under arrest!' Harry Goldsmith commanded, showing himself from behind a grassy bank, his musket aimed at Jack's head. Jack froze. He had half a mind to run, but with Kate so close by he couldn't risk her getting shot in the inevitable hail of musket fire that would ensue. He stepped back but saw he was dangerously close to the cliff edge.

'Jaaaack!' Kate screamed in alarm, her first instinct to run to him, but two boatmen leapt forward, grabbing her and holding her fast.

Jack raised his hands in surrender. There was no escape. 'I am unarmed!' he shouted as the excisemen stood up, surrounding him on three sides muskets trained on their target.

'Don't shoot him!' Kate cried imploringly. 'Jack!' she moaned tearfully, the sudden realisation she must have unwittingly led the lawmen to him suffusing her with guilt and regret.

'It's alright, my dunlin. Game's up, lass. Go home.' Jack smiled ruefully, when all at once a loud crack rang out, but not from direction of Goldsmith's men, who stared agape, watching in disbelief as the young man staggered back with a look of surprise now frozen on his face, then fell away without a sound, over the cliff edge.

Kate's scream of anguish echoed over the headland, as she watched Jack fall, as if in slow motion, the shock momentarily rooting her to the spot. A second later she wrenched herself free and ran towards the precipice, where her husband had stood only moments before. She looked over the bluff to see his body lying contorted and lifeless on the shingle below, sinking to her knees in horror-stricken despair.

'Jaaaaack, oh, Jack!' she cried. 'No, no, please God, nooooo!' She clutched her stomach as the agony of her loss overwhelmed her, and she let out a howl of wretchedness.

Harry Goldsmith approached and placed a hand on her shoulder. 'Kate,' he began kindly, any pent-up anger at his niece's deception now dissipating at the sight of her distress.

'Get off me,' she shouted, wrenching her shoulder away.

'It wasn't my men, Kate, the shot came from below,' he said quietly.

'Murderer!' she yelled, ignoring Harry, jumping up and running down the cliff path towards the beach, attempting to hold back heart-rending sobs as she ran, stumbling over her skirts on the steep track, the gradient almost flinging her headlong before she reached level ground, slipping and sliding as she encountered the shingle, her lungs fighting for air, her tears blurring her vision.

Upon reaching Jack's broken body she collapsed over him, attempting to embrace him, shaking his shoulders gently, hoping to rouse him, stroking his hair and kissing his bloodied corpse, peering imploringly into his eyes, now fixed and dulled, willing him to respond, as deep sobs caught in her throat. 'Jack, Jack, my darling Jack!' she wailed, pressing her face into his lifeless chest and weeping inconsolably. Her handsome sailor with his bewitching blue eyes and winning smile was gone, his heart pierced by a single shot, his body broken by the fall, his young life snatched from him before his time. She thought of Kit and her unborn child. Never would her children know their father. Never would he watch his son grow up or meet his unborn daughter, for Kate knew in her heart she was carrying a girl. It was too much to bear. Kate wanted to die, the thought of having to live without Jack too overwhelming, this all-consuming grief too burdensome, too painful.

Harry was equally stunned at what had just occurred, the scene now unfolding before him never having been part of his plan. He had simply meant to apprehend Howell and his gang and see them do their allotted time for their misdemeanours. He signalled for his men to follow Kate down the cliff path and onto the beach. *Somebody down there had committed murder and shot Jack Howell in the back!* He could not make sense of it. None of the smuggling fraternity would have shot one of their own and his men were all stationed on the cliff top, the command to shoot not having yet been given. Upon reaching his niece lying prostrate across her husband's lifeless form, he scanned the beach. In the far distance he could just make out a dark figure hurriedly disappearing into the dusk, his ambling gait lumbering his way along the shingle. Harry raised his musket and fired, several of his men following suit, but their shots failed to find their target.

'Go after him!' he commanded his men, but any hope of catching the murderer, given his considerable head start, was nigh on hopeless when attempting to run on deep drifts of sliding pebbles, and as the figure dropped out of sight in the darkness, they gave up the chase.

Having put as much distance as he could between himself and the pursuing boatmen, Charles Sawyer stopped to catch his breath as he reached the dunes bordering Dunwich Heath. He had covered nearly a mile and was utterly spent, his breaths coming in deep gulps, his throat raw from the cold air, his heart thumping wildly in his chest. He veered inland and flung himself down between the grasses, his eyes bulging, his legs giving way under him, but he smiled. 'You are avenged, my son! Howell is dead!' he breathed exultantly, hardly able to believe his one shot had found its target so perfectly, the days he had spent tracking first the excisemen, then Howell, finally paying off. With luck, he had got away quickly enough for the servicemen to be unable to catch up with him, there being no time to stop and stare at Howell's body, or to check to see if he was still alive, though it was fairly obvious he wasn't. As Sawyer lay exhausted, he clutched at his chest, his breaths still coming rapidly, the pain in his lungs increasing from the sustained effort of his flight along the shore. His ageing body and flour dust-infused lungs, unused to this kind of physical exertion, were struggling to keep him alive, but he almost cared not. His mission had been accomplished, his vow to his dead son now fulfilled. If he expired on this windswept shore, it mattered not; he had nothing more to live for, he concluded, as he closed his eyes. It was almost prophetic.

Almost immediately he was fully alert as the thump of a footfall only feet away reached his ear. He sat up with a start, turning his head towards the direction of the sound, but never even saw his assailant, as an iron grip grabbed his chest from behind and a razor-sharp blade sliced across his throat. He had no time to utter a cry as he flopped to the ground, his blood gushing into the sand, his mouth agape, like a fish gasping for air, his eyes bulging in shock.

'That's for Howell, ya cowardly scab!' hissed Ben, plunging his bloodied knife into the dune and wiping it clean on his breeches, before thrusting the miller's pistols into his belt, pushing the wide-eyed corpse into a hollow and covering the body with sand. As he finished and stood up, the old sailor stared across the water. The lugger and the fishing smack had gone, no doubt alerted by the gunfire. He would have to wait his turn. He spat in the direction of the mound he had just heaped over Sawyer's corpse. 'Go join yer boy in hell!' he sneered before trotting off in the direction of Minsmere.

Charles Sawyer had not been the only one tracking Jack that night. Ben Fosdyke was planning on joining his comrade on the *Sandpiper* and had been about to show himself to Jack, when first Kate then the excise turned up. Content to allow the couple enough time to say their farewells, he cursed when he realised they were not alone. *Yer losin' yer grip, old-timer*, he had scolded himself testily. His first impulse had been to shoot it out and rescue his friend, but the risk of being caught along with Howell was too great, so he waited. Crouching in a convenient crevice in the cliff edge, his movement had disturbed a rabbit, the same creature that had unnerved Jack and Kate, before a few moments later witnessing the shot that killed Jack, his shipmate's fall from the cliff and his assailant running away. Ben's reaction was instinctive. He didn't need to think twice, as he ran back along the headland, his target fixed firmly in his sights, the wheezing miller unable to match the pace of his determined pursuer. 'Sawyer's not gorn' to get away with this!' the old seadog vowed, gritting his teeth with wrathful fury. His young comrade's murderer would pay the ultimate price for his folly.

Further back along the beach, the boatmen were busy collecting Jack's body, while Harry rounded up Kate's horse and accompanied her back to the Bell. He could have arrested her for assisting a felon, but he felt she had suffered enough, a life as a single parent now stretching before her without her husband to support her. Besides, she had not harboured Jack, or facilitated his escape, simply rushed to say farewell to the man she loved. This was not the outcome he had imagined for his niece and he was not about to add to her misfortune, compassion for his dead brother's family playing on his mind. Soon the shore lay deserted and silent once more, a single dark red stain near the base of the cliff oozing through the stones, the only evidence of the spot where a young man had died, his blood erelong to be washed clean at the next high tide.

Chapter Twenty-Seven

Eighteen years later, a solitary figure stood motionless on the raised bank of shingle bordering Aldeburgh Beach, gazing out to sea. On the horizon silhouetted against a titian sky, between lumbering coal colliers and over-laden packet ships, a graceful three-masted schooner sliced through the waves. The woman watched, tears blurring her vision, as the elegant vessel carrying her son faded into the evening haze, its sails lit up by the oblique rays of the setting sun, while the light summer breeze wafting her hair across her face rustled with a melancholy moan across the marram grass of Slaughden Beach behind her.

Kate was still striking for her forty-three years, her long dark brown hair now streaked with grey at the temples, her eyes still a muted blue, her skin still taut but for a few tell-tale lines around the eyes and mouth, her lips still retaining a vestige of their youthful fullness. Many a local townsman had set his sights on her and attempted a courtship, but none came anywhere near the man she had loved and lost, and so she had remained a widow, content to raise her two children at the attractive brick house Jack had bought for her along the main street in Aldeburgh.

She was still known as Mrs Will Pallant, despite many folk knowing the truth about Jack Howell and how he had died. Many a time she would re-live the nightmare of that night on Dunwich Beach in her mind's eye, never quite having rid herself of the conviction Jack's death was somehow her fault. She could not erase the picture replaying in her mind: his last dispirited words, so full of bitterness and despair, 'Game's up, lass, go home,' repeating over and over, that sudden shot, his fall from the cliff, his broken body lying prostrate on the shore, his blood seeping between the stones to become part of the landscape he loved. For a long time she could not believe Jack was gone. Each time she awoke, she almost convinced herself it had all just been some terrible nightmare and her husband would still be beside her large as life, before reality sunk in once more confirming so cruelly his death was real.

Jack's murderer had never been found, but Kate couldn't help but speculate that somehow the strange disappearance of Charles Sawyer, Edward's father, had something to do with it. He had not been seen since that night, his Woodbridge mill lying empty and silent, while his unfinished mill near Blythburgh slowly fell into ruin. A skeleton had been unearthed on Dunwich dune about ten years ago, found when a pair of young smugglers were burying a cache. They had run off in fright, abandoning their haul, convinced they would be cursed for disturbing the dead, and shortly afterwards, the pursuing coastguard officers had come upon the scene. There was, however, no identification possible and it was assumed the bones were the remains of yet another anonymous lawbreaker, killed whilst carrying out his illicit trade. Of course, Kate had had her suspicions, given what she knew about Edward's death, but Ben Fosdyke had been on the wrong end of a soldier's musket ball some years back and his secrets had died with him.

Harry Goldsmith had kindly arranged for Jack to be buried in the graveyard at St Bartholomew's in Orford, his regret at having been partly responsible for his niece losing her husband, his wife's grandchildren losing their father playing on his conscience. Despite Jack having lived the life of a wanted felon, he had not wished such a tragic end for this enterprising young seaman. If only he had served his time, he would now be a free man, able to watch his family grow and with any luck might have been persuaded to pursue a more legitimate career.

Smuggling had gone on uninterrupted, of course, with many local folk unwittingly drawn into the subterfuge. Young women would continue to fall for loveable rogues and even ten years after Jack's death, Margaret Catchpole, a servant girl from Nacton, was convicted of stealing a horse for her smuggler lover William Laud and sentenced to hang at Ipswich gaol. She managed to escape, no doubt with help from Laud, but was re-captured and her sentence commuted to seven years' transportation. The Napoleonic War had offered a convenient distraction for the Navy but the construction of defensive Martello towers along the Suffolk beaches, each garrisoned by twenty-five soldiers, hampered smuggling activities, which nevertheless continued, employing increasingly ingenious methods of disposal and concealment. However, since his retirement Harry had ceased to concern himself with the nefarious activities of the starlight traders and was content to sit back, collect his pension and watch his great-nephews and -nieces grow, without risking his life after dark, much to Ellen's relief.

Every month to start with, Kate had ridden round to Orford to visit her husband's final resting place, but her visits had become less and less as the years rolled by. She would clear away the autumn leaves and in the spring would take fresh flowers picked from the waysides to lay against his tombstone. Kate would kiss her fingertips and touch his name on the *inscription. 'John (Jack) Howell, beloved son, husband and father 1760–1787.'* Kate had wanted to inscribe 'murdered in cold blood' on the stone but had to be content with a quote from the Lord's prayer, Harry deemed particularly apt, considering Jack's last occupation: '*Lead us not into temptation but deliver us from evil.*' Kate would sometimes bring her children to stand at their father's grave, Kit and Grace animatedly telling him about their life, but when she was on her own would sink to her knees and weep for the only man she knew she would ever truly love. The siblings could merely form an imagined picture of their father from what they were told of the dashing merchantman, who was resourceful, courageous and full of life. Kate's portrait hanging on the wall gave them an idea of his features but was a poor substitute for flesh and blood. Never would they look into his deep blue eyes, see his winning smile, hear his voice or feel safe in his warm embrace, as Kate had done. Despite the lawlessness of his chosen profession, Jack was a good man, mindful of the sanctity of human life, compassionate to those who opposed him or assisted him, sensible of the daily struggle we all face to survive, and Kate loved him for it.

His children would never really know the man who had given them life, run to welcome him as he came home, feel his touch, the stubble on his cheek brushing against theirs, the essence of the sea still fresh on his clothes, the look of love in his eyes.

After Ellen's initial shock at her daughter's deception, her sorrow for Kate's widowhood, and for losing the man she loved so deeply, came to the fore and she forgave her, knowing only too well the pain of losing a loved one, as well as a partner and provider. She adored her grandchildren, Kate's two being followed by two more from Becky and her husband Seb, but Ellen felt a special bond of care for Kit and his sister Grace, growing up without their father, his genes undeniably imbuing them with their striking good looks.

Now Kate had bade farewell to her only son, whose swarthy dark features were so like his father's, his intense blue eyes and engaging smile poised to melt the heart of many a young girl like his father before him. Two nights before, Kit had arrived home from Holland to his mother and young sister Grace, proudly presenting Kate with a bolt of French lace of the finest quality and each of them with silk stockings and a silver and pearl filigree necklace. Kate's face had fallen as she looked at his precious gifts. She knew they were illicit goods brought in under the guise of legitimate trading and guessed she was already too late to stop her son following in his father's footsteps. Recently a beautiful gold and ruby necklace had reportedly been turned up in the demolished ruins of the old prison at Dunwich Priory, no doubt a hidden cache awaiting collection in vain by a deceased free trader. Kate knew Jack had been held there briefly and she had oft found herself fantasising at the possibility the jewel had been meant for her. Now, however, she gazed at her son's gifts with a heavy heart.

'Perks of the trade, Mama.' He grinned, winking at his mother with a melting smile, so unfailingly reminding her of Jack.

'Oh, Kit! You shouldn't bring me gifts like this. I need nothing. Please don't get involved with the free trade, son – it only leads to misery in the end. Your father's proof of that!' she pleaded, knowing full well her words fell on deaf ears.

'I know what I'm doing, Ma,' he assured her, echoing his late father's words. 'Besides, you deserve it!' He had kissed her on the cheek and embraced her tenderly before settling himself down at the table. 'Something smells good, Ma! I could eat a horse!' he joked, attempting to deflect his mother's attention, patting his growling stomach and helping himself to the jug of ale Kate had just put down.

'Well, game pie will have to do, son. I'm fresh out of horse this week!' Kate quipped sadly, sighing in resignation as an image of Kit's uncertain future formed in her mind.

Now standing alone on the shingle, the sun having long since disappeared over the western horizon behind Orford, Kate surveyed the panorama before her. The sails of the *Lady Katherine* were no longer visible. Captain Nate Holdsworth would be setting course for Holland, teaching Kit the skills his best friend's son would need when he too would one day command his father's ship. A fresh tear welled up and travelled slowly down her cheek, as the lead weight of inevitability settled in her gut and a prayer formed on her lips. *Oh, Lord, keep my son safe. Don't let him go the way of his father. I can't lose him too.* As she turned to trudge along the pebble bank towards Slaughden, her feet sinking into the stones with a reluctant crunch, causing them to slide down the bank with an angry rattle, she heaved a heavy sigh. To her south the single beam from the new brick-built lighthouse at Orford Ness burst into life, the keeper settling down to maintain his nightly vigil over the oil lamps as the beam swung round, guiding ships past the submerged sand and shingle banks. To the east along the shoreline, the breakers' relentless pulse of ebb and flow merged like a backbeat in her ears, the languorously pounding surf a gentle backdrop to the raucous cries of the ubiquitous scavenging gulls as shore crabs scuttled for cover under the retreating waves, only to be washed up again moments later.

Surveying this empty coastline, Kate turned her gaze inland across the wide shimmering expanse of the River Alde towards Orford, where the bells of St Bartholomew's rang out for evensong and the imposing tower of the castle keep still dominated the skyline. She shuddered at the memories it revived: some happy, as she played around the tower in childish innocence with her siblings; some repugnant, as she pictured Edward's sneers and violent death; some bittersweet, as she saw again Jack's handsome face and felt his impassioned, powerful embrace.

It all seemed so very long ago now: another life, snatched away by a fickle wind, her memory of it constantly changing, twisting, evolving, illusory, like starling murmurations at dusk or an eerie roke, a swirling, formless turbulence of vapour, creeping sluggishly in from the sea, re-shaping everything in its path into ghostly phantasmal shadows. Oftentimes it seemed as if it had all been some strange dream from which she would awake, but real or not it had made her the person she was today and she would not swap her place with anyone. She would keep Jack's memory alive through his children and his life would become the stuff of legend, passed down with ever-increasing embellishment as each generation thrilled to tales of derring-do by their illustrious ancestor, the flash of a lantern, the whispers in the shingle, the footsteps in the sand – the illegality, brutality and roguery of real life eclipsed with the passing of time, by the romanticism of folklore and mythos.

Now she watched as a flight of dunlin took off from the riverbank and flew south towards the estuary, where the Ore spilled out into Hollesley Bay, while over the marshes the bittern's familiar call reverberated amongst the reeds and sedges. Her home, her refuge, this was the place she loved: the clean fresh air blowing off the North Sea filling her lungs with life, the soft muted colours of Suffolk perfusing her eyes, imbuing her soul with belonging and purpose, lifting her spirit but at the same time oppressing her subconscious with melancholy. *Oh, Jack, where are you? Why did you leave me? I miss you so much*, she murmured faintly, eyelids closed, pausing to listen for the voice she longed to hear once more, but no answer came, save for the perpetual surge of each crashing breaker and the swish of the tide as it ebbed and flowed in ceaseless rhythm.

She thought about their son's future. How history would repeat itself as he pursued his trade, tasting the thrill of illicit gains, still so temptingly available for those with enterprise and courage. Kit would find himself a lover and she would fear for him as Kate had done for Jack, watching and waiting for him to come home, straining her ears for late-night gunfire and dreading the knock on the door. How many more young men would have to die along this bleak seaboard, either upholding the law or opposing it in the struggle for a better life? How many more mothers, wives and lovers would pay the price for human avarice, fuelled by desperation and want?

Kate drew a long tremulous breath. Her life would endure, whether she willed it or no, the ghost of the man she loved walking beside her, ever-present, ever-elusive, ever part of this evocative landscape, until one day she would join him again. Two free spirits born under sweeping Suffolk skies, raised and nurtured by folk whose lives were bound by nature and necessity to a place of rich earth, whispering reed beds and teeming inland waterways, tied to the ever-encroaching sea until one or the other claimed its human toll. Two souls forever wafted on the salt-laden air, the sighing of the stones whispering their names, breathing in, breathing out, like the soothing words of a parent rocking a child in its cradle. Husssssh, husssssh... gently repeating, repeating, washing clean the blood of desperate men, while the shifting shingle banks perpetually preserve their time-worn secrets of lives lived and lost – lives once so vital, so sentient, now immured for eternity in voiceless mystique by the jealous reclusion of those dispassionate stones, perennially defining and re-shaping this desolate coastline.

It was time to go. Kate turned for home as the light began to fade and a thin crescent moon appeared in the eastern sky, a slender arc of silver suspended motionless over a serene sea. She paused, a wistful smile playing around her lips, as a fresh breath of wind soughed across the shingle, for within that mournful sound, she could have sworn she heard Jack's voice whispering softly in her ear... '*a perfect night for smugglin'*, *my dunlin*', as the murmuring drag of the relentless tide pounded its enduring heartbeat on the shore.

A Smuggler's Song

If you wake at midnight, and hear a horse's feet,
Don't go drawing back the blind, or looking in the street;
Them that ask no questions isn't told a lie.
Watch the wall, my darling, while the Gentlemen go by!

Five and twenty ponies,
Trotting through the dark —
Brandy for the Parson,
Baccy for the Clerk;
Laces for a lady, letters for a spy,
And watch the wall, my darling,
While the Gentlemen go by!

Running round the woodlump if you chance to find
Little barrels, roped and tarred, all full of brandy-wine,
Don't you shout to come and look, nor use 'em for your play.
Put the brushwood back again — and they'll be gone next day!

If you see the stable door setting open wide;
If you see a tired horse lying down inside;
If your mother mends a coat cut about and tore;
If the lining's wet and warm — don't you ask no more!

If you meet King George's men, dressed in blue and red,
You be careful what you say, and mindful what is said.
If they call you 'pretty maid', and chuck you 'neath the chin,
Don't you tell where no one is, nor yet where no one's been!

Knocks and footsteps round the house — whistles after dark —
You've no call for running out till the house-dogs bark.
Trusty's here, and Pincher's here, and see how dumb they lie —
They don't fret to follow when the Gentlemen go by!

If you do as you've been told, likely there's a chance,
You'll be given a dainty doll, all the way from France,
With a cap of Valenciennes, and a velvet hood —
A present from the Gentlemen, along o' being good!

Five and twenty ponies,
Trotting through the dark —
Brandy for the Parson,
Baccy for the Clerk;
Them that asks no questions isn't told a lie —
Watch the wall, my darling,
While the Gentlemen go by.

Rudyard Kipling, 1865–1936

About the Author

Bridget M. Beauchamp spent her childhood on the Suffolk coast. Fond memories of desolate shingle beaches, quiet waterways and huge watercolour skies stayed with her. Inspired by a love of nature, landscape, literature and history, she was inspired to write Whispers in the Shingle.